MIDNIGHT JUSTICE

BY

ROBIN DOBBINS

Gotham Books

30 N Gould St.
Ste. 20820, Sheridan, WY 82801
https://gothambooksinc.com/

Phone: 1 (307) 464-7800

Published by Gotham Books (May 3, 2024)

ISBN: 979-8-88775-722-3 (H)
ISBN: 979-8-88775-689-9 (P)
ISBN: 979-8-88775-690-5 (E)

DEDICATION

I am dedicating this novel to Janel, my loving wife and the smart one in this 57-year marriage. As my best friend, she word processed the manuscript, made the corrections, and edited along the way. All the long hours of deciphering my hen scratch, she worked rather inexpensively.

Secondly, I want to thank Linda Martin, a fitness pupil of mine, for cleverly coming up with the book title.

I offer this fantasy to every woman, man, and child who has endured a criminal attack and wants to inflict their own justice where the authorities have their hands tied or crafty lawyers figure a way to allow filthy criminals to walk free to harm some other unsuspecting individual.

Alexandria McCord's vigilante work will bring thrills, as you accompany her in dealing destruction to those predators who are unstoppable by the legal system. Are you too in the same grain as Alexandria McCord?

CONTENTS

Chapter 1

Dressed in a skin-tight one-piece navy blue Kevlar and leather suit with a matching full head mask, a sleek but muscular figure, poised stealth-like in the pitch black of night chambered seven Remington 870 slugs from a cartridge belt, and proceeded to blast two shots into the rear tires of a new low slung 1985 Lincoln Continental. With catlike quickness, he moved to the driver's side door and pulled a beleaguered youth from the car, slamming him face down on the pavement while binding his hands and feet with large tie wraps. Seconds later, four youths were making a frantic dash toward the car while firing shots in the direction from which they had come; a government housing project in the form of duplexes for those on disability and indigent retirees living solely on social security.

The mysterious intruder swiftly placed two more cartridges in his short stock 870 and emptied the magazine in rapid fire toward the unsuspecting assailants, taking down all four. With business-like precision, he quickly filled the cannon again and skipped across the shallow ditch in front of the houses to examine his handiwork. Finding the attackers on the ground screaming and clutching their wounds, he tossed their guns aside and confiscated the bags they used to carry the cash and social security checks stolen from those in the project.

By this time a crowd of old folks, donned in their sleepwear, was cautiously making its way to the scene. Speaking not a word, the masked marvel tossed the bags at their feet and began sprinting toward the back of the houses where a black 1971 Dodge Challenger awaited on the next street. No sooner had he hit full stride, police cars were converging on the scene at the front of the project, lights flashing and sirens blaring.

Upon reaching his getaway coach, two squad cars arrived on the backside blocking the roadway's only outlet; they had him penned. Taking a step to the side of his car, the crusader discharged several rounds into the police vehicles, knocking out their headlights and puncturing the radiators. Before the officers could react, he tossed the shotgun across the passenger seat and had the Challenger in second gear, plowing through the backyards. Moving between duplexes on the way to the front yard, he downshifted into first gear and forced the snorting 426 Hemi powered Dodge across the shallow ditch onto the pavement while passing the oncoming squad cars screeching to a halt in front of the Lincoln.

Two of the black and whites turned around and commenced giving chase, narrowly avoiding a collision with two ambulances arriving at the scene. By this time, Captain America had turned onto the boulevard in the direction of the freeway on-ramp nearing speeds of 100 mph. Seeing that the chase was futile, one of the officers radioed ahead for further assistance.

Moments after the ambulance attendants began their work, veteran Houston PD detective Mike Kinstley and his new partner, detective Sharon Murphy, arrived. Kinstley, a 5'11" amateur bodybuilder with evidence of gray amongst a head of thick black hair, was very deliberate in demeanor. Murphy was a marathon runner, standing all of 5'4". She was fast to react and like Kinstley, headstrong and all business. Although only in her third year as a detective, there was evidence of gray peeking through her short dark brown hair.

Approaching one of the uniformed police officers taking a statement from a witness, Kinstley immediately inquired, "Did he kill anyone?"

The officer turned his attention away from the witness and replied, "No, but one of the assailants did."

"Who?"

"Her last name is Carrington. We're actually standing in her front yard. Witnesses say she followed the assailants out of the house, screaming for help."

Kinstley stood scanning the scene and observed, "None of the bad guys may be dead, but it looks like Taub's emergency room will have their hands full. Who's giving chase?"

"Carter and Simmons."

Another officer walking toward his squad car remarked, "Detective Kinstley, you sure you want to apprehend this guy? I kinda like his work."

Puzzled, detective Murphy addressed her partner, "You know whose handiwork this is?"

"We don't know him by name; only his MO," he answered while wading through the crime scene debris. He stooped down to examine the wounds on the Carrington lady, pulling back the blanket covering her body

Further confused, Murphy inquired, "But what about a license plate check and witnesses? How can you not have a name? I don't understand."

Standing to watch paramedics place the gang members in ambulances, Mike explained, "He must have connections inside the DMV because none of the many plates he uses are registered. Witnesses have never seen his face because he wears a full head mask. It's also difficult to assess his build because he wears a thick full Kevlar suit that simulates an extremely muscular body. Anything else you want to know?" he gruffly inquired with a slight grin while turning in her direction.

Murphy persisted, "I get the strange feeling you don't want to catch this guy. Are we not talking about a common criminal taking the law into his own hands?"

Visibly losing his patience, Mike paused for a moment to maintain a respectful approach. "Murphy, there's nothing common about this guy. When he's not busy protecting old folks from being robbed of their social security checks and cash like he did tonight, he's finding time to rescue people from car jackings, robbery, assault, rape, and numerous other offenses against humanity. He once managed to avert a hostage situation at an all-night grocery. However, to set the record straight, I fully intend to bring this dangerous criminal to justice. Whatever that is. Personally, I think they ought to pin a medal on him."

Overtaken by frustration, Murphy placed both hands on her hips pleading, "But he's breaking the law! Police work is our job!"

Exasperated, Kinstley pointed to the crowd of old folks still mingling and giving statements. "Tell them."

Murphy then approached one of the officers investigating the crime scene, commanding, "I want to know the minute Carter and Simmons apprehend wonder boy."

"Sharon!" Mike hollered, "We're not going to catch him in an all-out chase, so don't get your hopes up."

"Kinstley, why can't we catch him? Does he have some sort of magical car?" she asked sarcastically while advancing toward him.

"Didn't your dad once race a drag car on the NHRA circuit?"

Puzzled, she asked, "What's that got to do with anything?"

He turned away and proceeded to amble toward their department-issued 1984 black Ford Crown Victoria. "Ask him the chances of us catching a blown 426 Hemi with a three fifty-five rear end."

Sharon paused for a moment to acknowledge the reality of his point, and then followed after him challenging, "I know all about engines and rear gears, Detective Kinstley. But you're going to tell me he can also outrun a Motorola?"

As he opened the driver side door, Mike turned and explained, "He makes wild stunt-like exits no one in their right mind would attempt, causing the chase cars to lose him. He then somehow manages to weave his way through the streets to wherever he holds up without being seen. Citizens in those neighborhoods are smart enough to not turn him in. Tonight, was our best shot to date at nabbing him. As soon as I call this in, we'll go to Denny's and finish this conversation."

The lonely stretch of Highway 59 south was suddenly shaken by the roar of a Dodge at full throttle attempting to increase the distance between itself and two Texas State Troopers giving chase.

Anxiety mounting fast and patience running thin, the lonely hero used the car phone mounted on the floorboard between the two front bucket seats to make a desperate call. "Come on Richard, answer the phone! Nobody knows this number but us...Hurry Richard!"

Just as the outlaw driver was about to slam the receiver back onto its cradle, Richard picked up on the other end. "Sorry to keep you waiting, Alex. I was preparing the paint booth for the car's next color. What's up?"

"I'm covered up in black and whites, that's what's up! I've got this elephant running a hundred sixty plus, but they're still in my rear-view mirror!"

"Where are you now?"

"I'm about five miles away. Surely, they've radioed ahead,

so I don't have much time to lose them. I need you to listen carefully. Open the gate and turn on the entrance lights. Stay on the line, because you'll need to turn them off and close the gate when I give you the word. Then immediately turn on the lights to the hangar door. Remain on the line and I'll tell you when to begin opening it. You'll also need to open the rear door, because I won't let off the throttle until I'm inside. That means I'll end up sliding out the back door for two whiles. You'll begin closing the front door just before I get there. Turn off the lights also. And Richard, please time it right."

"I know I shouldn't ask, but what are you planning?"

"I'm going to turn off my headlights about a half mile prior to that wide left turn just before the gate. When I come out of the turn, I'll go hard right and hope to slide through. From there it's full throttle again up the road to the hangar."

"That's an impossible feat! There's no other way?"

"No. I'm going to lay the phone down now but I won't hang up. It's time to prepare for this insane execution. If you know a good prayer, say it now."

Wedging the receiver between the seat and the console, Alex squeezed the pistol grip shift knob of the Borg-Warner four-speed transmission in preparation for the rapid downshifting needed to perform the desperate maneuver. Extinguishing the headlights, the fugitive forced the muscle car to straddle the center line in hopes the pursuing State Troopers would think the big Dodge had simply vanished.

Then a voice from the direction of the passenger seat broke

the silence softly saying, "I am answering your prayer, Alex. Have faith I will see you through this maneuver." But it fell on deaf ears. Downshifting with the precision of an experienced race car driver, Alex forced the vehicle to stay on the low side of the left turn, leaving room on the high side to perform the insane right turn angle slide through the gate. Then came the moment of truth.

Heart racing in overdrive, palms sweating, and hands shaking nervously, the Masked Marvel yanked the wheel hard right, sending the car into a skid. Steering the wheel in the direction of the skid and giving it full throttle allowed the tires to grab and the car to straighten out enough to slide through the opening. A violent collision with the fence posts at the entrance had been avoided.

Grabbing the phone, Alex hollered frantically, "Turn off the lights and close the gate!"

Poised beside the entrance to the hangar, Richard did as instructed, and then proceeded with turning on the lights to the hangar door. He informed Alex, "I've already opened the back door, so I'm waiting for the word to open the front."

"Now! Do it now!"

He reached over and thumped a large green button. "OK, it's opening as we speak."

The road from the highway to the old deserted county airport hangar was approximately one-half mile. As the mad driver approached within a hundred yards of the hangar, Richard turned off the hangar entrance lights and began the process of closing the extremely large door, hopefully having compensated for the speed of the hard charging vehicle. With fingers crossed, he waited anxiously.

Within seconds the Dodge bullied its way through the narrow opening, dismantling the driver side mirror. Immediately downshifting and braking, Alex brought the thundering vehicle to a screeching halt some 50 yards outside the back door, and began wheeling the car around slowly toward the hangar, stopping in front of the old offices turned into living quarters.

Emotionally drained and physically exhausted, Alex exited the car and placed both hands on the roof. "Did we lose them?"

Pushing the switch that engages the closing mechanism to the back door, Richard replied, "I watched the camera transmitting from the gate and never saw them. They must have given up when you turned off your headlights."

As Alex pulled off the mask, her long auburn hair fell well below the shoulders as she shook it from side to side. "I can't thank this magnificent car enough for my not getting caught tonight."

Richard, a slender six-foot South Korean with a Ph.D. in both Political Science and Philosophy, was Alex's 60-year old uncle and unwavering force in her life. Strolling across the Race Trac covered floor to the car, he leaned with his back against the front fender where his niece was positioned, and thoughtfully suggested, "Perhaps you may want to give God some credit."

Looking at Richard through tired eyes, Alex made a concession, "You're right. You're always right. The strangest thing happened after I extinguished my headlights. I could have sworn a soft voice spoke to me from the passenger seat. I took a quick glance, but no one was there, of course. I made that insane maneuver so easy; it was like someone else was driving."

Arms crossed and sporting a warm smile, he offered, "For the sake of your inner peace, I only hope someday you'll let the authorities and God handle justice. So, what did that phantom voice say?"

"I don't know; something about faith."

Puzzled, Richard replied, "Now you are scaring me. Better give up this night work and concentrate on the work God has planned for you at school and the youth center."

"I think they're on to me," Alex confessed as she ignored his offer of wisdom, and began to unzip her bulletproof Kevlar and leather suit. "The police were in that neighborhood tonight laying a trap. They know I protect the old folks in poor neighborhoods on Uncle Sam's payday. Tonight, they guessed the right neighborhood."

"It may be a sign from the Father. Your next stop could be jail. What would then happen to all those who need your guidance?"

Skipping over his plea, she said, "I think I'll spend the night here since it's Friday, and take the Jeep back to the house in the morning. I'll leave before sun up and get a few more hours sleep in my own bed."

Yawning, while rubbing his face with both hands, Richard commented, "I need to spend the weekend here and do some work on this car. The paint booth is ready. What color do you want this time?"

"White; in honor of Kawalski in the movie 'Vanishing Point'… I can't thank you enough, Unc," she said leaning her head on his left shoulder. You are the steadying force in my life. I don't know what I'd do without you. I don't tell you that often enough."

"What are uncles for? Want me to fix you something to eat before you sack out?" he asked, while bending over to pick up the driver side mirror that had been knocked off when the car squeezed through the entrance.

"No thanks, I'm not very hungry. My mind is racing and the adrenaline level is off the chart."

Placing the mirror on a nearby bench, he inquired, "Alex, why don't you give that Farley Fontenot guy a chance? The fact that you both teach history at the same school presents a pretty good foundation for a possible relationship. It would not hurt to have a man in your life. Maybe then you'll have something else to do with your life at night besides this insane stuff."

Shaking her head negatively, she replied, "I don't know, he's an ex-San Antonio Police Detective. It's almost like he sees right through me. It's an eerie feeling, especially when you consider what I do at night for fun. Besides, he's…"

Before she could finish her sentence, Richard interrupted while wiping his hands on a blue shop towel, "I know, he just doesn't measure up to Mike Koehl. Alex, it's time you have someone with which to share your life. At 40, you're not getting any younger. You're past an age world-class athletes start winding down their careers. For sure you can't do this forever."

"I'm going to go to bed.... Richard, I'm going to get those Lymko creeps next. They robbed hundreds of people's lifetime savings, yet they're still rich. They're gonna pay. From there I'm going after the airline executives who have the audacity to have the pilots and attendants take a huge cut in pay and benefits, while they pull huge bonuses and file Chapter 11. I'm going to get those squids."

Following her through the door, Richard exclaimed, "Alexandria McCord, are you out of your ever-loving mind? Those are the biggest of the big shots in this world. Tell me you're not."

She took a seat on a large sofa and begged, "Would you please pull off these boots? Pretty please?"

Unc succumbed to her charming child-like request, and while yanking on one and tossing it to the floor, he observed, "You get me. You're so gentle and caring at times, yet other moments you can turn into a cold-blooded administer of justice. A violent one at that. I'll never understand how you pull it off."

"I guess I was born that way. I remember watching movies where several guys would hold the arms of another fella while someone beat on him. It made me want to shoot up the bad guys right through the screen. I was filled with rage. When my parents were murdered while visiting some friends of my dad's parents, it did something to me. I know you remember how my heart was broken into pieces. Those thugs robbed the people of their Social Security checks at gunpoint. Then decided killing them and my parents would be fun. The woman lived long enough to give the police the ugly details. Hate filled my heart, and I vowed to hunt them down like the filthy dogs they are."

While tugging on the other boot, Richard rebutted, saying, "But that was ten years ago. You have not the slightest idea where they might be or even if they're still here. Maybe in jail or dead, for that matter."

She glanced up at her uncle and informed him, "Many bystanders identified them as the Grimm Reapers. At some point, I'm bound to run into them. Their leader back then was a young punk they called 'Willie Boy.' He's the driving force behind my renewed martial arts training and weightlifting. If steroids did not have horrible side effects and did not transform my appearance to that of a man, believe me, I'd be juicing. Someday they'll be illegal anyway."

Richard tossed the second boot aside and flopped down in a deep plush dark brown leather recliner. "Boy, would your students be shocked to find out about this Heckle and Jeckle side of yours."

With a sudden burst of laughter, Alex clapped her hands, correcting, "Heckle and Jeckle? Richard, it's Dr. Jekyll and Mr. Hyde. Heckle and Jeckle was a cartoon about two crows…Oh, you're so funny. I needed that… I needed a good laugh."

Unable to hide his embarrassment, a once in a century occurrence, Unc sheepishly responded, "Sorry, but I didn't watch much TV. In fact, we didn't even own a TV. I've always heard mention of Heckle and Jeckle, but didn't know what they were talking about."

Continuing to laugh, Alex said, "Oh, Richard, you're so priceless. As long as I have you, I can manage without a husband. Besides, can't you just imagine Farley amping out when he sees me suiting up to go out on one of my nighttime missions?"

Eyelids sagging, Richard replied, "Sounds like the perfect time to quit, considering he's friends with Mike Kinstley, the renowned homicide detective here in Houston."

Smiling in Richard's direction, she assessed, "Doesn't look like you can stay awake much longer, so what do you say we continue this far-reaching conversation when we're both not so tired?"

Richard simply rolled his head to one side and allowed his eyelids to close. Leaning back in a recliner late at night would have been certain comatose for most anyone.

Alex rose to her feet, entered the bedroom and opened the closet door, pulling a blanket off the top shelf. She then reappeared, placing the blanket over her uncle to his chin. Placing a kiss on his forehead, she softly whispered, "Good night, my precious friend."

Returning to her bedroom, she closed the door and kneeled at the foot of the bed, placing her elbows on the mattress with her hands clasped. She began to pray:

"Father Almighty, keep your vigilant watch over me, protecting me from harm. Make my hands steady and my aim true. Keep me on the narrow path. Let me continue to be an instrument of protection in the lives of the oppressed and the deliverer of justice to the oppressors. Keep me strong and keep me swift,

Father. Let me be stealth and let me be wise. Father, let me be the teacher and mentor my students need. Thank you, Father, for Richard's undying love and loyalty. Your humble servant, in Jesus name I pray. Amen."

While sitting in a booth at Denny's Classic Diner with a view of the boulevard, detectives Kinstley and Murphy scanned the late-night menu.

Mike placed the menu back in its holder and announced, "Murphy, I think I might just order breakfast. Pigs in a blanket, hashbrowns, three scrambled eggs, and a large glass of milk should do the trick."

Sharon looked up commenting, "I would never have guessed you indulged in such a calorie loaded choice this late at night. My, I'm really perplexed."

"Murphy, what do you say you let me eat my way, and I'll let you eat your way? Perplexed? Where did you come up with that word?"

Yielding, she responded while hiding behind the huge menu, "I don't care how you eat. I was just surprised a fit looking guy like you would carb up so late at night. I didn't mean to start a war…I was just trying to make conversation for God's sake. Man, you are so grumpy."

Stupefied by Sharon's declaration, his voice flexion heightened, "Grumpy? You're calling me grumpy just because I want to eat something without being made to feel self-conscious or guilty? I brought you here to help us both relax and begin to get to know one another. And this is the thanks I get?"

Continuing to use the menu to avoid eye contact, she fired back, "You're blowing this all out of proportion. I do appreciate your seemingly sincere effort. And I do mean seemingly. It would be a big boost to our working relationship to better understand each other."

Kinstley reached across the table and pushed the menu down low enough to look into her eyes. "I'm going to the bathroom. If the waitress comes to our table, order for me. You know what I want." Standing erect, he ambled in the direction of the restrooms.

When Mike returned to the booth, a smile swept across his face upon gazing at the plate of sausages wrapped in pancakes placed next to a dish loaded up with hashbrown potatoes and scrambled eggs flanked by a large glass of milk. Looking at Murphy while she was busy slicing and dicing an egg, ham, and potato omelet, he playfully quipped, "Hey, you remembered. Maybe we'll get along after all."

Sharon shot a return volley aimed to inject some humor and lighten up the atmosphere, "It's certainly an impressive beginning. Seeing how food's so important to you."

Placing the cloth napkin in his lap, the detective retaliated, "You have potential, Murphy. God forbid I should find myself fond of your company. Anything is possible, I suppose."

Determined to maintain some semblance of combativeness, she launched another salvo, "Kinstley, you have such a tender way of putting things. Makes a girl really feel appreciated."

"A girl? You're a girl? Ha! Ha! To me you're a police detective. Like me, I'm just a police detective. There's no time to be a man or a woman," Mike answered, wiping his mouth with a napkin to hide an admiring grin.

"You will need to change your approach if you want me to throw myself at you."

Embattle from the onslaught of exchanges, Kinstley surrendered, saying, "Somehow, this conversation needs a more meaningful direction. So, what made you become a police officer? Why law enforcement? Huh? You're no bigger than a minute. Geez, with your looks you could have made a ton of money modeling or pole dancing at a high-class gentlemen's club. It'd be a lot safer."

Caught off guard by his sudden switch, she responded, "Wow, did you change gears!"

"You bet I did. I'm puzzled," he replied looking down at his plate while chomping on a mouthful of hashbrowns and stabbing his fork into a bite of pancakes and sausage.

Mortified at the thought of disclosing a lifetime of hidden hurt to someone seemingly insensitive, was not the limb she was willing to climb out upon with such weak reassurance that her confidence would not be betrayed. After a moment of reflection, she faintly pushed back, "My, you sure can put away the food quickly. I've never seen it done quite like that…Kinstley; it's not something I've related to anyone. Besides, it'd just bore you."

Not so much as slowing down the consumption process nor looking up, he encouraged, “Sharon, I would not have asked you, if I was afraid of being bored to tears. So, try me.”

Reluctantly showing signs of conceding, she hinted, “It hurts. Most people’s attention span and caring range does not exceed twenty-five words or seventeen seconds. I’m not much for watching someone yawn while I spill my guts; especially someone like you. No offense.”

He dropped his fork on the plate and looked up, bewildered. Choking on some food he had not quite swallowed, the hardnosed detective asked in earnest, “Someone like me? What does that mean?”

“You are not exactly a sensitive kind of guy it seems, when dealing with anyone. I guess all the years of tracking down perverted criminals have hardened you. Maybe I’ll become the same way someday. I certainly hope not.”

After a momentary loss for words, the veteran detective looked into her eyes sincerely and offered, “Look, I’m sorry if I have been hard on you. I’m really not as insensitive as you may think. I just have a habit of keeping people at arm’s length. Please, hurt and all, long story, I’ll give you my undivided attention. I promise.” Further attempting to console her, he pledged, “Sharon, whatever you tell me will stay between the two of us. I am a lot of things to a lot of people, but I never break a promise.”

Convinced Mike was sincere, Sharon thought for a moment before revealing, “My father was a detective in San Antonio. Growing up, he gave most of his attention to my younger brother,

Frank. I guess he figured mom was who I was supposed to be with. When Frank died of leukemia my senior year in high school, dad became distant from both mom and me. I thought by majoring in criminal justice at Sam Houston State he'd take an interest, but I was wrong. So, I joined the police force with the idea that if I could become a detective, he would then bond with me; you know, talk shop. The loss of Frank was more than he could bear. The doctors said they could have saved Frank if they had gotten to him sooner. Dad blamed mom's obsession with her clothes designing business for not recognizing Frank's symptoms sooner."

She paused for a moment to gather her wits before continuing, "Alcohol abuse forced his early retirement from the force. He took his pension and disappeared. Never saw me become a detective. It's been eight years and no one knows where he is or even if he is alive. Mom died in a car crash three years ago. The two emergency room surgeons said mom wasn't hurt that bad, but she just didn't have the will to live. I can't tell you how much I just wanted to drink myself to death. Even hoped a bullet would find its way through my forehead. Still cry myself to sleep many nights. So, there you have my life story, Mr. Kinstley." She then took a drink from her water glass and stared out the window as though her mind was somewhere else.

Uncharacteristically solemn, Mike softly inquired, "Do you still want to check out?"

Tears beginning to stream down her cheeks, Sharon answered, "In honor of my father and mother, I want to be someone they can be proud of. My love for them – to keep their life from being in vain, I have chosen to be the best I can be in everything I do."

Overcome with empathy, he confessed, "Your story has deeply humbled me. I thought you were just another rich brat. I'm really and truly sorry I misjudged you."

Sniffling, she turned to face him, asking, "Does that mean our working relationship will be a real partnership?"

He nodded his head while looking directly into her eyes, confirming, "Yes it does. But also consider me your friend."

"Now you're going to make me cry more than I already am," she informed, wiping her tears with a napkin.

In an attempt to comfort her, he explained, "We're going to be connected at the hip, Murphy, for many years to come."

"So that's the plan, all of a sudden?" she asked, blowing her nose on a napkin.

"Yes. And while we're on such a high note, I'll take you home and pick you up in the morning. It'll save you a drive into the office." He then slid out from the booth and stood looking down at her.

She motioned for him to sit back down. "You didn't tell me about yourself. You heard my story, now I want to know yours, if we're going to be partners and friends."

Having stood up to grab their coats, he sat down again. "Murphy, there's not much to tell. My dad was a cop; ten years on the beat then another thirty-three as a detective. All right here in Houston. He and mom do a lot of traveling, and I pick his brain when we're not fishing or hunting. There you have it. Not too terribly interesting."

"Mike Kinstley, have you left out something? Or just don't want to be as honest with me as I was with you?"

Rolling his eyes and letting out a huge sigh, the detective hesitantly revealed, "Sarah ran off with her boss. She was an executive secretary to a Lymko chief officer. You know, the company that cheated its employees out of their pensions and 401Ks? He made her an offer I could not match. End of story." Picking up the check, he urged, "So, come on, let's go home. We have a busy day tomorrow, partner."

Sharon asked, while scooting out from her side of the booth, "We gonna work on catching tonight's wonder boy?"

After assisting his new-found friend slip into her coat, he informed, "We have to. The mayor's putting pressure on all the precincts to bring this guy to justice. Doesn't want his administration to look bad. Are you happy now?"

"Are you?"

"No. I'd like to meet this legendary hero and talk him into retiring before he gets caught," he admitted, nudging Sharon toward the door.

"I knew it! You don't want to catch him!"

Leaving a tip for the waitress, Mike further revealed his feelings, "He's accomplishing what I wish I could. There, I admitted it. So, let's not talk about this anymore."

Chapter 2

The Saturday morning sun poked through a small opening in the drapes covering the bedroom window at one side of Alex's king-size bed. Just as she rolled over to avoid the pesky rays, the phone rang. Frustrated, she thought out loud, "Can't get any sleep on Saturday morning. If it's not the sun, it's the phone. Gotta fix those drapes." Reaching toward the nightstand, she picked up the receiver and rolled over on her back answering, "This better be good."

On the other end of the line a voice asked, "What if it's not?" It was Farley Fontenot, a fellow history teacher at Centennial High School. Farley was Alex's self-appointed mentor, being it was her first year of experience at an impoverished inner-city school in Houston, Texas.

"Oh, hi Farley. Sorry. I haven't had much sleep."

"It's noon. How much sleep do you need? Anyway, I called about three times last night but got only as far as your answering machine."

Stalling for a moment to conjure up an explanation for her whereabouts, she petitioned, "You got my answering machine? Is that what you said?"

An attempt at being facetious, he countered, "Yes ma'am, I think that's what I said. One of us can't hear too good, I'm afraid."

Gathering her wits, Alex explained, "I turned off the ringer. Had a bunch of research papers to grade. Still not through."

"What a shame. I had a bottle of wine begging for CPR. Wanna try tonight?"

Through a deep yawn, she replied, "Let me call you later. I need to wake up and get my bearings. I wouldn't mind doing something, so I'll call you in a couple of hours. Sorry again about last night."

"Hey, you'll love this: Captain America struck again. He put the big hurt on four of our finer citizens who had been a reigning terror for several months on the elderly in the Gulf Gate area. My friend at the Post, Buddy Hodges, says his boss actually doesn't care if they ever catch him; this guy sells newspapers. In case you don't know, Buddy is a renowned investigative reporter."

Alex feigned ignorance asking, "What are you talking about? Who's this Captain America? I haven't kept up with the news lately."

Steadily spinning a basketball on his index finger, Farley leaned back in his chair and placed both feet in cross-over fashion on top of a roll-top desk. Astonished at her lack of knowledge concerning this vigilante's exploits, he informed, "The guy has been elevated to folk hero status. The mayor wants him brought to justice before he makes fools of everyone. Does all his work under the cover of night. He's really legendary for protecting senior citizens who depend on their social security checks. When the dude guesses correctly where the bandits will strike, he leaves the perpetrators lying in a pile crying while licking their wounds. Once the police arrive, they simply call for the ambulances. So far, this incredible masked man has managed to spare the lives of all the desperadoes."

Continuing to probe, she asked, "Why is he so difficult to apprehend? Is he magical?"

"According to Buddy, his license plate is always different, and the car is never the same color. This means law enforcement can't look out for him in advance. Not to mention the car's unbelievably fast, and his driving skills are unparalleled. Also, for your information, few people know Hodges is an ex-Oklahoma City police detective."

While glancing at the clock on the dresser, Alex advised, "Well, let me go, so I can start waking up. I promise I'll call you in a couple of hours. I assume you'll be at home?"

"You are quite correct."

"Good, so let me go."

"Alex, I just had a thought."

Exasperated, her eyes rolled, and her head shook side-to-side while asking, "What?"

"Meet me at the Cadillac Bar & Grill in Kemah. Four hours. Don't keep me waiting. I'll be outside on the top deck sitting at a table as near the water as I can find."

"OK. OK. Let me go so I don't keep you waiting." Replacing the phone on the cradle, she sat up on the side of the bed, mumbling, "I am so not in the mood for this. Oh well, it might be interesting to hear more about my own exploits. Maybe find out some useful police information."

No sooner had she reached the kitchen and pulled a canister of Dave Draper's famous Bomber Blend protein from the pantry, there was a knock at the back door. Peeking around the corner, she recognized her best friend, Laura Reynolds. "Come in, it's not locked."

Opening the door and stepping inside, Laura announced, "Have you seen today's paper? You made the front page, girl. Someone, somehow snapped a picture of you standing over one of the guys you shot. That special suit makes you look really muscular. I'll bet it makes you look thirty pounds heavier. No wonder they think you're a man."

"Let me see," insisted Alex as she set the protein canister on the counter and reached for the paper. "This is scary. Who could have taken that shot? I can't feature any of the old folks bothering to carry a camera with them to the scene…I've never had my picture taken before."

Laura advised, "I'd be afraid to think how close that person might have been to enable his taking this shot."

Continuing to stare at the picture, Alex remarked, "Yeah, the picture was shot from behind me. Kinda eerie."

"You still don't drink coffee?" Asked Laura out of frustration after picking up an empty coffee pot.

The question fell on deaf ears as Alex was too engrossed in the newspaper article about her heroics the night before.

Rummaging through the cabinet above the coffee maker, Laura continued, "Oh, I guess you still only make it for Richard when he visits. I'm about to have a caffeine fit here…My God, you don't even have some coffee a girl could brew up for herself. Don't even propose one of those nasty protein shakes."

Still oblivious to Laura's babbling, Alex set aside the paper and offered, "I'll make you a protein shake if you like. I'm going to make me one right now."

"Thanks, but no thanks," she answered, while rolling her eyes.

After dropping the ingredients of her protein concoction into the awaiting blender, Alex jokingly mused, "In case you ever want to make yourself one, I use Bomber Blend, one banana, frozen strawberries, ground flax seed, dark chocolate cocoa, honey and milk. Bear with me while I turn on this loud mixer."

Laura took a seat at the table and advised, "Alexandria, we've been best friends since the third grade. As the only person besides your uncle Richard who knows your other identity, I truly believe it's time for you to quit this stuff here."

Alex turned off the blender and poured the contents into a glass. Taking a seat on the other side of the table, she asked while sipping from her drink, "You did not come over here just to tell me that - did you?"

Embarrassed, Laura let her head fall straight back and stared up at the ceiling confessing, "For heaven's sake, Alexandria, I'm a hypocrite. In one breath I'm telling you to quit this action stuff you do, and in another I'm going to ask you to do your thing at least one more time…I can't believe I came over here to ask this of you. I'm so ashamed."

Alex leaned back, crossed her legs and urged, "Out with it girl. The anticipation is killing me."

Elbows on the table and both hands now cupping her face, she explained, "We have trouble at the center. It began about two weeks ago. Four guys looking like gangsters put together by an affirmative action committee, cruise out front terrifying the girls as they stroll along the sidewalk. A couple of guys from the Center, who started accompanying the girls along the way, were found beat to a pulp. They could not identify the attackers, but said they drive a dark blue Mercedes Benz, and to make matters worse, police say they have to catch the creeps in the act. There's no law against their cruising around the center. Many kids have stopped coming for fear they'll be next."

In an effort to console her friend, Alex reached out and gently touched Laura on the arm, explaining, "I'm so sorry. I've been completely covered up in activities at school the past several weeks, and I've neglected my work for you at the center…I'll take care of this, I assure you. You'll never see those dirt bags again."

Looking up at her beloved friend, Laura confided, "I didn't know who else to turn to…"

"You came to the right place. What are friends for? This is what I do, protect those in need. However, I must go get ready so I can meet Farley Fontenot for an early dinner. I've got two and a half hours to make my presence at the Cadillac Bar and Grill in Kemah."

"How's that relationship shaping up, if you don't mind my asking?"

Ambling toward the sink to rinse out her glass and the blender, Alex revealed, "It's OK. Nothing special. He's a great guy, good looking, smart, kind and considerate. He's got it all."

Laura rose to her feet, slid the chair in its place under the table and proclaimed, "But he's not Mike Koehl, right? Alex, no one will ever be Mike. You have to find a way to let go for your sake. I'd take that Farley guy in a minute. He has character and is as honest as the day is long. I could really learn to love that guy. But he wants you."

Alex gave some thought to that and said, "Maybe someday. I do like him a lot, but I must go upstairs and get ready. Thanks for coming over. I really do cherish our friendship. You and Richard are all I have. Please know that."

Heading toward the door, Laura informed, "I feel the same way about you. I can't thank you enough for offering your help with those hoodlums. …Alex, there's a high school kid that comes to the Center and works with the younger ones on various physical fitness skills. You may know him; his name is Johnnie Wimbush. He's an all-state, all-world basketball player for Centennial. The kid lives with his grandfather, who has been a wonderful influence on him. I wish you would somehow add to that. A rather large gang of thugs is putting pressure on him to quit school. Lord, Alex, the boy has scholarship offers from Duke, North Carolina, Villanova, and Syracuse, to name of few. His neighborhood, however, lives in fear of this bunch who calls themselves the

Grimm Reapers. Seems he'll need to help his grandfather pay for protection."

Grabbing Laura's hand, she shouts, "Wait a minute! Did you say this gang calls themselves the Grimm Reapers? For real?"

"Yes, why?"

"That's the name of the gang who killed my parents! I've been searching for them ever since that night. You bet I'll talk to that kid! He's one of my students. I even love basketball, so we'll have a lot in common."

Sighing, Laura thankfully said, "You are so wonderful. I'll let you go now so you can get ready for your dinner date."

The Cadillac Bar & Grill was one of many upscale restaurants comprising a portion of the Kemah Boardwalk. The establishments were laid out side-by-side with a deck extending out over the water. Numerous shops selling jewelry, clothes, and accessories to go along with a hotel and theme park dot the landscape. Several restaurants present live bands, and the grounds, sculptured to an immaculate tropical setting, have several outdoor stages where music groups also entertain.

Alex made her way up the stairs to a wooden deck overlooking the waterway leading out to the bay from Clear Lake. Lined against the railing at the water's edge were several tables, one which Farley occupied in the far right-hand corner. Seeing him waving his arms back and forth, she weaved her way between the other tables en route to the cozy little spot.

Taking a seat across from Farley, she commented, “Well, I’m a little ahead of time. Does that surprise you? Why did you choose such a remote table?”

Pointing in the direction of a cluster of sailboats, he explained, “It has the best view of the setting. Besides, it is the most isolated. We can converse without anyone being able to hear what we’re talking about. You know, some chance to be more intimate.”

“I didn’t know we shared anything that’s so private,” she countered, attempting to hold back a face-stretching grin.

“Well, if I could get a chance to see you more, maybe our relationship would evolve enough to have some more intimate things to talk about.”

Alex winked and offered a slight ray of hope. “Don’t give up; you never know what might develop.”

Farley chuckled before commenting, “You know, if I didn’t know better, I’d say you were married once, and it was not a very good experience. But I’m not going to ask at this point. Someday, I just hope to see a softer more compassionate side of you I’m certain resides way down deep inside.”

Placing a napkin in her lap, she hinted, “You might just see that side someday…So tell me more about this mysterious nighttime man of justice.”

At that point, a waitress approached and distributed two menus. She placed a basket of tortilla chips in the center of the table and asked if they wanted to order something to drink while looking at the menu. Farley chose a frozen Margarita and Alex picked a Pina Colada.

Clutching a few huge corn tortilla chips from the basket, Farley informed, "Not much to tell that I haven't already. A trap was set last night in a neighborhood near Gulf Gate where the police thought he might be on that particular payday. It's a government housing project for those on disability and others who exist solely on social security. He hadn't been to that locale, so it seemed right. The police were four blocks away, and he drove right by four patrol cars on his way out. Two black and whites reversed their direction and gave chase, but had to radio ahead for assistance. Two State Troopers picked up the call and had him in sight but lost him somewhere on 59 South heading toward Wharton. They claimed he just vanished into thin air. Everyone thinks he must be holding up somewhere in that area, so the search is on. To date, that was the closest the police have come to nabbing him."

Reaching for a chip and dipping it in picante sauce, she continued to probe, "What are you going to do next? Investigate on your own?"

"I'm going to look over this menu and decide what I might like to eat. Why don't you do the same? People talk better on a full stomach. I read that somewhere. To answer your question, I am out of that business. It's just fun to keep up with his activities. I do have a theory the masked man might be a woman."

"Gee, now I'm really beginning to become interested in this guy!"

Scanning the menu, he said, "You can't be all that interested. Why don't we talk about you and me and my chances of breaking down that wall you have erected? For two months now we've managed to solve the world's economic, social, and political woes during our lunch period. We've even attempted to change the weather."

"What then would we say or talk about?"

Looking up from the menu and focusing on Alex, Farley suggested, "What's your favorite song for instance? What kind of music do you like? Do you like movies, and what kind? What sort of things do you like to do? You know, the really complicated subjects too deep to cover in one night."

Alex placed the menu face down and glared back at Farley, saying, "Well, let's see. My favorite song is 'Talk to Me' by Sunny and the Sunglows. Little Willie John also sang the song. In fact, he recorded it in 1958, two or three years before the Sunglows. My favorite music is the old 'Doo Whop' of the early 50s, along with the original Rock' n Roll. The only group I go see now is Johnny Dee and the Rocket 88s. They play that stuff so good, it's like I'm back in the 50s again. And Johnny Dee has the most awesome voice with unbelievable range. He sings Elvis and Louis Armstrong as good as they sang. I go see the band every chance I get. They make me feel alive again. When the 88s retire, a piece of my life will go with them."

Slamming his menu on the table, he abruptly announced, "That's it! Our first real date will be a night of dancing to Johnny Dee and the Rocket 88s. Name the time and place."

"OK, Mr. Fontenot," she replied, looking into his eyes searching for sincerity. "But I hope you like that kind of music. You can take me to Burnet, Texas for the Bluebonnet Festival. They play in the town square Saturday night, April 8th. Today is February 3rd, which leaves you a little over two months to find us two rooms."

"Consider it done. This does mean we will be in the same car? Just the two of us?"

"Of course. Separate rooms don't chase you away? It has all the others."

Taking a large swig of his margarita, Farley revealed, "I'm not all the others, I'll have you know. Besides, I don't really care to sleep with someone until I decide if I like them. That may sound corny or fake, but that's me. I have to like someone, and to do that, I have to get to know them."

"Well, how many dozen or so have you liked?" She asked while reaching for another chip and taking a sip from her drink. "Surely they were able to, shall we say, connect without a marriage license."

Offended, Farley took a deep breath, stared directly into her eyes and said with conviction, "Marriage comes first, and I've only liked one enough to marry. Just one. If you think connecting is what I'm about, you can consider this my last intrusion on your precious time."

Shame and embarrassment raining down on her, Alex showed some compassion for the first time since they had met. "I'm sorry, I shouldn't be so tacky. You've been more than a gentleman. Perfect in fact."

Farley smiled and said, "Apology accepted."

Leaning forward with both elbows on the table while placing her chin in cupped hands, she looked into his eyes, quietly asking, "So tell me, Farley, what are you about? Where did you go to high school? What college did you attend? What do you do for fun? The usual questions on any application for a real date. Or shall I say, a real relationship."

Taken by surprise, he choked on some chips while responding, "Wow! You used the word relationship. I'm stunned. But somehow I feel this is just a cross-examination of some sort."

"It is," she laughed.

"Alright then," he granted, "I graduated from high school at Port Arthur Jefferson. Earned a degree in criminal justice from Sam Houston State. Quit sports my junior year in high school to spend more time learning how to sail. Wanted to race in big time regattas like my father. Dad owns Quantum Sails in Seabrook and travels all over the world racing and inspecting the factories that make the sails he sells. How's that for a tongue twister? It's a great life my father has. He's got more free time than I have right now. Certainly, more than when I was a detective. One of these days, I'll find a reason to accept my dad's offer to join his company and someday head it up. At 45 years old, I need to make a decision in the next year or two. I also love old muscle cars. Hope to have the time someday to restore one or two. Would love to go on those Hot Rod tours and nighttime cruises on Woodward Avenue in Michigan... Holy cow, listen to me. I didn't know I could talk this much. I better shut up."

Fashioning an admiring smile, she softly pleaded while reaching into the basket for another chip. "No, please, go on."

"I love to go to movies. Not much on shoot 'em ups and cars exploding. That happens every day here in Houston, so it's boring. Ha! I loved *North to Alaska, Smokey and the Bandit,* and the *Rocky* movies. I like just about all love stories…So there, you have it."

Gazing at his upper torso, she commented, "Looks like you lift weights. Would I be wrong?"

"No, you're not wrong. You've just now noticed? Wow! I'm 5'8" and weigh one ninety-five."

"I'm kinda hungry now. What do you say, we order?"

"I'm for that," he agreed while signaling to their waitress. "I'd almost forgotten we hadn't."

The two spoke very little while picking over their food. Alex had blackened red snapper and Farley favored the beef fajitas plate. Taking a sip from his drink, he asked, "Have you ever had someone special? You claim two rooms always chased away the guys. Surely one somewhere along the way was special."

Wiping her lips with a napkin, Alex laughed before lying, "No. I've never spent any appreciative time with someone I could even trust. I'll admit the jury is still out on you."

Taking another sip from his drink, Farley nodded saying, "I don't quite follow the humor, but I guess that is some sort of encouragement."

"Who was that one you once liked?" Alex inquired while slicing off a piece of fish. "What happened? Or should I mind my own business?"

"No. That's quite alright…Her name was Ramona Poole. The last time I saw her was two days after our high school graduation dance." Staring past Alex but not focusing on anything in particular, he said with a somber tone, "She informed me she was moving to some place in Africa with her parents. Some kind of missionary work. Neither of us saw it coming. Her parents didn't want to ruin graduation ceremonies or the dance that night, so they didn't tell her until the day after. Ramona couldn't stop crying. I managed to pull myself together for her sake. Told her not to worry, that I'd find her when the time was right. Promised her as a mater-of-fact. Went home and cried a river…She and her parents were killed in some sort of uprising before summer was over. The only way I found out was from her aunt who seemed to like me."

Overcome with empathy, Alex could hardly speak. "I'm sorry. You must have really loved her. Just seems there's no justice anywhere."

"There's a reason for everything, Alex, whether we like it or not. That's our only comfort. It may take years to discover the reasons. Who knows what kind of woman she might have become, or for that matter, what kind of couple we would have evolved into. Young couples must grow together in the same direction or the union perishes. In the long run, we may not have been a good match. It's a long way from young love to adulthood and marriage."

"Is that how you reconciled closure?"

"I haven't reconciled anything. Ramona's dead and there's nothing going to bring her back."

Sticking her fork into some broccoli and assorted vegetables, Alex posed a question. "What if by some miracle she could be brought back?"

Farley glanced at some sailboats passing by before saying, "She'd have to come back as that same eighteen-year-old girl I knew, and somehow I'd have to be transformed into that eighteen-year-old boy she knew. And that ain't happening."

"But what if that were possible? Would you do it?"

He looked into her eyes and answered with conviction, "Without hesitation."

Looking down at her drink while stirring it with the tiny straw, Alex mumbled, "At least you're honest. There's something to be said for that." Another dish of humility sorely needed.

Before she had much time to mull over the surprising disappointment, Farley countered, "Tell me about your one guy. I know you had one, it's written all over your persona...Did I say that right?"

With much reluctance, she confessed while continuing to stir her drink. "Mike Koehl. He was killed in a car wreck the night of our high school graduation. It's an understatement to say I've never gotten over him. I also can't believe I've related this to you. I've never told anyone. Only my Uncle Richard and lifelong friend Laura Reynolds know this."

"If he came back today, would you pick back up where you left off?" Farley asked, holding his breath.

With unyielding conviction, she too answered, "Without hesitation."

Attempting to lighten the mood, Farley laughed, saying, "We have more in common than I thought. We could build on this. What do you think?"

"I think we'd each be just second best. Rebounds are good in basketball, but not in relationships."

Farley gulped down the last of his margarita and placed the glass firmly on the table and proclaimed, "That old saying about it's better to have loved and lost than never to have loved at all is a bunch of B.S. if you ask me."

Smirking, Alex added, "Whoever said that probably never found anyone to love. So how would he know about any of that?"

Farley thought for a moment before disclosing, "So I guess the real problem is finding someone else to love who can love you back. Wouldn't you say?"

"Maybe we all should just love our work so we don't have to face losing again, either by death or divorce."

"Our work won't love us back. It won't be the smiling face that cheers us up when we're down. It won't embrace us, when we need a certain loving touch. It won't put the toilet paper on the holder when we need it most, nor will it share anything with us. And it certainly won't know what we want for Christmas."

Gazing past Farley, Alex took a long sip from her Pina Colada before saying, "Touché."

Chapter 3

Monday morning Alex addressed her first period American History class. Sitting behind her desk, she informed, "This week we will be focusing on current events in America. That's not exactly related to where we are in our text, but I occasionally like to see where my students are in terms of at least keeping up with what's impacting the news. You're old enough to begin forming opinions, so that when the day comes for you to vote, you can do so as a somewhat informed individual. Looking around the room, she asked, "Anyone want to start a discussion or voice a concern about something current?"

Silence pervaded until a student earnestly related, "The Lymko Corporation lay-offs and pension cutting. My mom's best friend worked there twenty-three years and was two years from retirement. She was laid off and lost her pension. The year before, she lost her husband to cancer. It took all the life insurance money to pay his medical bills and bury him. She has nothing and no one will hire a 60-year-old woman. Yet the corporate chiefs took millions in bonuses."

Inspired, another student blurted out, "How about the airline company that cut wages and benefits to supposedly stay out of Chapter 11, and yet their top executives took bonuses in the millions? People's lives are being ruined and yet executives are being rewarded beyond belief."

"Your names are Sarah Hill and Sue Staton, are they not?" asked Alex gazing down her roll sheet. "I'm still trying to learn your names. I don't usually have courses that begin in the spring. Besides, you haven't said much until now. ...So, class, what do the rest of you think about these types of corporate actions? Here's a thought for you to contemplate: In a slight stretch of the imagination, could these corporate leaders be considered 'traitors' to the welfare of our nation?"

Jose Gonzales spoke out vehemently, "We need another revolution like 1776. The big guys are getting rich off the little guy's sweat and blood. I can see us being a third world country someday at this rate. I guarantee you, our forefathers would not have done this."

Honor student Chuck Gooden sounded off, "I don't believe in 'give-aways'; people should work to better themselves. I believe in capitalism, because it's the only system in the world that works. It gives people the opportunity to explore individual initiative. There's nothing wrong with a person becoming wealthy from hard earnest work; honest work. Those guys pay the bills and take the financial risks. But their lack of character, coupled with oppressive strategies, make for third-world poverty and the disappearance of democracy and ultimately the demise of individual initiative."

Mike Stillwell stood and proclaimed, "They'll have to take our guns first. Once they collect all the weapons, we're finished. The next step is to keep our children from learning to read and write. An unarmed illiterate people will be hard-pressed to do anything but acquiesce. The Soviet Union made a huge mistake allowing select university students read western books."

Surprised by their sudden eruption, Alex sensed the grossly excessive compensation for corporate executives had hit a chord. "Sounds like you feel these corporate leaders are truly 'traitors.' What can the rest of us do to prevent their betrayal, if anything?

Scott Barton, a burly 6'4" 270-pound All-State offensive lineman on the football team, stood up to make an announcement. "Paul Getty, the CEO for Lymko, is having dinner and a meeting with his lawyers at the Benihana Restaurant tonight. He's rented the whole place so they can have privacy and get the royal treatment. I'd love to see someone put a slug in his forehead."

Leaving her seat and maneuvering around to the front of the large wooden desk, she counsels, "Isn't one of the things that separates our nation from the many others is our non-violent system of justice and the changing of regimes? Would executing people before their day in court be a good way of handling those charged with crimes? Isn't that similar to lynching? Wouldn't Stalin and Hitler be examples of such an approach?"

Dexter Hill tossed a new ingredient into the mix. "How else would you remove Hitler or Stalin in an effort to save the world?

In this case, to save America, a nation in danger of being bought out or in an uglier term, sold down the river? You don't want us complacent, but you don't want us to take action either. What do we do to get the attention of both the judiciary system and those that own it?"

"Dexter, your point is well taken," advised Alex, now sitting on the front edge of her desk. "Can anybody answer that? There is one other important consideration in my mind. What would God have us do?"

Dexter fired back, "Jesus committed the ultimate act of defiance against the Jewish leaders. He refused to deny his heritage even at the cost of a horrendous beating and crucifixion on the cross. He made them commit the unpardonable sin, which leads to eternal death. So, you might say they were dealt the death penalty indirectly by Jesus for their sin."

Mike Vincent questioned, "So apply that to us today. What do we do, Dexter? And by the way, for your information, you could get expelled from school along with Miss McCord for talking about God, or even referring to him."

Laughing while interrupting, Barton revealed, "I don't want that huge a production. I just want to put a bullet in their foreheads as a warning to the rest of 'em who want to be oppressive. It'll work. You may buy your way out of punishment from the system, but you can't buy your way around my plans for your filthy corrupt self. As a nation, we need to deliver that message."

As the class bell rang, Alex exclaimed, "This is the best discussion in a class of mine since I've been teaching here. Let's have this carry over. See you tomorrow."

Upon entering the faculty lounge at lunch time, Alex spotted the dynamic trio of Jerry Walker, Jack Klam and Ed Hughes sitting around a large octagonal table. Walker, entering his second year as the head baseball coach and history teacher, was a former Major League Baseball pitcher who prematurely retired due to an injury and a sure bet to enter the Hall of Fame. Klam, an advanced math teacher who played Major League Baseball for a short time, voluntarily helps coach the baseball team. Hughes, whose father pitched in the Big Leagues for the old Brooklyn Dodgers in the 50s, is a small black man with a wealth of baseball savvy. As Walker's assistant, he's being groomed to become the head coach. During the previous 13 years, none of the other coaches allowed Ed to do anything but take care of the field and the players' laundry. Walker elevated him to assistant coach with specific duties of working with infielders and making the game lineups. It was a dream come true for Hughes. The team went to the play-offs last year and was ranked in the top ten in the greater Houston area.

Approaching their table, she addressed Jack, whom she maintains an ongoing ritual of exchanging fun-poking remarks, "May I sit down?"

Jack, reading the sports section of the newspaper, looked up saying, "Might as well be invaded by a pretty history teacher versus some boring accounting instructor."

Pulling a chair away from underneath the table and taking a seat, she quipped, "You're really funny, Jack. Not bad for a narrow-minded math teacher."

"Hey, I only teach the advanced math courses. You know, geometry, trig, calculus. You, on the other hand, deal with the middle-class side of the spectrum; American and World History. Those are courses all students must take. Very few are capable in my arena. It's for the elite."

Sliding her chair closer to the table, Alex retaliated, "If you're so elite, why are you teaching at this impoverished school in a room two doors down from mine?"

"I consider this missionary work. My sacrifice for the good of mankind," he added while preparing to take a bite from a grilled cheese sandwich he purchased in the school cafeteria.

Alex confessed sarcastically, "No wonder my heart palpitates when I'm in your royal presence. It's a wonder there's not a statue of you beside the flagpole. Maybe it should have you nailed to a cross for such a noble sacrifice."

Laying his sandwich on the table, Jack finished swallowing a huge bite and surrendered, "I believe you out did me this time. I hope you'll give me a rematch."

"I'm stunned a man of your caliber would give in so easily."

"I must confess the mouth best serves my interests when it allows food to go down the throat to the stomach."

Walker pushed aside the list of students in the baseball program to change the subject of discussion. "Alex, would you like to co-chair the committee for inspiring students to better understand and appreciate our heritage?"

"Gee, I'd love to. This is the first I've heard of such."

"I'm trying to work out the details with our new principal, Dr. Long. I'll get with you when something materializes. Ed's going to help if I can get his head out of that book he's reading about baseball's great managers."

Ed spoke not a word, but kept reading, while continually reaching for pieces of grilled chicken his wife, Sandra, had prepared the night before. Only a slightly hidden grin indicated he might have heard the mention of his name.

Alex informed, "It's funny how you bring this up now. My first period class is extremely interested in our heritage. They're not liking the direction the country is heading. They're afraid it's becoming an elitist society that will at some point become something similar to a third world regime of the rich and the poor. Rape of our nation's companies by top executives has them agitated. Namely the Lymko Corporation and the airlines cases." She then proceeded to remove the lid to a canister holding a protein shake she brought from home.

Jack chimed in, "What about that tool company located in a small Massachusetts town that moved to Arizona to increase profits. They had been making money forever, and practically speaking, everyone in town was employed there. So instead of being satisfied with making a good profit, they moved to Arizona and paid the employees on the average $6,000 a year less while leaving the town in Massachusetts to dry up. No conscience."

Jerry added, "Are you surprised? The people running our corporations are the same ones who promoted 'me, myself and I' in the late sixties and early seventies. They have no loyalty except to themselves. Such a culture ultimately will not survive. I sadly must confess it's my generation. We need a peaceful revolution."

Alex perked up asking, "How would you like to put together a dissertation on the subject of a much-needed peaceful revolution and present it to my first period class so they can digest it and ask questions? It might be a dynamite session. Thought provoking, to say the least. What do you say?"

"I'm sorry, but you won't be able to reel me into yours and Klam's cult-like shootout club. I'm not biting."

After drinking the last of her protein shake, she explained, "No, that's not it at all. I'm serious. I'd love for you to prepare an argument for a peaceful revolution. My class would enjoy it immensely. Could drum up some good discussion."

"I'm flattered, but baseball has me stretched over a rainbow. Graduation depleted our team, and the three of us are having to coach more than manage…I'll give it some thought, though. Might actually be fun."

Snapping the lid on her container and placing it in a satchel, Alex said, "I'm going to keep the invitation open." Glancing at her watch, she informed, "Lunch is over, so I'll see you good ole boys later." She stood, pushed the chair under the table, and marched out of the lounge into the hall.

No sooner had she departed, Jack remarked, "I wish I could get to first base with that girl."

Ed finally broke silence with a cunning remark, "Gotta step up to the plate first."

After school, Alex immediately called Richard to check on the car. "Richard, is the paint dry enough to make a run tonight?"

Dragging the phone into the paint booth, he replied, "Barely. I can't believe you're ready for another adventure so soon. What's the occasion?"

Leaning against the kitchen wall where the phone was mounted, Alex revealed, "I'm going after Paul Getty to deliver a message. Somehow a student of mine found out he'd be at Benihana's tonight. That pompous jerk wanted some privacy, so he rented the entire place. I'll be outside waiting for him."

"You've got to have a death wish to keep this up," Richard said, closing the door to the paint booth so the paint could finish baking.

"I'm going to get in a quick workout and head for the hangar to get the car. You don't have to be there this time. I'll carry the remotes. I already ask too much of you."

Turning up the heaters, Unc informed, "I'll be here in case the pieces need picking up." Then pleading, he added, "But after tonight, please give it and myself a little time off."

"I've not been pumped up like this in a long time, Richard. You should have heard my students' displeasure with those warts. It's the hand of justice for Getty tonight."

Paul Getty, the top executive for Lymko, exited the Benihana Restaurant after a lengthy meeting with his team of lawyers in an effort to defend his corporate actions to the media. The man's facial expression reeked with a pompous smirk and his swagger exuded confidence, the cock of the walk. Owning the best legal department money could buy, he expounded, "The world is right again, because the natural order of things is falling back into place; the haves have and the have-nots have nothing. The have-nots were simply casualties of a system where the superior eventually have everything. Nature's survival of the wealthiest is both confirmed and justified; nothing personal, just business. I'll tell you, fellas, this is what America's about. It's what makes this such a great place to live, don't you think?"

Strolling along the sidewalk, he turned to his eight-man corporate law entourage saying, "Those disenfranchised hearts don't realize big business is for those who work to get to the top. They should feel lucky to have a job. In fact, not only are we not responsible for their retirement, they're lucky we pay them a decent wage. Other countries' labor forces don't have half the standard of living these chumps do."

One of Getty's attorneys quipped, "We're taking some real heat over the pensions being eliminated. The huge lay-off was bad enough. All of this came on the heels of the bonuses and salary increases for you and the others. It'll be next to impossible to smooth that over with the media."

Irked at his attorney's remark, Getty reminded, "That's what I pay you guys for. The system will absorb those we laid off. They'll find some kind of job. They're like insects, they'll adjust. They'll just keep making baby insects to insure a labor force." Laughing he added, "In fact, we shall refer to the insect fetus as a janitor in a drum. Ha!"

"Just stay away from the press. Let us handle your statements," yet another attorney advised.

"Who cares?" replied Getty. "The day is coming when their children will be forced to work beside their parents because public education will cease to exist. It'll be easy to manipulate the poor and illiterate. Along with that will come pay cuts. Those are cruel hard facts, and I'll do my best to take advantage."

Suddenly, one of the younger attorneys in the group yelled out, "You can count me out! I can't believe I went to law school under the symbol of the balanced scales of justice to work for the ends of a douche bag like you and your fraternity brothers! I'm out of here, and I hope they string up guys like you! I'll catch a cab."

The rest of the entourage stopped in their tracks as Getty turned and screamed, "That's just as well! You're gutless! A weakling sticking up for the scum!" Addressing the remaining team of lawyers, he pronounced, "He'll never amount to anything. Anyone else want to leave, go now. I can get a dozen more tomorrow who know what Capitalism is all about. I thought they teach you guys to get all you can at any cost – at least in the Ivy League where he came from."

No one else muttered a word as they continued their walk toward Getty's new Mercedes Benz limousine, parked on the next block.

The CEO, walking on the outside nearest the street, suddenly became aware of a white slow-rolling Dodge Challenger to his right. Without looking over his shoulder, he quietly alerted the others to pick up the pace. The Dodge kept abreast; leaving little doubt in their minds they were being stalked. The limo was sitting approximately 90 feet away, just the other side of the crosswalk. Hearts racing, all eight men broke into a panic sprint toward the crosswalk. The stalker followed in taunting fashion.

Leaping from the curb, all the power brokers were certain trouble was about to be avoided. But with the far curb out of reach, the Challenger made a hard left, blocking their path. Immediately, the window slid down and a pump shotgun emerged from inside. An electronic voice commanded, "Stay where you are, or they'll be picking up your body parts all over the street. So, listen carefully."

While his attorneys were trembling hysterically and backing away for their own safety, Getty feigned some courage, interrupting, "What does a punk like you want? Why don't you take off that mask?"

The Darth Vader-like voice commanded, "Resign and give back employee bonuses. Have your cronies do the same. Also, rehire those you laid off and restore the pensions."

Abhorred, Getty shouted in anger, "You're out of your mind! Everything I have I'm entitled to! They just have to face being casualties of big business!" Calming down, he added, "Nothing personal."

Before Getty could exhale the last syllable, he heard the universally terrifying sound of a shotgun chambering a slug. Seconds later he heard another horrifying sound as he was knocked to the ground while screaming in pain. The others sank to their knees crying and begging for lenience.

The driver exited the car and chambered another shot.

Standing over Getty while the man grabbed his left knee crying, the night-time administrator of justice warned, "You'll either do as I instructed or you will not be able to enjoy the fruits of your despicable ways. It was rock salt this time. Next time you won't be so lucky. Tell your other officers they too will be dealt with in the same manner. I have no patience, so you have one week to make the announcement on TV and in the local papers. One week is all you have. The police cannot save you."

Turning his attention to the other five, the masked marvel warned, "I'm holding you equally responsible for his carrying out this command. Fail, and you seven will face the same judgment."

Crying out, Getty pleaded, "Who are you?"

Placing the shotgun barrel on the CEO's forehead, the masked marauder informed, "A Monster." And he slipped back into the car and disappeared down the street, leaving Getty yelling for his associates to call for help.

Several minutes later, two black and whites, and an ambulance arrived on the scene, followed by detectives Kinstley and Murphy.

Addressing one of the paramedics who had been working on Getty, Kinstley asked, "How bad is he?"

"Not bad at all. Just some severe lacerations caused by rock salt."

Murphy asked Kinstley, "Is this another of wonder boy's work?"

Nudging his partner toward the ambulance tailgate where

Getty sat, the now patient detective said, "Let's ask our victim for a description."

Approaching Getty, Kinstley inquired, "Did you get a good look at the guy who did this to you? Did he say anything?"

Wincing in pain, Paul Getty replied, "He wore all black or blue leather with a mask. Didn't say anything."

Murphy chimed in, "Any prominent features?"

"He was about 5'9" and weighed maybe 195 pounds. Sleek muscular body."

Pulling Kinstley off to the side, Murphy asked sarcastically, "Tell me what this man's crime is?"

Placing both hands on his hips, he asked, "Ever heard of Paul Getty?"

"The Lymko guy?"

"Are you able to figure the crime now? Does it come together for you? Huh? Hold that thought." Nodding in the direction just off her right shoulder, Kinstley announced, "Here comes Buddy Hodges, the one and only ace investigative reporter for The Post."

Turning to look, she asked, "Where?"

"Behind you."

Hodges caught up with them and greeted, "Hey, Detective Kinstley." Staring at Murphy from behind, he informed, "I don't believe I know this young lady."

Pointing toward his female partner, Mike said, "Buddy, meet detective Murphy."

"Hi, detective Murphy," he said while ambling around from

behind to shake her hand.

Murphy simply nodded, not knowing what to think about the working or social relationship of her partner and the newspaper reporter.

Looking around, Hodges inquired, “Another piece of work by the Masked Marvel?”

“Definitely.” Laughing, Kinstley mused, “Getty looks real good sitting on the ambulance tailgate don’t you think?”

Buddy commented facetiously, “Might look even better flat on his back. Ha! Get a description of the car and its color?”

“White,” interjected Murphy. “That is according to Mr. Getty’s associates over there. None of whom were harmed.”

“And not a body shop in all the Houston area can ever remember painting the car,” added Hodges. “Wow.”

Kinstley noted, “We’ll probably be doing this exact same thing three more times.”

“Huh?” asked Murphy puzzled.

“Lymko has at least three other executives defending their actions.”

Laughing, Hodges revealed, “Maybe this guy will give ‘em what the legal system will not be able to.”

Kinstley remarked, “I wish he’d do it soon if that’s his goal. I can’t quite figure out why he spared Getty by using rock salt.”

Hodges answered, “Must be some form of warning. Probably wants Getty to resign. Wouldn’t doubt it if he wants Getty to give back all that bonus money. I’ll bet my career I’m close. What’d Getty say anyway?”

Kinstley smirked, “Claimed the assailant didn’t say a word. He’s lying.”

Hodges scanned the scene and informed, “Well, there’s no further reason for me to be here. Call me or keep me posted somehow. I’m outta here. Nice to meet you, detective Murphy.”

Mike looked at Murphy. “Come on, I’ll buy you some coffee or something. You look puzzled. This may be a little overwhelming for a pup.”

Shaking her head in dismay, she confessed, “I am totally lost here. This isn’t the way I expected investigations to be performed. I feel so useless. I signed on to catch the bad guys, and you and that newspaper guy simply laugh it off.”

Both hands in the pockets of his beige London Fog overcoat, Mike Kinstley spoke with a trace of compassion, “Come on, I’ll take you to Alfredo’s Diner. I’ll try to make some sense of this for you. We’ll call this part two of your training.”

Taking Murphy by the arm, he led her to the squad car and opened the passenger side door. “I’ve never held the door open anywhere for my past female partners. I’m not sure why I’m doing this for you, but consider this a compliment of some sort.”

Once at Alfredo’s, the two found a booth near a window facing the street. Kinstley always liked to eat next to a window. He hung his overcoat on a hanger near the front row of booths and helped Murphy remove her coat and hang it up.

Sitting across from the bewildered young female detective, Mike offered some encouragement. “Even after our heart-to-heart talk at Denny's, you still allow yourself to stress over this. Murphy, we can only do so much, so it's not good for you to fret over what you can't do."

Slumped in her seat, Sharon meekly replied, "Yes, you're quite correct. But right now, I just feel like I'm not doing my job. I'm not doing all I could."

The often-brusque veteran detective, showing the tenderness and understanding he promised, leaned across the table and put his hand on hers consoling, "We will catch him sooner or later. And when that time comes, it'll be a sad moment. So far, he's doing what we all wish we could do legally. I will also miss the hunt. He's not a bad guy, and this hunt is both fun and interesting. It's a welcome change of pace from hunting society's meanest, cruelest dregs. You have to have some humor or lightheartedness in your life."

Staring out the window, she revealed, "I just expected faster action with more intensity. This is my first case with you and it feels so laid back. Almost like no one wants to catch this guy."

"Murphy, the pressure is mounting more everyday on the Commissioner for us to bring this guy in. It's the media we have to thank for that. This do-good vigilante has the public singing his praises right now, but it's been my experience he'll fall out of favor, because he will begin to kill people instead of wounding them. He's going to kill an innocent person one of these days. Right now, he's making our work easy. But power corrupts. I want to catch him before he crosses the line. Don't worry, things will tighten up."

Continuing her gaze out the window at the activity taking place in the street and on the sidewalk, Murphy confessed, "I guess I haven't figured out how all this works at the subcultural level."

Handing her a menu, he said, "Order yourself some breakfast. I'm buying again. You are totally messing up my style, you know that don't you?"

Looking over the menu she mumbled, "Maybe I ought to do you a favor and go back where I came from."

Placing a napkin in his lap, Kinstley encouraged his partner, saying, "Murphy, you have a lot of savvy and energy. Someday you are going to be really special. You'll be sitting right here giving this same speech to your pup. It just takes time to know when and where to channel all that energy."

Continuing to flip through the menu, she asked, "So there's hope for me?"

"Without a doubt." After some introspection, Mike shook his head while reluctantly opening up his inner feelings, "I'm going to make a confession here. I chose you from four others. Your dad was a detective with an impeccable reputation. Your resume too is impressive. I love your work ethic, and your spunk wins me over. But you need to allow some of my lesser charming remarks and demeanor to roll off your back."

"I'll try, but…"

"There's no buts. Just toughen up and continue to be exactly who you are. But be alert to the ever-changing rules. For now, let me be your compass."

"Are we doing all we can to catch this stupid folk hero?"

"Yes. He's unbelievably talented with gobs of savvy. Truth is, if he doesn't increase his activity, we'll never catch him. Admittedly, I really do hope he lessens his activity and eventually quits. If that happens anytime soon, it won't be long before we'll be taken off the case and asked to solve something more conventional. The captain will put a new pair of faces on this chase if it drags out much longer."

Placing a napkin in her lap, Murphy revealed, "I must admit, that'll probably be a huge lift for me, to chase someone neither the public nor the media adore."

"Murphy, there's another reason I want to catch him...He's embarrassing me."

"Thanks, Kinstley, for the encouragement. I feel a little more comfortable knowing there's growing evidence you are human with the capabilities to be considerate. I'll try to let you keep the lead and just follow and grow."

Smiling while looking into her eyes, he said, "You're already improving your approach. Now let's order. I'm starving. By the way, please call me Mike in private."

Chapter 4

Alex, tail-feathers spread like a peacock in all their brilliant colors, pranced triumphantly down the runway toward her first period class basking in a glorious marquee performance from the night before. Just as she began acknowledging the standing ovation from the throng of adoring fans, Scott Barton swooped in behind her, seemingly out of nowhere, shouting, "Hey, Ms. McCord, have you read the morning Post?"

Swiftly she yanked in her feathers and swirled into a Kung Fu stance of the tiger, ready to strike a deadly blow.

Shaken by the suddenness of the lightning fast move and intimidated by the striking pose, Scott dropped his books while leaping backward. Arms crossed in front of his face, was the big guy's only other defensive maneuver.

Alexandria relaxed her position and gave a deep sigh of relief upon recognizing the perpetrator was simply one of her students. "Oh, Scott, you scared me. I was totally somewhere else."

The lad's pulse rate was off the chart, and his voice reverberated as he choked out, "Wow! What kind of move was that? I'm blown away." Stooping to gather his books, the hulking youngster added, “I never in a million years would have dreamed you were such a deadly killer. Where’d you learn that karate stuff?”

“It’s Kung Fu. The move is one of the Tiger…Saw it on television one time,” she explained while handing him a book she retrieved beside the water fountain. Hustling toward the classroom with Scott at her heels, she apologized, “Forgive me, Scott, I was a little jumpy. And to answer your question, no, I didn’t read the morning Post.”

Sporting a wide grin while towering over her, he related, “Last night that Marvel Comic Book character shot Paul Getty in the knee with rock salt. My guess is the guy threatened Getty’s life if he didn’t correct his wrongdoing. Ain’t that something? Man, I wish I had been the one who nailed that squid. Only I wouldn’t have used rock salt that’s for sure. Funny how we were discussing him in class yesterday, and the next thing you know, somebody busts him.”

As they approached the classroom door, she replied, “Yeah, sure is. Well, stranger things have happened, I’m sure.”

Puzzled, Scott asked while opening the door, “You don’t seem too impressed. Actually, you still seem preoccupied with something. Did you do it? Ha … Just kidding.”

Entering the room, she looked over her shoulder and said, “Thank you, Scott. And thanks so much for your concern.”

“Think nothing of it,” he replied, shaking his head out of confusion while weaving his way toward his assigned seat.

Alex sat on the front edge of her desk and addressed the

class. "Did any of you read the morning Post? Scott just informed me someone attacked Paul Getty last night." Chuckling to take the edge off her anxiety, she asked, "Was it one of you?"

Susan Gredvig remarked, "I'll bet it was that superman who goes all around the city rescuing people from criminals. My dad said they ought to pin a badge on him if they catch the guy."

Suddenly, from the back of the room came a resounding declaration. "I don't think it's a man. I'm almost certain it's a woman."

"Are you stupid?" shouted Chuck Gooden, trying to overcome the noise of the class cackling and snickering.

Karen Austin, undaunted by Chuck's remark amidst the class reaction, cleared her throat, taking time to savor the moment of undivided attention. When the laughter began to cease, she laughed out loud while shouting, "I think it's Ms. McCord!"

Except for Scott Barton, the class again began laughing and making fun of Karen's declaration. Alex noticed Scott was not joining in, so she felt a real need to quickly divert the discussion. "I hate to change the subject, but tomorrow we need to discuss some of The Federalist Papers. So, take your book home tonight and begin reading. Meanwhile, let's take up our discussion on current events."

As the class settled down and resumed discussing current events that directly affect them, prayer in school was a major issue. Interest and intensity took off like a runaway stagecoach until the dismissal bell, with the students filing out of the room while continuing the discussion. Many were still laughing at Karen Austin's seemingly foolish accusation concerning Ms. McCord being the masked marvel.

Preoccupied with her attack on Paul Getty, Alex marched toward an awaiting second period history class when suddenly someone grabbed her by the arm from behind. Startled, she turned and blurted out, "Farley! You scared me. I was in deep thought."

"I'm sorry, but I wanted to catch you early to ask if you'd meet or accompany me to the basketball game tonight. We're taking on our arch rival, Washington. It'd give you a chance to see one of your students play."

"I love basketball. Who's the student I have that plays?"

"Johnnie Wimbush. He's the Houston area leading scorer in the Five-A division. He also ranks fourth in rebounding and eleventh in assists. At six-foot seven, he can even bring the ball up court. So, you want to go?"

"Sure. I'll meet you at the entrance to the gym and pay your way."

Jubilant, Farley informed, "Great, but I'm paying; for both of us."

"Have it your way. What time?"

"Game starts at seven, so meet me at six-thirty."

"OK. I got to run to beat the bell. See you at lunch."

Skipping down the hall unable to contain a sweeping grin, Farley mumbled, "Maybe she's finally taking a liking to me." Looking over his shoulder to gaze upon Alexandria making her way to class, he banged squarely into the chest of Principal Long.

"Oops! I'm sorry Dr. Long, I wasn't aware anyone was in my path. I'm sorry, are you alright?"

Also caught by surprise, the principal answered, "Sorry, Farley, I guess I didn't turn back around in time to avoid a collision. I saw you coming, but was a little slow adjusting. I was waving at a student."

"Well sir, I guess we both just were meant to say 'good morning' in some kind of way."

Dr. Long quipped, making fun, "I saw you grinning from ear to ear. Judging from seeing you look over your shoulder, I assume you had a pleasant conversation with Alexandria McCord. Nice looking with a big heart and a wealth of intelligence. Hope she's grinning too for your sake."

Caught off guard by his keen perception, Farley had no place to go, but the truth. "You are perceptive, Dr. Long; quite so. Yes, sir, I too hope she's grinning, if you know what I mean."

Placing his hand on Farley's left shoulder, the principal offered, "I'll put in a good word for you when the moment presents itself. That is, if your intentions are honorable."

"Yes, sir, they're most honorable."

"Going to the basketball game tonight? It'll be my first since accepting this job. I don't have a clue what kind of team we have."

"I'm meeting Ms. McCord there. One of her students, Johnnie Wimbush, is the star player. That's the understatement. He's a shoe-in for All-State recognition."

"I had no idea we had someone of that caliber. Can't wait for tonight then. Thanks for telling me…Oops, you better go, the tardy bell just rang. If you need a written excuse to give your class, come see me. Ha!"

By 6:15 p.m., Farley had purchased two tickets and was anxiously pacing back and forth inside the lobby near the ticket booth as energetic students began filling the stands. The Centennial Cavaliers were holding on to third place in the Metro League with a 9-4 record while their opponent, the Washington Generals, was on top with a perfect 13-0 mark. In the previous meeting on the Generals' home court, the Cavaliers lost 76-70.

Slightly before 6:30 p.m., Alex made her appearance. She spotted Farley and slipped in behind him shouting above the crowd noise, "I'm early! How about that?"

Spinning around to face her, Farley shouted, "We better hurry, the good seats are disappearing fast."

"OK, I'll follow your lead."

Farley grabbed her hand and made a move toward the entrance to the gym. To his surprise, she made no attempt to release from his grip. Navigating through the crowd, he found seating in the fourth row near mid-court, right behind the Cavs' bench, to the left of the scorers' table.

Farley looked at Alex, declaring, "These are great seats. Can you believe this atmosphere? It's electric!"

"Kinda like a play-off game, huh?"

"You can say that again…Here we go, there's the tip."

Centennial had a 6'10" center handling the opening tip, swatting it to Johnnie who drove toward the bucket and dished off to Larry Brown, the team's speedy point guard who laid it in for a 2-0 lead.

Brown turned and stole the inbounds pass, bouncing the ball to Johnnie deep in the corner, and the Cavs' All-State swingman knocked down a 3-point shot, hitting all net. The Cavs were up 5-0 with less than a minute off the clock, causing the crowd to work its way into a frenzy.

The Generals wasted no time regaining their composure, and the first quarter ended with the Cavs clinging to a 24-22 lead.

Throughout the second quarter, the teams exchanged baskets, with the lead changing hands numerous times. Johnnie hit a pair of 18-foot jump shots and a free throw within 20 seconds of halftime, lifting the Cavs to a 46-40 lead. He had 24 points and 8 rebounds to go along with 6 assists.

Washington was led by their 6'11" center, Hal Schofield and point guard Gene Ellis with 19 and 13 points respectively. Schofield had 11 rebounds to go with 6 blocked shots. College recruiters were scattered about the stands scribbling notes, in what could be called a recruiter's feeding frenzy.

Both teams came out in the third quarter where they left off, each hitting over 60% of their shots with Washington on top 70-66. It was a replay of their first meeting, but there was still a fourth quarter left. Johnnie Wimbush scored but 6 points on 4 shots while attempting to get more of his teammates involved in the scoring. It turned out to be a strategic mistake.

During the end of the third quarter break, Alex, asked Farley, “Do you think we can come back? I mean with Johnnie not taking any shots?”

“He’s got to take over the game. Somehow, he has to overcome their double teaming him. No one else can hit besides Brown. It’ll come down to defense in the fourth quarter. Our big man just isn’t much of a shooter. The kid guarding him is also helping out with the double team on Johnnie. We’ll see.”

But the fourth quarter belonged to Johnnie. He did the one thing few high school players can; he took shots off the dribble and nailed them, putting on a clinic showing how to beat the double team. Instead of waiting for a teammate’s pass in the spots he likes to take his shot, he would dribble away from the defenders and take running jumpers or drive the lane, drawing crucial fouls. The defining moment came as he drove along the baseline and performed a magnificent two-hand slam on a reverse move with his back to the bucket.

With Johnnie contributing a scorching 15 fourth quarter points, the Cavaliers rallied to a convincing 91-82 victory. His totals for the night were 45 points, 16 rebounds and 9 assists. The Centennial quintet tightened the defense in the fourth quarter, shutting down the Generals one-two punch.

Farley walked Alex to her car after the game. Both were ecstatic over the performance Johnnie had displayed. “I can’t believe that quiet guy in my history class does this kind of stuff in his off time. He's never mentioned his basketball prowess. No wonder everyone in class lights up when he arrives. I couldn't figure it out."

Farley added, "If they all could be so humble." He opened her car door and said, "I'll sleep good tonight. I'm worn out emotionally. Drive careful."

"Thanks for getting me to come to the game tonight. See you tomorrow, Mr. Detective."

He stood waving as she pulled away from the curb and motored out of sight.

Silas Wimbush and Johnnie arrived home after the game slightly before midnight. Silas asked, "You want something to eat before you sack out? I'll warm up some of this roast and vegetables if you like."

"That'd be great Gramps. I'm starving," informed Johnnie as he collapsed on a chair at the kitchen table.

Opening the refrigerator door, Silas remarked, "If Duke and North Carolina weren't impressed tonight, then nobody would suit them. You just might have had one of the greatest high school games in basketball history. "

Slumped against the kitchen table, Johnnie responded, "I don't know Gramps, that guy from New York back in the 60s was awesome every night from what I've heard."

"His name was Lew Alcindor from Power Memorial High School. You know him as Kareem Abdul-Jabbar," Silas said while pulling a large deep pan from the refrigerator and placing it in the oven. “He was a foot taller than everyone else. You’re not. I’ve never heard of a kid play both No. 2 guard and power forward on offense at six-foot seven and set up down low on defense.”

Bringing the discussion back to reality, Johnnie interjected the awful truth, “It’s all for nothing Gramps. Any day now Willie Buchanan will pay us a visit and say the time has come for me to quit school and get to work.”

Silas continued to prepare Johnnie a plate of roast with carrots and potatoes, placing it in the small toaster oven. Disappointment in his voice covered the room. “I won’t lie to you, son, it kinda shakes a man’s faith. The Almighty is in control, but I don’t see the good in all this. He gave you many gifts, and basketball is one of them. You have a good mind for school and a wonderful heart. You could really do some good things for this world.”

“God has blessed me more than a lot of people, so who am I to question this fate?”

As he remained leaning against the countertop next to the toaster oven, Silas offered, “Somehow, God must be punishing me for something I’ve done. To do that, he’s denying my only living family member a chance at life. If I only knew what to repent for. God may strike me dead now, but I wish someone would kill that evil young man who is destroying this neighborhood.”

“Maybe I will, Gramps. Then you’d be free.”

“I’ll never be free if you’re in jail for murder. Don’t even think like that son. Please don’t.”

Dejected, Johnnie said, “Neither one of us is free now. In

case you didn't notice, Willie Boy was in that black Chevrolet Monte Carlo following us home. No one can help us, and better yet, no one will even try. We have been warned about that."

"It would take a mighty big person to get us out of this mess. I'm not afraid for my life, but I am yours," explained Silas.

"Same here."

Silas paused for a moment while staring at the floor before thoughtfully saying, "Son, when your grandmother died, I thought there wasn't much to live for anymore. But you came along and brought joy to my life. I had a reason to look forward to the next day. So, I owe you for the kind of young man you have chosen to be."

"I won't let you down, sir. You have saved my life."

"I think God will forgive us for not reading our nightly scripture, don't you think?" Silas remarked while placing on the table the pan of roast surrounded by potatoes and carrots.

Piling the goodies onto his plate, Johnnie said, "It's by grace we're saved anyway, huh?...I know our deeds must reflect our faith."

Silas thoughtfully replied, "I wasn't going to say a thing. I know you knew that fact."

The morning after the game, Alex immediately addressed her first period class. "I would like to know why it was never brought to my attention we had a great athlete amongst us other than Scot Barton? I'm talking about the basketball exploits of our own, Johnnie Wimbush." She waited patiently as no one spoke up until Johnnie himself stood to explain.

"Ms. McCord, it's my wish to remain anonymous as possible. It keeps my focus on humility; grounding myself with the Word. The Lord is my shepherd and I want for nothing that is good and necessary."

Deeply moved by such an unselfish young man, Alex was left speechless for a few moments before praising, "You are a breath of fresh air to be such a renowned athlete. I saw you play last night. Words can't describe what I saw. You and Scot are a tribute to the character of young people."

Johnnie nodded his head while sitting down, saying, "Thank you, ma'am."

Alex directed the class toward their current study of the Federalist Papers.

"These were a series of 85 articles written by Alexander Hamilton, James Madison, and John Jay. They appeared in a New York journal with the purpose of persuading the Constitutional Convention voters and later the general public of the necessity of replacing the Articles of Confederation. That old government was inefficient in helping the new government realize the ideals of justice and the individual right. As a new nation facing the rest of the world, the Articles were not as encompassing as what was now needed. These papers were collected and printed in a book by John and Archibald McLean in 1788 under the title, 'The Federalist.'"

"Just to jog your memory, fifty-five delegates from the brand new thirteen States met in Philadelphia from May of 1787 to about September of that same year. They hammered out what became our Constitution. The ratification process was long and hard. The papers written by these three men played a huge role in giving what you people enjoy today; individual freedom as the world has never seen. The emphasis here is on a level the world had never seen. Get it?

"I want each of you to read one of the articles and write your interpretation of that article. You have all weekend to do this for Monday's class discussion. I will call on some of you to read your papers. The bell is about to ring, so be gone."

Monday morning following the huge victory over rival with Washington on Thursday night, Johnnie Wimbush was missing from his usual seat at the back of the room beside Karen Austin. Alex marked him absent and moved on to the topics of discussion, which entailed the students having prepared a short interpretation of one of the 85 Federalist Papers. However, it would not be Johnnie's last absence. By the end of the week, he had not made a single appearance.

Then the following Monday after class, as Alex latched up her satchel, a voice broke her concentration. "Ms. McCord, I didn't mean to accuse you of being that guy last week." Alex looked up just as Karen Austin continued, "I wish you were though. Johnnie Wimbush needs some help, bad."

Placing both hands on the satchel, she looked straight at Karen, asking, "How so?"

"You know he dropped out of school."

Alex was not entirely stunned, as her friend Laura from the Community Center had recently warned of this moment. But the disappointment was still there as she replied, "Dropped out of school? Tell me you're kidding! I just thought his absenteeism was due to some illness or other difficulty. It makes no sense! Why?"

"Ms. McCord, he didn't drop out because he wanted to. There's a gang that terrorizes his neighborhood. They threaten people and make them pay for protection. Johnnie's grandfather owns a small grocery store and can't afford the payments. Johnnie's working full time to pay for his grandfather's protection. They've even threatened Johnnie if he goes back to school."

Pausing to gather her thoughts, Alex reassured, "OK, I'll see what I can do. I'll let Dr. Long know about Johnnie's situation. Maybe we can put our heads together and come up with something. I'm just too shocked right at this moment to even have something intelligent to say. Let me digest this."

Karen added, "I just felt like somebody should know. He's such a nice guy. Lives with his grandfather because his mother's in prison for murdering his father. He's had so much bad luck. Yesterday I saw him sitting on the ground behind his grandfather's store, crying."

Placing an arm around Karen's waist, she assured, "I promise Dr. Long and I will look into his situation. Now go on to your next class and don't let this be a distraction for what you're here to accomplish. Understand?"

"Yes, ma'am."

Sitting in a chair in front of Principal Long's desk, Alex related Johnnie Wimbush's dilemma. Always dressed very stately, the six-foot 195-pound principal took over the school helm in January, a job vacated by the beloved Bill Saddler at the end of the previous school year.

"Alex, I really don't have an answer right this minute. This is extremely disturbing. I saw him play basketball a couple of weeks ago. He's a phenomenal talent. Every college in the country will be seeking his services. What do you know about the boy's grades? Well, let me call up his grade reports. I'm just curious if he's a serious student. You say he's a junior?"

"Yes. So, if he's not a great student, you don't' want to help him? Well that's wonderful! All that should matter is he wants to stay in school. You never know how someone will turn out. Might go to college and prove to be a late bloomer."

Scanning student records on the computer, Dr. Long ignored her remarks, saying, "Look here. He's a solid 'B' student who has no prior absences until this year. He has never been disciplined."

"Dr. Long, I hardly know him. I also was in attendance at the game, and he is an exceptional talent to say the least. He's in my first period history class, and until I recognized his game exploits Friday, we've never exchanged dialogue. He asked to remain anonymous. That's awesome in the character department, and he owns enough humility to give the whole school some of that attitude."

Exploring further, he exclaimed, "Wow. He is the teams' leading scorer with 41 points a game! Furthermore, last year he was first team all-city, second team All-State. Now we might be able to recruit Coach Ed Ramsdale to help solve this predicament. I wish I could have seen this kid play more. Admittedly I am a basketball junkie."

Ears pinned back, Alex challenged, "Dr. Long, I hope I'm way off base, but surely his basketball prowess will not influence how much help, if any, you give him. I mean…."

"Ms. McCord," interrupted Dr. Long, "You've now challenged me on two fronts. Perhaps if you'd throttle back and give me a chance, you'd discover yourself way out in left field. I'm serious about education and every child's right to one. I appreciate athletics so long as their value is kept in proper perspective. In Mr. Wimbush's case, I see a kid with a chance to have his college education paid for through his basketball skills. To rob a kid of a chance to get an education should be a crime, as should refusing to lend a hand or turning one's back on a kid in need of help." Leaning forward, elbows on the desk and glaring into her eyes, he asked, "Are you clear now on my position?"

Ears back up and refreshed by his perspective, she answered, "I'm thrilled to know that, actually. It's a big relief knowing you value the person's education above athletics. It's also a relief to know he doesn't have to be a great student for you to offer assistance."

Leaning back in his high-back leather chair, he challenged, "Let me ask you this: Are you anti-athletics? Because if you are, consider changing your perspective."

"And if I were?" Alex fired back.

The principal rolled his chair back from the desk and stood up. "I'm not ignoring your question, Alex, I'm just going to walk over here and pour myself a cup of coffee. Would you like one?"

"No thank you."

"A lack of support for any legitimate extracurricular activity could lead to non-support of others, including ones you may favor," added Dr. Long, returning to his chair. "My goal is to have every child at Centennial involved in some activity so they can bond with the school. School should be a place where students experience respect and receive support from each other. Self-esteem and a place to belong are hard for many kids to come by; more than you'd think. Athletics can play a positive role. If Johnnie uses basketball to have his way to college paid for, then he'll be an inspiration for the next kid with some kind of talent. Can you understand and support that idea?"

Crossing her legs while pulling down an already modest skirt over the knee, she exclaimed, "Boy, for a minute I thought I was listening to Jerry Walker. But I agree with you. I'm just tired of athletes being pampered. There are college students living in shacks and working two jobs while keeping their grades up, and you have athletes who don't go to class, live in plush accommodations, and have everything handed to them. They can break the law and every school rule, but it's OK if they can perform well in their respective sport."

"Alex, I'm on your side," he concurred while taking a sip of coffee. "Let's also not forget we're here to see what we can do for Johnnie. It's just a thought, but we could consider home schooling him until we can solve this. I'm afraid the police can't escort him to school and no one in the neighborhood is going to rat out the gang who's terrorizing everyone. Wish I knew how to get in touch with that Masked Marvel or whatever they call him. You wouldn't happen to know of such a person, would you?" he asked while chuckling.

Rolling her eyes, she replied, "Maybe. They call him an assortment of names. Captain America, for one."

"Good, then if you discover someway to reach him, arrange a meeting for the three of us. Meantime, how would you like to write the speech I have to give the student body tomorrow? Tomorrow is Wednesday isn't it?"

"As a matter of fact, it is. No, I don't want to write the speech or give it for that matter. I'll be there, though. It should be interesting. I've never heard of a principal giving a state of the school address."

"Neither have I. But back to our problem. How would you like to volunteer to take Johnnie's schoolwork to him and pick it up?"

"That'd be fine. Is that the route we're going?"

"For now, until we can come up with something else."

Alex warned, "You better figure a way to get him to school before basketball season next year. That is if you want to see him play."

Crossing his arms, the principal smugly asked, "Ms. McCord, do you know how many high school kids in the greater Houston area will average 41 points a game at the 5A level? I know you don't, so let me tell you – five maybe. How many will average 41 points and have his grades? Probably two or three. I shall repeat myself for the sake of your skeptical self: Johnnie is being cheated out of doing what God put him here to do."

"OK, I'm convinced you're altruistic, so when do we start this homebound program?"

"Tomorrow we'll pay a visit to his grandfather and get a feel for the atmosphere there. We'll go right after school if you're free to do so."

"Suits me. Can't wait for your speech. It ought to be one of the year's real highlights."

"I'm still working on it. See you tomorrow."

Alex rose to her feet and thanked Dr. Long again for his commitment and left the office.

Later that evening while at the kitchen table grading papers, Alex decided to take a break and call Richard to ask for a special favor. Sliding her chair over to the wall where the phone hung, she reached up and dialed his number. This particular request would require his best effort to date.

Uncle Richard was at his desk scratching out some notes for a new book manuscript, when the phone rang. Leaving his chair to answer the call, he muttered, "This could only be Alexandria."

Picking up the receiver, he answered, "What do you need now?"

"I'm going to need another car. I have a pressing project and don't want the police to know the same guy is doing this one."

"I don't think having a different car is going to throw them off track. Your MO is consistent. You never kill anyone, and you leave the bad guys tied up waiting for the police to arrive...What kind of project do you have in mind?"

"There's a boy who dropped out of school because he's being forced to do so by some gang. This gang terrorizes his grandfather, who owns a small grocery store in the hood. They demand protection payments that he can't afford, so his grandson, a student of mine, works full time just to meet the payments. The grandfather is raising the boy. Now get this: The boy's mom is in jail for murdering his father. Now guess who this evil gang is?"

"Oh my God; the Grimm Reapers. Alexandria, you just keep getting involved in these entanglements. Where is it going to stop? Jail or the cemetery? Oh well, why do I waste my breath … So, what kind of car are we looking at? Or are you asking me for a suggestion?"

"I guess I'm asking for a suggestion."

Richard removed his eye glasses and thought for a moment before asking, "What does the car need to do performance wise?"

"I plan to terrorize the gang members. It'll need to be quick out-of-the-hole, but with lots of 'top-in' for the straightaway. I'll need some armor, though. The tires need to be protected from the sides and front to back. I'll also need the fuel tank protected. Oh, bullet proof glass. Can you make driver side and passenger side doors non-penetrable?"

Returning to his desk, the magic car builder begged, while closing a reference book, "Please don't tell me you need this done today."

"Funny Richard," she replied while continually wrapping the phone cord around her fingers. "Can you find me a car to fix up? It'll need to be able to carry a passenger or two, plus some artillery."

Scratching his scalp with the free hand, he answered, "I'll need some time to think this one over. Off hand, you're probably looking at a 1969 Plymouth Road Runner 440 Six Pack. You'll get great gas mileage in the city because it runs on the center two barrel, but on the highway or at full throttle, the other two carbs kick in – six throats pouring gas down its intake to the cylinders. You'll need both horsepower and monster torque to tote around that armor-plated beast. Your other option would be a brand-new Buick Grand National. It's fast. Has a turbo charged V-6. On second thought, cancel that. It doesn't have the torque to haul the armor, especially a quick getaway from a standing stop. Give me a few days."

"Thanks Richard. I owe you so much."

"You don't owe me anything. You owe God and yourself, in that order. God has a perfect will for your life, but you must ask that it be revealed to you. That you haven't done. You've asked His guidance for your intentions, not His. The end result of His permissive will never ends with the same success. It's written, you should be careful what you ask for."

"What do I do then if I feel like I'm the instrument of His will?"

"That's not for me to answer. That's between you and God. You have to ask yourself honestly if you've petitioned the Father to show you His will for your life."

"Am I supposed to put aside my own personal desires? Am I not entitled to pursue my own convictions? If not, what's the point in living?"

"Alexandria, God did indeed give you a free will. He wanted you to choose Him on your own accord. However, the Father knows the evil one you are up against, far better than any mere mortal. That's the difference. That's why he wishes you to follow His guidance so you'll have eternal victory. You can't beat the evil one on your own."

"Richard, the police can't do what I can accomplish. I am not shackled by rules that favor the criminal. I can administer justice by going around the scuzbucket lawyers and hamstrung court system. I can make things right. You know that."

"So does the Father, but your real adversary is not the Grimm Reapers; it's the evil one. The Reapers are his instrument for destruction. They are guided by Satan's wishes. If you don't have the blessing from God the Father, then you'll meet your end someday. God says, justice is His, so you better make sure you are truly His instrument. If so, you'll prevail, because inside the will of God, there is no failure. That too is written."

"So, if I ask God to reveal his perfect will for my life, I must ask Him to guide my steps until it's revealed to me? Until I receive a sign that I don't have his blessing for my actions, I'll stay the path."

"That approach would be a considerable improvement. Bringing God into your equation and placing the burden on Him is what it's all about. The answer it seems is seldom what we want to hear. But based on His 'all seeing' and 'all knowing,' we'll understand why someday if we keep our mind alert and listen to our heart."

Rubbing her forehead and yawning, Alex admitted, "I'm tired, Richard and you're getting complicated or too deep. I haven't decided which it is. I really need to hang up and go to bed."

"Let me leave you with one last thought. A sun room addition manufacturer came up with the idea of portable rooms made specifically for cats you can put on a patio. The room will contain things to climb on, water to drink, a food bowl, and a soft bed to lie in, etc. The structure is all Plexiglas with holes for breeze to flow through. It contains everything they could possibly need to have fun and yet be protected from any predator. It also prevents him from wandering off and entering places that can only do him harm. Think of God's will for your life being in that shelter. Outside the shelter, sooner or later, the cat will meet its end at the hands of an instrument for the evil one. There's nothing outside the shelter that's better for you. Your inquisitiveness is all that's satisfied, and nothing of substance accomplished that."

Yawning, Alex said, "OK, my brain's fried and I'm about to fall asleep here at the table. Hold those thoughts. Good night."

"Good night, Alexandria."

Hanging up the receiver, she grabbed a picture frame from the bar while collapsing in a chair against the wall under the phone. She proceeded to place her feet atop the kitchen table and gaze into the photo of herself and Mike at the graduation dance. Wiping tears from her eyes, she sobbed, "You promised we'd be together always. Why did you have to leave me? Maybe I'll get lucky and somebody will kill me some night. If it weren't for all these needy people, my life would have no meaning. Mike, I'm so lonely. Sometimes it's unbearable. Friday after school I'm going to Victoria and put some fresh flowers by your headstone. For my own sanity, I need to let you go. But I don't know how."

Chapter 5

Wednesday morning, beginning first period, the entire school gathered in the auditorium for Principal Long's inaugural speech, addressing the student body and any parents who wished to attend. Teachers stood lining the walls to monitor behavior.

Standing behind the podium, Dr. Long began. "I want to thank you for your orderly assembly, and apologize to the faculty for disrupting your planned curriculum, although many of you students are glad for the break. I'll try to keep this at about fifty minutes. I'm sure you all wonder why I've decided to such an address. This is seldom done anymore in modern times. However, due to the environmental changes I intend to install here at Centennial, it's imperative to give you substantial notice concerning these changes. Centennial High School will pursue a new, more positive horizon.

"I believe in the public-school system that has helped make this a great nation. The past several years it has come under much criticism for doing a poor job of educating our young people. I would go a step further and add we haven't done a very good job of motivating.

"There are several reasons for what I call the collapse. One is the focus on tests, tests, and more tests. We now teach you how to pass some arbitrary exam designed by a board which many of its members have never been in the classroom nor have been a parent. Another failure comes from allowing certain students to not only disrupt the atmosphere required for learning but to intimidate others into pulling back from reaching their potential or from pursuing their goals. That falls under the category of letting the prison inmates run the prison. It's time adults took back control of the schools, so that you young people can do your best.

"Every child deserves a chance to explore both his potential and his interests. Some learn faster than others, but that does not mean the slower learners cannot catch up or even eventually surpass the faster learner in the long run.

"My goal is for every student who sets foot on this campus to feel glad to be here. Not only glad to be here, but feel a part of this school. This should be a place of sanctuary. A place one can belong and receive support. It should be a place where compassion for one another is in abundance. It's a tough enough world out there without kids killing kids. Without kids ridiculing kids and forcing others into a poor behavior model.

"So where are we, here at Centennial, headed? Here's the essence. No longer are we going to have an alternative school for those who insist on being habitually disruptive or a physical threat to the well-being of those who desire a favorable leaning atmosphere. Such behavior will find them off campus and out in the street. This will save the school a significant amount of money that can be channeled back to where it can do some good. That money saved will go to those who want an education. It'll go toward helping each student discover his talents and find a direction that will eventually lead to a career. It'll put faculty members back where they belong – teaching instead of babysitting. The additional faculty members back in the classroom of learning will help lower the teacher to student ratio.

"The additional resources will allow the launch of a new program of mine that will encourage every kid to join some extra-curricular activity. You'll be asked to take a survey to identify interests. I want industrial arts to rise from the back of the bus. All shop classes will be upgraded. My goal is for every student to belong, even if we have to create a new curriculum."

Uncustomary silence and attentiveness permeated the gymnasium, as he continued, "You can thank Coach Jerry Walker for convincing me to immediately implement this agenda, regardless of district support.

"Traditionally, athletes and gang members dominate the school and determine the rules and decide who may have self-esteem. After high school, few athletes will go on to play at the college level and fewer will participate professionally. I don't mean to downgrade athletes. They do entertain us and provide some inspiring moments. But let's not forget the contribution made by the guy who loved industrial arts such as shop and automotive. He offers a service that many have no ability to perform themselves. Remembering a long touchdown run will not repair your car. It won't drive an ambulance or help the underappreciated EMTs or paramedics save the lives of loved ones. It won't unplug a backed-up sewer or build a slab for a patio. It won't write the books your children read or the novels you read. It won't play the instrument that contributes to a band's concert we all attend and enjoy. It won't sing the songs, paint the pictures, teach the children or nurse the sick back to health. And so on.

"There is only one point of view that has any credence: We all contribute equally to make this a great nation in which to reside. There's no place for the pompous or the arrogant. Not here at Centennial.

"The only characteristic that makes someone special is their willingness to help a fellow human being in need. A society of vultures will eventually eat itself into extinction. A society of nurturers will only expand and prosper.

"Beginning right now, as students, you have an obligation to respect your teachers or hit the highway. On the same token, you can earn respect by giving it.

"I will go the final mile for you, but you must give me something to carry. To me the greatest accomplishment this nation can be proud of is that public education has been a major contributor to its success.

"I want each and every one of you to put your hand out to those that need an encouraging word. I can't change the direction America seems to want to go, but I can change what happens here. It may never happen, but my goal is to have everyone graduate who so desires. There are many of you here right now who will do your best to prevent this plan from succeeding. I am convinced the lack of love and a feeling of belonging both at home and at school is the real culprit that motivates this destructive behavior. You're striking back at heartache and disappointment; disillusioned with the world you've been handed. I wish I could both undo it and change it. But because of your circumstances and experiences, many of you don't trust my intentions. I'm sorry. You may now dispense to your next scheduled class. Thank you."

Much to the surprise of Dr. Long and the faculty, there was scattered applause. Not to be ignored were the skeptical remarks concerning both the principal's sincerity and his authority to carry out the promises. At any rate, there was a reaction, much of it positive, some of it skeptical, but the mainstream feeling was one of hope as the students and teachers scattered and in an orderly fashion moved to their respective classrooms.

Dr. Long made his way through the crowded hall in front of his office. There he was met by his secretary, Amanda Blinn, a slightly overweight but pretty 19-year-old. "I hate to tell you this, but Max Wedge is waiting for you. He heard your speech, and I'm afraid this will be a closed-door session."

Tapping his left hand on her desk, he agreed, "You're probably right. When the school district superintendent visits, it's never good. Been nice knowing you, Amanda. You're a real treat to work with day-in and day-out."

With a wide grin on her face, she looked at him sincerely and offered support. "Keep your chin up. He can't fire you. Nobody wants this damn job. He also has the audacity to sit in your chair. Just so you'll know."

Shaking his head affirmatively, he waltzed through the door, closing it behind him. "Dr. Wedge, what a pleasant surprise," he said reaching out to shake his boss's hand.

"Sit down, Long, this is not a social visit," the superintendent informed, pointing to a chair beside the principal's desk. Placing his feet on the desk, Dr. Wedge added, "I thought assigning you to this underachieving, oppressed school would be enough to break you of those lofty do-good ideals. That you'd finally figure out what high schools are for. This is the last assignment before a person like you is told to make like cow shit and hit the trail. That speech of yours was atrocious.

"You can't and won't carry out any of that nonsense program. Thanks to you, I'm going to have parents knocking my door down, and those aspiring a superintendent's job here hoping you'll at least launch this policy of yours long enough to get me run off. So, you better call another meeting with your faculty and call this off. You don't need to tell the student body anything. Do I need to give you anymore instructions? Do you fully understand what's at stake for you?"

Quickly rising to his feet, Dr. Long took back control of his office, opening the door and commanded, "Get out of my office, Max, and don't come back unless it's to apologize or fire me. Send me those parents you expect to cause trouble. I'll set 'em straight. It's time we take back control for the kids' sake. So, until I'm fired, stay out of my way. Go take care of the schools where the principals have no guts and don't care about the kids."

Appalled, Dr. Wedge stood up and aid, "You're gone, Del! You hear me? Gone!" Grabbing his umbrella, the superintendent marched out of the office, heading for the main door.

Before the angry administrator could leave the reception area, Dr. Long hollered, "And stop legislating out common sense and wisdom, Max! You liberal fascist!" He then proceeded behind the desk and collapsed in the huge, plush leather chair, propping up his feet on the low two-drawer file cabinet.

Stumped, Amanda wandered into the principal's office and took a seat. "Wow! Where did that come from? I wanted to give you a standing ovation, but I need this job you so graciously gave me."

Visibly stressed, Del confessed, "I didn't graciously give you anything. You're honest, refreshing, appreciative, pay attention to detail, and just plain effective. Besides, I like looking at you. Takes the pressure off a bad day to see you so cheerful and vibrant."

Smiling with a look of larceny, Amanda teased, "Admit it Dr. Long, you do like my big tits, don't you?"

Laughing out loud, he admitted as much. "You nailed me, Amanda. You nailed me. Unashamedly and most certainly, I do appreciate beautiful mountain peaks."

Winking at her boss, she asked playfully, "Would you have me for a wife? Huh? Or am I too overweight for you? There are plenty of single shapely teachers here."

"Amanda, I'm going to be serious now. It's been three years since my wife died. I'll always love her. A day doesn't go by that I don't miss her. But a day doesn't go by that I don't wonder about asking you to fill that void. You're the only one I've dared think about in those terms, but you need someone your age to learn and grow with. You'd be good for me, but I wouldn't be that great for you. After I remind myself of that fact, I fall back to earth."

As she stared into his eyes looking for the truth, she asked, "But do I stoke your inner fire?"

He looked into her eyes without a blink, "Uncontrollably."

Never losing eye contact, she revealed, "This lust goes both ways. Kinda neat, huh?"

Continuing eye contact, he offered, "Makes for a fun day, don't you think?"

Standing up abruptly, Amanda said, "I better get after some of my work. Feel free to steal a look now and then or every chance I give you." She then waltzed into the reception area and sat at her desk.

Mumbling to himself after she left the room, he said, "Going to miss her when Wedge fires me."

Alex quickly dismissed her last period class and promptly marched down two hallways to the principal's office. The two of them were going to pay a visit to Johnnie Wimbush's grandfather. Knocking on the open door, she said, "I liked your speech."

Pulling his coat from the hanger, Dr. Long replied, "Thank

you. I only hope I didn't alienate any of the faculty members. Max Wedge was mad. Probably going to fire me."

"Who does he know that would covet this school? Anyway, I felt your sincerity. I really think the kids did too. But now you have a titanic job ahead of you. You're taking on more than I imagine one person should. I'll be pulling for you. Anything I can do to help, please call on me."

Grabbing his briefcase, the principal said, "Let's go pay a visit to our boys. I'll drive. I looked up both the house and the grocery store on the map. We'll talk to gramps and see if we can find out when Johnnie gets off work. Maybe find out where he works."

Thirty minutes later, Dr. Long brought his 1985 GMC ¾ ton 4 x 4 pickup to a halt in the small parking lot beside Wimbush's corner grocery, across from Tesse's Lounge on the same side of the street. On the other side of the grocery sat a liquor store and a Hi Lo Auto Parts house.

Exiting the truck, the principal and Alex entered the grocery where they spotted a big burly man behind the meat counter slicing T-bone steaks. He appeared to be in his seventies, but wielded the huge butcher knife with speed and accuracy. Packed with amiable intentions, the two wondered over to the counter and introduced themselves.

"Hello, I'm Del Long and this is Alex McCord. I'm the principal at Centennial High School and Ms. McCord is one of our history teachers."

Never looking up from the task at hand, he cautiously replied with a low bass voice, "I'm Silas Wimbush. I assume you are here on behalf of Johnnie. He's sixteen, so it's legal to quit school."

Addressing Silas, Dr. Long asked, "Mr. Wimbush, we'd like to arrange for Johnnie to get his schoolwork at home. Ms. McCord would bring his assignments to the house and pick them up. There are several kids who do homebound schooling."

Sticking the huge knife into the meat block, he glared at Principal Long and firmly answered, "The Grimm Reapers have their hangout across the street at Tesse's Lounge. If they thought he was getting schooled, they'd hurt him and tear up my place. You best leave him alone. Don't come around here causing us any more trouble than we already have. You hear me?"

Relentless, Principal Long retaliated, "Mr. Wimbush, it won't require him to quit his job. He'll just do his schoolwork at home on his off hours. Surely they can't monitor that or even care."

Leaning over the counter, Silas firmly repeated, "Stay away from Johnnie and me. Don't come around here again. Being here right now is gonna cause me trouble."

Alex interrupted, "Can't you go to the police?"

"Tried. They don't care nuthin' 'bout a black man havin' trouble with a Mexican gang. They said they'd have to catch them committing a crime. Otherwise, it's my word against theirs. Besides, the Reapers have paid off the police who patrol this area.

So, if you want to help, butt out. Now leave my store."

Looking at Alex in disbelief, Dr, Long said, "OK, Mr. Wimbush, we'll leave for now."

"Mr. Long, Ms. McCord, I truly appreciate your efforts to come over here. But you don't know the fear we all live with. These guys are evil like none others. We have to trust in God to get us through this. So, please don't cause us any trouble. May God bless you two for your concern."

Reversing their path back outside, they paused on the sidewalk out front. Dr. Long informed Alex, "For two cents, I'd have a look inside that lounge. For what reason I don't know. I feel like bribing them with extra money to let the kid at least do homebound so he could finish school."

"They'd probably keep raising the ransom until you were broke. I don't know where we go from here. Mr. Wimbush made it pretty clear the consequences and there is no police help."

Hands on his hips looking at the surroundings, he said, "Where's Captain America when you need him. He could probably fix this somehow. If only we could find someone with a direct connection to the guy."

Concealing her grin, Alex said, "Lots of luck. Shall we leave before we get into trouble or better still, cause Mr. Wimbush any?"

"Yeah, I have to really think this out. I can't figure out why that gang cares if Johnnie goes to school, so long as he can work and pay the protection payments."

Trudging around the corner to the parking lot, both were startled to see the windshield of Principal Long's truck shattered. As the two inspected the damage, a voice hollered out. "Looks like you need a new windshield, man. If I was you, I'd get outta here before your other windows get broken."

Dr. Long quickly turned to see who was addressing him. It was a man appearing to be in his late twenties, perched on a short brick wall running along one side of the small parking lot. Accompanying him were six of his associates.

Shaking his head at the sight of the broken windshield, the principal instructed Alex, "Stay here while I get a closer look at the turd."

Principal Long quickly advanced toward the group demanding, "Why do you not want Johnnie Wimbush to go to school? Why would you do that to one of your own kind?"

Hopping off the wall, the short muscular leader confronted the principal from within a few feet. "He needs to keep working so he can make his grandfather's insurance payments. We don't want anyone in this neighborhood thinking they can just leave and become a white wanna-be. In case you don't know, I'm Willie Boy, the warlord in this neighborhood. Leader of the Grimm Reapers."

"What if I pay you some extra to let us bring his school assignments to him and pick them up? He could still keep working and pay you. My money would be just that much more."

Shoving Principal Long several steps backward, Willie Boy said, "Hey, man, who'll pay us if he goes off to college? If he moves out, these other punks will think they can do the same thing. There are those who are the prey and those who are predators. We're predators, and we need prey. It's the natural order of things."

Reasserting himself, the principal retraced his steps, positioning himself directly in front of the militant youth. "How can you just let this boy miss out on an opportunity to better himself?"

"You better get out of here before we tear up your pretty truck some more."

Visibly disgusted, Dr. Long lost his composure and pointed at Willie Boy warning, "You won't get away with this. That boy is not going to throw his life away for scum like you. You're not going to ruin his life or any other kid's. Somehow you're going down."

With that, Willie Boy signaled to one of the other gang members who quickly waltzed over to the truck and stuck his knife into the driver's side rear tire.

Turning in time to see the youngster pull his knife out of the tire, Dr. Long glanced back at Willie Boy shouting, "You lousy punk! If you didn't have all your entourage, we'd see just who the real man is!"

"You better get out of here while you still have three tires."

"I can't put my spare on?" demanded the principal in disbelief.

"You have five minutes to get out of here or we'll cut another. You're lucky we haven't messed you up or your lady friend. Now get out of here. If we see you so much as pass through this neighborhood, you'll find the old man's store trashed. And I can't say what will happen to Johnnie and gramps."

Recognizing his being overmatched, Dr. Long returned to the truck addressing Alex, "I appreciate you not getting involved over there."

"It didn't take much restraint on my part, believe me. Did he say his name was Willie Boy, leader of the Grimm Reapers?" she asked hiding her new felt joy.

"Yes. Do you know him?"

"No. Just curious as to whom we're dealing with."

Both climbed into the truck, and the principal drove the vehicle through the streets with one flat tire until out of sight of the Reapers. He then pulled over into a K-Mart parking lot and changed the tire.

Alex wasted no time informing Richard after all these years she had finally made contact with the Grimm Reapers, the gang that murdered her parents and their friends. "Richard, Willie Boy himself was there. I'm so pumped. There is a God watching over me."

Placing a coffee cup in the sink, he declared, "That gives a new meaning to this bionic car you want me to build. I have mixed emotions. I have a hunch you're now going to devote your life to dealing them misery. It could get ugly, Alexandria. You may be overmatched against such a large group that's battle tested and probably has the local patrol officers bought off. You've never faced this kind of a test."

"You're not going to spoil my great mood, Richard. This is a dream come true for me. So, I'm going to hang up so you can concentrate on that car project...You're a sweetheart!"

The remainder of the week passed quickly with Dr. Long and Alex speaking very little about the incident. Both agreed to take a week or two to give some further thought to another strategy.

Farley Fontenot managed to convince Alex she should have dinner at his place Thursday night. She had taken the first step toward trusting him. Wearing a knee-length black leather skirt, black open toe heels, and a white long-sleeved turtleneck sweater, she entered the old Rice Hotel which had been reconstructed into a stable of lofts. Boarding the elevator, she traveled to the 8th floor and proceeded down the hallway to apartment No. 806. After banging the brass doorknocker, she heard Farley yell, "Come in."

Entering the open living area-kitchen, she spotted Farley pulling a roast from the oven. He confessed, "I'm really not surprised you accepted my invitation, because you know my reputation as a great chef."

Standing next to a countertop near the stove, she took a bite from a piece of garlic bread and replied, "I was unaware of your legendary reputation. Truth is, I didn't have anything else to do. Thought I'd give you a chance to show me you're really a gentleman and want to get to know me better for something other than sex."

Lifting the roast from a deep pan and placing it on a large serving plate, he retaliated, "I got to hand it to you, Alex, you cut to the chase. I'm patient. But there's more to me than even you can imagine. Then again, there's more to you than you'll let anyone know."

"You may be right. You may be the first to know, if you play your cards right. It's possible I might learn to like you. I do like the fact you're not pretentious."

"Well, everything's ready, so let's dig in." Pulling out a chair for her to sit, he said, "Ladies first."

Lowering herself to the chair, she offered, "Smells so scrumptious, Farley. Maybe you are a chef after all. So far, I'm impressed."

Laughing while moving around the table to a chair opposite Alex, he replied, "They always said I'd make a woman a good wife; even a stay-at-home mom."

"Who's they?"

"My parents mostly."

"Where did you pick up the culinary skills?" she asked while placing some broccoli and rice on her plate.

"Mom. I was fascinated with cooking." Watching Alex take a bite of roast, Farley asked, "Well, what do you think? Huh?"

"It's as delicious as it smells. You do have possibilities a girl might just appreciate."

Farley reached across the table to fill Alex's wine glass while asking, "What kind of possibilities would you be looking for?"

She took a taste of wine and thought for a moment. "Have you ever gone shopping for an article of clothing but didn't have a preconceived idea of what you were looking for? You'd just know it when you saw it?"

Shaking his head while expressing confusion, he answered, "Not often. But I guess I understand. There must be some basic elements a guy or an article of clothing must have."

"Yes, there is. The article of clothing or the guy?"

"The guy, of course."

"He must value closeness. Must be of impeccable character. It would help if he was the active, dashing type, a hero at heart. Must love old rock'n roll, as I have already revealed. Must love slow dancing. Being romantic is a must. That's a start."

"You call that a start? It eliminates most guys," he smirked while placing a bite of roast in his mouth.

"I'm afraid so. Are you still wanting to go to Burnet on April eighth? Or is that trip off? She asked while sticking her fork into another piece of roast, while taking note of his expression between giggles.

"No, but those are huge shoes to fill. Too bad the key to a woman's heart isn't her stomach."

"Who says it isn't a factor?"

Overwhelmed, Farley gulped down his wine and changed the subject. "Would you like to attend a play sometime at the Hobby Center? The *King and I* comes to town next month."

Smiling, Alex countered, "Boy did you come up with a diversion…Yes, I love plays."

The rest of the evening was less ground-breaking, spent sitting on the floor looking at and listening to his collection of old 45rpm records and long-play albums. When she was about to leave, he asked her to attend a big sailing show at the George R. Brown Convention Center on the weekend, but she declined saying, "I'm going to Victoria after school Friday to visit my aunt. Haven't been down there in a long time."

Falling backward until he was completely stretched out on the floor, he exclaimed, "I'm crushed."

Maneuvering to a standing position, Alex informed, "Farley, I had a wonderful time, but I really must be going. School starts early. You're lucky to not have a first period class."

Farley sprung to his feet and accompanied her to the Jeep, opening the driver's side door. "Hey, be careful, please."

Tossing her purse onto the passenger side of the vehicle and sliding into the driver's seat, Alex assured, "I promise. I won't even pick up hitchhikers."

Closing the car door, he tapped on the roof while saying, "Well, I guess I'll see you when you get back."

Placing the key into the ignition, she looked up saying, "Thanks, Farley. I feel like I know you so much better. You seem to be a genuine guy. Time will tell. Bye."

He stood in place waving while watching her drive away. "Please be careful driving to Victoria tomorrow. I have feelings for you I thought I'd never experience again."

Chapter 6

The three-hour drive south to Victoria along State Highway 59 carried Alex through such small towns as Wharton, El Campo, and Edna. In between towns, late night traffic was almost non-existent as were service stations open for business. Farmers notoriously turn out the lights and go to bed early, so the setting was not ideal for a traveler with car trouble. It was so pitch black, one could not see a hand in front of their face. The only lights outside the city limits came from the very same dance halls that served as her and Mike's stomping grounds in junior high and high school.

Listening to the great Johnny Dee and the Rocket 88's on the cassette player called up wonderful memories from those days. The parking lots were crowded this night, just as back then on a Friday night. Passing by those old wooden buildings brought tears to her eyes, as she remembered dancing with Mike back when all was right with the world.

As she reached across the center console to grab a Mounds candy bar lying on the passenger seat, she took her eyes off the road just long enough to begin tearing off the wrapper. The dark chocolate covering coconut treat was Mike's favorite. Tossing the paper on the passenger side floorboard, she looked up just in time to see the Jeep's headlights spotlighting on a terrifying sight; a little boy dressed in but a pair of jokey underwear, a cowboy hat, and extremely oversized cowboy boots. There was not a prayer to avoid running over his little body. Panic stricken, Alex screamed, "Oh, God!" while slamming down on the brake and jerking the wheel hard right.

Her right leg locked in the extended position, frantically ramming her foot on the brake pedal. It seemed as though the propelling vehicle would never stop. Anxiety was choking the breath from her, anticipating the inevitable horrifying sound and vision of the young boy's small body thumping against the front bumper and flipping up against the windshield.

After a lifetime of flashbacks, the relentless vehicle finally succumbed just off the shoulder of the highway in a cloud of smelly burning rubber. Shaken, Alex was astounded the little boy was not a bloody mess lying against the windshield. Trembling uncontrollably, her hands dropped from the steering wheel. As the smoke cleared, she began fumbling with the door latch, when the passenger side door swung open and a voice yelled out, "Did you think He was gonna let you hit me? Not on your life. I have a mission to carry out."

Trembling while engulfed in shear horror, Alex yelled, "Are you crazy? What are you doing out here on the highway? Who are you, anyway?"

Calmly pointing toward the sky, he said, "I told you. I'm a messenger from Him. I'm here to take you to Mike Koehl. That has been your wish for twenty years, so He's rewarding your persistence, I guess. If you ask me, it's stupid. And the reason for this get-up I wear would only scare you."

In total disbelief, she asked, "How can you take me to Mike when he died in a car crash on the night of our high school graduation? And how can you even know about my life back then, you sick little sawed-off shrimp? This is somebody's sick joke! You hear me?"

"It's no joke, Alexandria McCord. Time's a wasting," he proclaimed rather nonchalantly while climbing into the passenger seat and closing the door. Pointing straight ahead, he informed, "Keep on 59 here for another four miles. You'll take the Business 59 exit. Just do as I ask, or this magnificent gesture of mercy and grace from Him will be revoked. Don't be such a hardhead and get this vehicle on the road to your dream."

Still confused, Alex pleaded, while steering the Jeep back onto the highway and throttling it up to speed, "Please tell me what this is all about. How can he be alive and where?"

Looking directly at Alex, the little boy revealed, "He's alive in a time warp in Victoria. Tonight, he's waiting for you at the Optimist Club Dance, the one you used to attend every Friday night. Honey and the Teardrops are playing just like always. We must hurry so you can get there for that first dance."

"I don't get it. Is he an adult my age or what?"

"When you exit right up here on Business 59, you'll pull over into the parking lot of one of your old hangouts, the Jet Drive-In restaurant. It'll immediately be 1962 again with you two in the ninth grade at Crain Junior High."

Still trembling and overwhelmed, she pursued, "Am I actually going to be fourteen again? How long will this last? Do I ever go back to Houston? Tell me something!"

Ignoring her plea, he instructed, "Stop, this is where I get out. Right up ahead is the Jet Drive-In parking lot. When you enter, the engine and headlights will shut off, so coast into a parking spot. As soon as you exit this vehicle, you'll find yourself one block from the old Optimist Club dance hall. Mike will be inside waiting for you. You will be the only one there who knows what's going on."

Climbing out, he handed her a small metal blue and silver saucer-like object. "Here's something that you should put in your purse and keep with you. This is a clicker; when you want to leave, press this button twice and you'll instantly appear beside your car right here in the Jet Drive-In parking lot. A minute or two later, I'll appear. From there, I'll help you back on the road to Houston. This won't be your last trip, so use the clicker on Sunday afternoon and that will correspond with Houston time. From there I'll give you further information. Time's up, I gotta run." Climbing out of the car, the little boy said, "Bye for now." An instant later he disappeared.

Apprehensive, Alex slow-rolled the Jeep another two blocks before pulling into the restaurant parking lot. The headlights turned off as did the engine. Visibly afraid, she stepped outside the Jeep and waited for the magical moment. Mumbling to herself, she said, "I'm shaking so bad, I can hardly walk. I can't believe I'm doing this. In fact, I'm downright scared, that's what I am."

Just like the kid had said, no sooner had I walked into the dance hall, I was in Mike Koehl's arms slow dancing to one of our favorite songs, *You Belong to Me* by Bobby Helms. Honey and the Tear Drops sang that song so great. With Mike's arms wrapped around my waist and mine around his neck, my cheek was just under his chin. Nothing in the world compared to this. I wanted so badly to just breakdown and cry for happiness. I was on my tiptoes trembling while melting in his embrace. I never wanted this moment to end. Memories just flashed through my brain like a fast-moving slide show.

I saw myself cheering on the sidelines after Mike would drop back and heave one of those long passes to Jimmy Joe or make a long run down the sideline like he did against city arch rival Patti Welder in the last game of the season.

When he would hit a long jump shot in basketball, we'd cheer out "and the score goes up another notch. Rah, rah, Koehl!"

And those magnificent games he'd pitch in the summer. He could just throw that ball right past the hitters. He was so handsome standing on the pitcher's mound like an invincible warrior. Seemed like everyone loved Mike Koehl.

I just know he felt me shaking as I cried tears of happiness when he squeezed me tighter. The tears found their way down my face as Honey and the Teardrops played Mike's favorite song, *Mountain of Love* by Harold Dorman. But it took me back to that fateful night after our high school graduation dance.

He had taken me home and drove straight to Lee Yariger's dad's Gulf Service Station to uncap his headers so he could race Bill Kratz. Mike's '57 Chevy was considered one of the fastest in all of Victoria County, but Kratz, who graduated two years before, had a '56 Ford that was causing quite a stir.

They raced down the Cuero Highway at the far end of town. Onlookers said Mike was pulling ahead when a car driven by an old couple pulled out from a stop sign in front of him. He swerved off the highway to avoid them and rolled over several times before hitting a culvert. He died at the scene. I knew then I could never love again – there was nothing left of me to love with. I remember wanting to die so I could be with him in Heaven. All I could remember thinking was 'why did you have to leave me here by myself?'

Just then Mike leaned back while still holding me. We just stopped moving on the dance floor when he looked at me asking, "What's the matter, sugar?"

Never looking up, I just mumbled, "Nothing really. I'm just so happy to be here with you."

Flashing that irresistible smile, he reassured, "I'll always be right here with you." And he pulled me closer and we continued to dance. The world never felt so good.

After the dance, I was back sitting next to Mike in that gorgeous turquoise and white Chevy. We always sat hip to hip with my left arm around his neck, placing frequent kisses on his ear. We were headed to Ferguson's Drug Store in the Town & County Shopping Center. It was a hangout that always stayed open a couple hours after our dances or a school function.

The whole gang was there - Jimmy Joe and Judy; Craig and Karen; Lee and Diane; Ronald and Georgia; Ray and Dorothy; and Arthur and Pat. Jimmy Joe put a quarter in the jukebox and the old familiar tunes rang out. It was so great to all be together again. I couldn't help but wonder why everyone was in this warp. I knew why I was here, but why were they? I was so glad they were though.

The night ended with Mike driving me home. That was really strange. Times were really neat back then, because you could get your driver's license at fourteen. You took Driver's Education after the eighth grade during the summer. That gave you a learner's permit and from there, you could take the test to receive a full-blown driver's license once you turned fourteen.

As we embraced on the porch, my dad turned on the light above the door. That was the ten-minute warning. Pressing myself against Mike, I kissed that guy like there was no tomorrow.

Mike always managed to pull from my grasp before dad had to open the door. I guess that was one reason dad liked him so much. Walking down the sidewalk Mike looked over his shoulder to let me know, "I'll pick you up at six-thirty tomorrow for the YMCA dance."

Leaning on the porch post, I waved and softly said, "Good night."

I turned and entered the house, climbing up the stairs to my bedroom. It was an awesome sight to see it just as it was twenty something years ago. I threw myself on the bed and lay on my back looking around the room. The bed was a present on my thirteenth birthday. My mom saw me eyeing this same canopy bed with a pink and white comforter sprinkled with embroidered hot pink roses. We were standing in Kaymin's Furniture Store while dad was buying mom a new davenport.

The walls were adorned with pictures of Fabian, Connie Frances, Frankie Avalon, Annette Funicello and Troy Donahue. But the best picture of all was Mike and me at the YMCA Christmas Dance. On my dresser, stood a picture of us taken during the ninth-grade athletic awards ceremony.

Then there was the junior high cheerleading outfit and pom poms hanging on the closet door. The skirt was a green pleated one and the long sleeve sweater top was white with a big green 'C' on the front. We were the mighty Crain Comets. Draped over the chair by the dresser was my green and white school jacket.

On a shelf by themselves were the foot-high porcelain dolls – Rhett Butler and Scarlet O'Hara from *Gone With The Wind.* That was really Mike and me, but only I knew that.

The next morning, I awoke to the smell of mom cooking breakfast. It would be a day spent helping her clean house. That was one of our ways of bonding. We were close and sharing the chores brought us closer. Nothing pleased dad more than seeing mom and me working together in harmony. We were his two most favorite ladies he'd always say. It was all I could do to keep from crying. To be with mom and dad again was something I hadn't thought about until now. It was wonderful.

Mike always arrived thirty minutes before our date to talk to dad about sports, cars, or whatever else they could conjure up. We were surely destined to be the happiest couple in Victoria or anywhere else.

As always, Mike and dad would talk until I came down the stairs. Mike stood up and proclaimed, "Wow. You look sensational."

Dad moved up behind him and put his arm on Mike's shoulder. "Doesn't she though. And that's the way I'm sure you'll bring her home. Know what I mean?"

Without looking back at dad and never taking his eyes off me, Mike replied, "Yes, sir, I never intended different. Just so you'll know, my dad already covered that for you."

I saw the strangest sight as we entered the YMCA building. Johnny Dee and the Rocket 88s were on stage ripping out their first song. Though they always dressed 50s, they were not around back then, but no one acted like they knew any different. Besides feeling funny in a fourteen-year-old body, this was certainly peculiar. How could this be?

I had the weirdest feeling Johnny Dee was looking right at me the whole time during their first set. But their presence made the night even better, especially when they sang 'Earth Angel' by the Penguins. Johnny Dee did say once they were his favorite group.

When Mike went to the bathroom during the band's first break, I walked over to the table where the huge punch bowls rested. While pouring a glass for Mike and myself, a deep voice called my name. "Having a good time, Alex?"

I almost dropped both glasses while looking back to see who addressed me. It was Johnny Dee himself with his lovely wife Marylyn standing next to him. Now I was really confused. "How'd you know who I am?"

"You come to most of my shows. I signed a picture for you a month ago and a shirt before that. I'd never forget you."

Barely able to respond while trying to figure out what he was doing here, I said, "How can you be here?"

"I'm here for you. Just got in town this afternoon. I've been asked to play at the dances you and Mike attend. Didn't have an opportunity to be here last night, but I won't miss any more. The Man wants me to keep an eye on you."

"Now I'm really mixed up."

"Honey, everyone here came for a specific reason. Jimmy Joe and Judy were having trouble with their marriage and prayed for a chance to go back and find each other again. They will progress up the ladder to adulthood again and hopefully grow together this time. There are numerous reasons for starting over and true love is the best one of all. None of them even remembers their prior adult life. If they could, those memories would block a true second chance to start over. They'll all grow out of this dimension someday with fond memories, hopefully."

He continued, "You're the only one aware of the reason you are here. Only you know the final outcome, should you decide to visit this dimension again. Mike is not aware of his fatal accident. It's like it never happened. You'll have approximately three and a half years to relive those wonderful moments you've never gotten over. Honey, if it were me, living through Mike's accident would not be something to repeat. You might want to never come back after trip number three. Anyway, the little guy will fill you in on the details.

"Craig and Karen are here because she was diagnosed with a fatal cancer. They'll at least have a chance to relieve their life up until her time is up, and hopefully they'll do a better job of caring for each other this time."

Terrified and confused, I asked, "Mike's going to die again? I'm blown away! But why? Why can't I just stay here with him forever?"

"I can't answer that one. Here comes Mike. I better fade. Hey, I learned that song you like. I'll be playing it next. Hope you like it."

The band broke into my favorite song by Sunny and the Sunglows, *Talk to Me*. I just couldn't hold back the tears. I started sobbing, and the next thing I knew, a full-blown crying spell took over. Poor Mike was at a loss for words. I just whispered in his ear, “Please don’t ask any questions. Just hold me tight.”

Like a true prince, he never asked a single question, but held me like it’d be the last time we’d see each other. Johnny Dee somehow knew all the right songs to play from that point on; all upbeat or fast, bringing me out of my misery in time to salvage the evening. Now I know what he was sent here for. I can’t imagine waking up some morning to the realization that he and the Rocket 88’s have retired. No more of their great music.

When the night was over, Mike took me home. We all had Sunday School and church in the morning, so I was required to be home immediately after the dance. Mike gave me a kiss after opening the passenger door, and I ran up the sidewalk and waived to him as he drove away. Much the same way he did that fateful night years ago.

Overwrought with hurt, I decided to bypass Sunday, so I clicked for that little boy and found myself standing beside the Jeep with him sitting in the passenger seat.

Opening the door, I slid into the driver’s side asking hysterically, “Why didn’t you tell me Mike is going to die again! That even if I stay here forever, he’s still going to have that accident?”

“Geez, Johnny and his big mouth. Your prayer was to spend a few moments. I think three and a half years is generous. I was going to tell you about that, but you were already too overwhelmed. Now is when I had planned to tell you.”

Not responding to his answer, Alex drove until the boy gave

her the word to stop.

"I get out here." Climbing out of the car, he consoled. "I'll see what He says about your case. I'll put in a plea on your behalf. Keep your fingers crossed. Now drive home safely by keeping your mind on your driving. If you have a fatal accident, then we have a real problem. So would Johnnie Wimbush. I'll tell you more on your next trip."

"How do you know who Johnnie Wimbush is?"

"Everyone where I live knows who you are and what your everyday life is like. Don't you get it? The Him I am referring to is God! You know, Heaven – the place I'm from?"

"OK. Ok. What day will it be when I get home?"

"Same as now. The next time you want to see Mike, simply do as you did this time. I'll be at this spot waiting for you. But you must come on a Friday night. Oh, I almost forgot, you have three visits to decide if you want to live out those final three and a half years. You have two more. If you go back a fourth time, you're there for the duration. Now scram, you have work to do back in Houston," he ordered while closing the door.

Chapter 7

Wrapped in a long purple satin robe while sporting fur high heel house slippers, Alex ambled into the kitchen early Sunday morning and pulled a small cast iron pot from a cabinet under the stove and half filled it with water. Reaching for the cardboard container of Quaker Oats, she poured ½ cup into the pot and placed it on the stove before turning on the gas burner. She had oatmeal for breakfast every morning, adding walnut halves after cooking. That's in addition to the usual protein drink she would concoct once the oatmeal was inhaled.

Physically and emotionally exhausted, Alexandria would forego church. Instead she plopped down on the sofa, stretched her feet across a coffee table and commenced eating the oatmeal while watching the television ministry of Charles Stanley, entitled *In Touch*. Pondering the prospect of confiding in Richard the incredible miracle of Friday and Saturday dominated her thoughts. He would surely not believe one single word of the tale. For crying out loud, she was having trouble believing what happened. The need to tell someone was so overpowering, perhaps Laura might be the better choice.

As Dr. Stanley signed off, Alex wandered back into the kitchen to blend up her usual protein and strawberry shake to go along with the oatmeal. This day, she was going to add local honey and some whole almonds to the oats. Poor nutrition leading to failing health was a constant fear.

Returning to the couch with the cold, thick drink, she concerned herself with the task of substantiating the episode really happened. Placing her fur covered feet back on the coffee table while taking another gulp of liquid nutrition, a flash of light illuminated the darkness. The "clicker" gadget given to her by the little messenger boy lay in the Jeep's front seat passenger side. It was the breakthrough she needed to convince Richard without his being totally skeptical or unbelieving.

Leaping to her feet, she placed the glass on the coffee table and waltzed through the kitchen and out the back door to the garage where the Jeep was parked. Opening the passenger side front door, she spotted the blue and silver metal "clicker" right where she had left it. Shouting for joy, she yelled, "Explain this away, Richard!"

Quickly shuffling back into the kitchen and grabbing the receiver from the wall cradle, she sat in a chair at the table while dialing her uncle's phone number. Placing the "clicker" on the table, she began mumbling while the phone rang. "I hope you're sitting down, uncle."

Moments later, a voice on the other end of the line answered, "Hello, Alex, how was your trip?"

"How'd you know it was me?"

"You're the only person I know who would call me this early on Sunday morning. So, to what do I credit this call?"

Taking a deep breath in an effort to keep from bursting out in laughter from nerves, Alex blurted out, "I saw Mike this weekend."

Silence pervaded on the other end of the phone line for several seconds before Alexandria continued, "Richard are you still there? Are you sitting down?"

"I'm still here. As a matter of fact, I'm at my desk working on a paper for a professional journal. But I'm now trying to figure out what 'Mike' you're referring to."

Placing her elbows on the table, she answered, "There's only one Mike, Richard. This is not a prank. I have this awful need to share a miraculous experience with someone. You and Laura are the only ones I trust. You're the only ones who know how I feel; how to relate to this."

Sliding his chair back from the desk, Richard asked, "Alex, you do know people don't come back to life after twenty years, don't you?"

"Could you possibly tear yourself away from what you're doing and come over here? I have something to show you as proof."

"Give me an hour and a half."

"I'll be waiting Unc. I'll be waiting."

Professor Kim arrived almost to the minute of the hour and a half promised. Alex opened the back door, as Richard always drove all the way up the driveway to the back of the house between the kitchen and the detached garage. Closing the door after he entered, Alex pointed toward the table where the clicker lay. "Ever see anything like that before?"

Approaching the table, he picked up the blue and silver metal object, observing, "Sure is heavy for its size. The metal is unbelievably dense." Looking at Alex intensely, he asked, "So I assume this is the proof of your encounter?"

"Let's go into the living room and I'll tell you all about this encounter that I know you won't believe. Please hear me all the way through before you start in with your 'It's impossible' speech."

Sauntering into the living room, Alexandria slumped on the couch with her feet stretched across the long coffee table, while Richard found a plush leather recliner. He encouraged, "I'm a captive audience, so blow me away. I'm all ears."

Alex proceeded to recall the entire experience in explicit detail. Richard listened politely as agreed, uttering not a word. Concluding the story, she solicited his opinion, "What do you think? Give it to me, both barrels, while I'm assuming the position of a patient in my shrinks' office."

Leaning forward, bringing the recliner to the upright position, he was almost at a loss for words. "My gut feeling believes you, but my intellect totally rejects the plausibility. Quite frankly, I was afraid I'd arrive and see that you had flipped out."

"Sorry to disappoint you. It'd have been much easier that way."

"I agree with you there."

"If I had flipped out, neither one of us would have to deal with this seemingly impossible happening. We could just disregard the statements conjured up by a crazy woman."

"Alex, the real question is: 'What are you going to do?' And I can't believe I'm asking that question regarding such an absurd episode. Surely this isn't really happening."

"I'm going to play it out for a while until I can comprehend what's happening. Richard, I went through it and can hardly believe what took place. To say it's kinda scary is an understatement."

Looking around the room, Richard sighed, saying, "Alexandria, this year your life is getting way too complicated. You've gone from an occasional job rescuing old people, to full-blown war on crime with your life on the line, and now the supernatural. I really do wish you could just walk away from all this and concentrate on teaching. Maybe even have some fun."

"My life has meaning now, Richard. I just know God has chosen me to serve justice in His name. We all have a need to be needed or have a purpose. You have your writing and speaking engagements. Heck, South Korea offered you the number three job in their government. For all of that, you get to be my stabilizing force. Ha!"

Standing up and stretching his arms above his head yawning, Richard informed, "I can't tell you how relieved I am you didn't flip out. But I must get back and work on that paper for American Political Science Quarterly. I have to sleep on this, believe me."

"I'm going to spend the remainder of the day letting this soak in and preparing for school tomorrow," she said popping up off the sofa. "I have to come back to earth. If I don't, those kids will see right through me. They'll know something's up."

Richard waltzed through the kitchen to the back door with Alex following suit. Grabbing the doorknob, he advised, "You better figure a way to keep Farley from sensing his competition comes from the spirit world. He'll likely be the one to see right through you if you're not careful…Please don't forget your prayers. Never stop asking Him to let his perfect will for your life manifest itself. You hear me Alexandria McCord? His perfect will for your life without you monkeying with it."

"I always do. Sounds like you don't trust me, Unc." Closing the door, she hollered, "You do the same you hear?"

Waving back at her, Richard climbed into his 1971 silver and black Ford Mustang Mach 1. Backing out of the driveway, he honked once before steering the pony car down the street and out of sight.

No sooner had Alex closed the door, the phone rang; it was Laura Reynolds with some news about Johnnie.

"Alex, I'm at the Center. Johnnie just showed up, and he's shooting some buckets. You might want to come down here, that is, if you want a chance to talk to him alone.

"Yes! Holy cow, Laura, do what you can to keep him there. I'm gonna throw some clothes on and be there in 30 minutes tops."

"I'll do what I can."

Within thirty minutes, Alex had arrived at the Community Center. Exiting the car, she raced toward the entrance where Laura was waiting, holding the door open. "He's still doing some drills and taking shots. It's heartbreaking just watching knowing he's giving up his future."

Rushing through the door, she said, "It's not over yet."

As Alex walked into the gym, Johnnie stopped what he was doing and stood facing his teacher. Fumbling with the words to explain his dropping out of school, he offered, "I guess we know why you're here."

Never hesitating, she answered, "You're quite correct. You're having to throw away your dreams and those of your grandfather. He didn't raise you to let that scum rob you both of happiness. Myself and Dr. Long are going to do everything in our power to save you and your grandfather."

"Gramps said you and Principal Long dropped by the store. The Reapers control the entire neighborhood. I have no doubt they will kill us if you don't just walk away. They'll make an example out of us for those who also might have plans to leave or better themselves."

The realization of Johnnie's statement was undeniable. Conventional law enforcement could not act on a threat nor protect them both. There was also the question of police manpower to watch over the two until the Reapers act. The only way for law enforcement to act is after-the-fact; when it's too late to save Johnnie and Silas from the hands of Willie Buchanan.

Then it occurred to her to ask Johnnie about home school. "Would you be willing to do your school work at home? I could get the assignments from all your classes and bring them to you. Then I could pick them up and give them to your other teachers. That way you could at least graduate."

Pausing for a moment, he replied, "What's the use? I'm stuck working at the tire shop four blocks from the store. The Reapers got me that job. Part of the deal is I can't leave the neighborhood. This place here is as far as I can go. Any farther, they'll kill gramps and me. He's been my whole life; my compass. I wouldn't know what love is without him."

Puzzled, Alex inquired, "You live two miles from here, so do you have a car?"

"Gramps lets me use his seventy-two Chevy Cheyenne truck. He bought it brand new, and it still looks new."

"Johnnie, I'm going to spend all my waking moments to come up with some way. I'm not going to give up, ever. I gotta go."

"Miss McCord, thank you for caring. But I doubt there is a way out. I thought about taking out Willie Boy, but the Reapers are many, and they'd retaliate. Can't kill them all. Even if I did, then I'd go to jail. Who'd look out for gramps? Face it, there is no solution."

After a moment of reflection, she offered while walking away, "We'll see. I have a friend who handles stuff like this. You are seeing this through the eyes of a seventeen-year-old. I am old enough to see a much larger picture. I am going to leave here and immediately start working on your future; the one you and Gramps dream about."

Monday was hectic. Alex had no time to reflect on the most wonderful, yet startling weekend of her life since that fatal night Mike died in a car crash, let alone the heartbreaking meeting with the ever-elusive Johnnie Wimbush. Her first period class was in a feeding frenzy for knowledge of the Forefathers' stance on prayer and the role it played in the formative years of America. Led by Scot Barton, they had been in the process of forming a student delegation proposing to challenge the no prayer in school decision by the U.S. Supreme Court.

However, on this particular morning, the class was buzzing over some big-time breaking local news. As Alex entered the classroom, Scot shouted, "Ms. McCord, someone killed that Getty guy! Can you believe it?"

Placing her satchel on the desktop, Alex leaned against the front side of her desk asking in disbelief, "Is this your idea of a joke?"

Lee Zimmerli stood up and yelled, "No ma'am, it's the gospel truth. Someone shot him last night!"

Scot added, "He got what he deserved. He was warned by that Captain America guy, but ignored the warning. Good riddance to him!"

Caught off-balance by the news, Alex was at a loss for words. Who could have done this? Pulling herself together, she managed to say, "I'm blown away by this. I don't know what to say, actually."

Scot added, "It's time to party! Wow, there is justice in this world sometimes. Some guy out there is my hero. He's a superhero in fact. Belongs up there with Superman, Batman and Flash Gordon!"

Karen Austin informed, "My dad said he read where all the employees would be reimbursed and their pensions reinstated."

As the classroom echoed with students' joyous celebration, Alex could not take her mind off wondering who could have done such a deed. It was somewhat scary to think another figure is involved. She was going to give Getty another week before taking action.

Alex managed to use the moment to have a class discussion concerning taking the law into your own hands. She asked them to think very deeply within their conscience if Getty actually deserved to die. There have been times in world history where courts sentenced a man to death for a similar act against society. Although it could be argued justice was served, was such an act by the assailant still murder, punishable by a court of law in this country up to and including the death penalty?

When the class bell sounded, Alex let the students rush through the door before trekking to Principal Long's office as requested.

Appearing in the doorway to Dr. Long's office, the principal acknowledged, "Alex, have a seat please. The reason I called you in here was to get some background on this movement Scot Barton is leading. There were two cases that killed prayer in school; the *Engel v. Vitale* case in 1962, and the other was *Madalyn Murray O'Hair v. Curlett* in 1963. She was an evil woman filled with bitterness. She wanted revenge on God."

Slipping into a chair in front of his desk, she explained, "Dr. Long, it has grown out of our study of the Founding Fathers and their writings concerning the basis of a wise government. When you read the letters and speeches, as well as prayers, you'll wonder how our Supreme Court could possibly have rendered such a seemingly poorly thought out decision. It's had such a negative impact on young people especially."

"I agree. Most of the Court's decision was influenced by Jefferson and Madison. Jefferson was misconstrued on a term called 'wall of separation,' which he himself later explained was misconstrued. They all prayed before each session of Congress. The liberals of this country want to tear it down. Democracy and freedom as we know it today is going to be a thing of the past. Madison simply was reacting to the situation in England with the State religion. I'd like to turn this into a full-blown school forum. It'll give the students something to rally around. Know what I mean, Alexandria? Together?"

"Yes, sir, I do. I assure you I do."

Changing the subject, Dr. Long revealed, "I must confess I haven't given much thought about Johnnie Wimbush lately. I've been busy putting this new plan together I outlined in my school speech. That, and my working on the budget. Quite frankly, I'm at a loss for any ideas concerning Johnnie."

Alex wasted no time divulging, "I saw Johnnie yesterday.

The Reapers have threatened to kill him and his grandfather if Johnnie so much as leaves the neighborhood except for work to pay they're protection demands. The Reapers actually got him a job at some tire shop four blocks from Silas' grocery store. He rejected the idea of home-schooling quite naturally."

"Our hands appear to be tied. I'm willing to listen to any ideas you come up with. We'd have to relocate Johnnie and his grandpa, along with the grocery. And we know that's impossible."

Standing up she smiled saying, "Maybe God will have an angel appear in my sleep delivering His solution. Maybe the answer is to relocate the Grimm Reapers."

Puzzled, Dr. Long said, "Huh? I'm afraid you've lost me."

"Just a knee-jerk thought. I'll let you know as soon as I unlose myself. And by the way, someone shot and killed Paul Getty last night. My first period students are elated. We had been discussing recent events that aroused their feelings one way or another. The Lympko Corporation rape of their employees topped their list. Shooting Mr. Getty was their unanimous response. And it happened. Interesting, huh?"

The principal had no reply, but his facial expression was worth a thousand words as the saying goes.

After school, Alex drove home and called Farley, leaving a message on his voice recorder to meet her in front of the book checkout counter inside the public library downtown at 7 p.m. The message conveyed a sense of urgency, so she planned to be there if he did not call her.

Entering through the revolving door, the ever-faithful Farley showed up and immediately spotted Alex standing near the front desk and made his way through a maze of display standees to slip in next to her. "This must be mighty important for you to ask me to meet you at the library. I can't imagine what could be so urgent. Hopefully this is a good sign; you need me for something."

Motioning to a nearby table, she said, "Please sit down. I didn't want to go to some bar, and dinner is out of the question because I have no appetite. And yes, I'm quite surprised myself, so it's apparently a good sign. I have a big problem, and I'm turning to you."

Pulling a chair from under the table and taking a seat, Farley remarked, "How could I possibly help you? Get lost? Ha! ... OK, shoot."

"Johnnie Wimbush and his grandfather are in deep trouble. A gang called the Grimm Reapers terrorizes them both; the whole neighborhood in fact. The boy had to quit school and work full time to pay for his grandfather's protection insurance...from the Grimm Reapers."

Interrupting, Farley informs, "Did you know the Grimm Reapers are on the big list of dangerous gangs. You're probably going to ask the police to do something. Well, they can't. Not until a crime is committed. Detective Kinstley would love nothing more than to put them away, especially their leader, Willie Buchanan. But no one will testify against them."

"I was about to say, they will not even allow us to home-school Johnny. Any attempt to continue his education in any form will bring harm to them both. I need your help getting him back to school."

"Alex, I don't have the slightest idea right now. It'd take some time to work up a plan. Off hand, I'd say the only way would be to set the gang up. Be waiting for them to attempt harm on Johnnie and his grandfather. Maybe have Johnnie attend school with a tail on him and a stakeout at the grocery store. But you have to catch Mr. Buchanan himself. Without the man himself in jail, you have not accomplished anything. In fact, even in prison, Willie Boy can direct the gang to do Silas and Jonnie as much harm as he wishes. To put this in perspective for you, some wonderful administrator of justice, untouchable by the law, would have to kill Willie Buchanan and at least half of the rest of the gang, and we both know that ain't happening."

"OK. I agree, but we have to try something. So, what would we have to do to get that stake-out arrangement?"

"My friend, Buddy Hodges, could talk to Detective Kinstley. I think I told you before, those two guys have a close friendship. It'd be a major operation since most of the local patrolmen are paid handsomely to look the other way."

"Maybe I'll visit Silas and Johnnie after school tomorrow. I could see if they would be willing to give it a try. It'll be tough to convince Silas. How are we going to coordinate this?"

"I'll talk to Hodges tomorrow. You know you've bitten off an impossible assignment. I hate to see you go there tomorrow just to set this up. If Detective Kinstley likes the idea, maybe you should let him take it from here."

"What if Detective Kinstley is not interested? From what I've read, the mayor wants him to concentrate on bringing that dangerous Masked Marvel to justice."

"I just wish you wouldn't go into that neighborhood anymore."

"Why?"

"The gang left an old poverty-stricken neighborhood on the northwest side. It had become void of any small businesses to hold hostage for protection payments. They relocated to our school's area to terrorize a more affluent neighborhood with a greater number of young people who could be forced to become members. That is as long as Centennial stays open. Right now, the Reapers are fully entrenched there. They rule with as much violence as any gang we've seen. I hate to admit this, but you're quite correct; with the Masked Marvel causing such a stir, the Reapers are not the highest priority right now. So, please stay off that turf."

"I may be the only one who can talk to Johnnie. If I can't convince him and his grandfather to cooperate, Detective Kinstley can save himself a trip. I get the feeling what you're really saying is, there's probably no help in sight. Am I correct?"

Looking up at the ceiling and sighing, he regrettably replied, "There's very little hope with the department's focus on that masked man. The media coverage supporting Mr. Marvel's efforts is an embarrassment to both the mayor and commissioner. But I promise to approach Buddy about your problem."

Reaching across the table and touching Farley's hand, she said, "Thanks, for meeting me. I have a bad feeling the grandfather will not have any part of this. If not, Johnnie probably will not attempt to go back to school. It's like a death sentence. The only hope is for me to be able to promise police protection, and that probably won't happen according to your assessment. We're not just talking about Johnnie, but all the kids in the neighborhood of legal age to work now and in the future."

"You're right, so there's no reason to go until I talk to Buddy."

"I still have to ask Silas if he'd cooperate with police protection. I just need to know. Don't ask me why, because I am not sure."

Sliding his chair from the table, Farley rose to his feet. "Well, I guess we'll forgo the hug and kiss in public. I have one major question: Is this the type of work we, as teachers, are supposed to be doing? Ask yourself that question."

Looking up at him, she winked, "Bye, Farley. I'll cross my fingers."

"Pray instead."

Predictably, Alex motored toward the Wimbush neighborhood the next day after school. She guided her car along the roadway until she came up beside the corner grocery store and turned into the small adjacent parking lot. Exiting the Jeep, she walked around to the front side of the building and pushed open the door.

Looking up from his work, Mr. Wimbush shouted, "I thought I told you not to come back here! They weren't too happy with your last visit. They broke the windshield on my old truck. No telling what they'll do this time."

Alex responded, "Mr. Wimbush, I think we have a plan to put those boys in jail. I would like to explain."

"All I want you to do is explain yourself right out of here as fast as you can," Silas ordered. "If you have any sort of feelings for me or Johnnie, please don't come back!"

"Don't you want to put those guys away and free yourself and Johnnie?" Alex pleaded. "Heck, free the neighborhood?"

Becoming more irate, Silas stepped toward Alex pointing toward the door, yelling, "Get out of here! Beat it! There's nothing you can do!"

"We can have a police stakeout and catch them attacking you or Johnnie. Detective Mike Kinstley wants the Reapers bad. You can help."

"Leave my store now before I throw you out," he yelled while raising his hand as if he were going to physically push Alex out of the store.

Convinced it was hopeless, Alex maneuvered out the door and headed back to the parking lot. Approaching her vehicle, she saw a group of the Reapers leaning against the fenders and hood. One of them was the leader himself, Willie Buchanan. For the first time, she felt the reality of the situation.

"Hey teacher lady, I thought we already expressed our concern for you being here? Huh? Didn't we tell you not to come back?"

Not knowing what to say, she instead chose to remain silent and see what their next move would entail.

"What's the matter? Cat got your tongue? You too good to talk to us?"

Standing in place, Alex couldn't help wishing she had thought to bring her .45 automatic. Hindsight revealed the mistake she made by not returning home from school to fetch the handgun before entering into this neighborhood. Bluffing, she remarked in desperation, "You don't think I was so stupid as to come here alone, do you?"

Walking toward her waving his arms in the air displaying provoked anger, Willie said, "Hey, I don't think anyone knows where you are." Motioning for the others to follow him, he added, "We're gonna have to teach you a lesson for your own good. It's gonna hurt a little bit. But not near as bad as the next time you show your once pretty face around here."

Fear gripped Alex as she had never known. A single Kung Fu artist whipping several assailants all at once only happens in movies. After all the times of inflicting the fear factor, she was now on the receiving end; should have heeded Farley's advice. The only question now was how bad they were going to hurt her. With no viable exit for retreat, she was suddenly overcome with anger and hate. Unadulterated hate for the man who killed her parents and their friends would propel each and every blow she could manage to strike. Taking the Kung Fu stance of the tiger, Alex readied herself to strike the first blow with every intention of making as many of them pay as possible for their intentions.

Just as Willie Boy and the others were poised for the attack, a black 1970 Boss 429 Mustang roared into the parking lot, and the driver stepped out wielding a .357 Magnum, firing four booming shots toward the antagonists, hitting one in his left shoulder and another in the thigh.

Quickly withdrawing their attention from Alex, they grabbed their badly wounded comrades and fled across the street while returning fire and disappearing into an alley. The driver refrained from further discharging any shots for fear of hitting any innocent bystanders.

Turning to see her savior, a wide grin swept across Alex's face. It was Farley! He was such a welcomed sight. How he knew she was here could have only been the work of the Lord. Now she would have to feign being the helpless maiden in distress, although she was most certain to have come out on the short end of the assault.

The hero hustled over to see what kind of condition she was in and was jolted off balance from the death grip Alex put on him, wrapping her arms around his neck. "I can't believe you're here! I've never been so glad to see anyone in my life!" That part was real.

He returned the embrace, replying, "It's OK, they're gone. They're gone, Alex… Let's get out of here. Come on, climb in your Jeep and I'll follow you home."

"OK. Let me get the keys out of my purse." Fumbling with the snaps on her purse, she finally managed to reach in and grab the key chain. "My hands are still shaking."

Holding open the door while she climbed into the seat, he asked, "Are you going to be able to drive?"

"Yes, but you stay close you hear?" That part was fake.

"I'll be right on your bumper."

Turning on the ignition, she repeated, "You better stay close Mr. Fontenot." That part was also feigned.

"I promise. Shall I follow you home or do you want to talk this over at dinner."

"Dinner, I guess."

"OK. That'll be fine."

Sitting in a booth at Los Jocales Restaurant on Lyons Avenue, munching on a blooming onion while waiting for their dinner, Farley reminded, "If you'll remember, I asked you not go into that neighborhood alone."

Thinking about how different the situation might have been had she at least brought her Colt .45, just burned a hole in her stomach. Next time the mighty Reapers would be looking down the barrel of a Remington 870 pump shotgun. She could not help thinking how satisfying it would be to have a chance to take on Willie Boy one on one.

Reaching across the table, Farley touched her hand saying, "Alex, are you somewhere else? Can I bring you back?"

Snapping out of her hypnotic state, she shook her head saying, "I'm sorry. What did you say? I was still thinking about what a close call I had."

"I thought I lost you for a moment. I said, do you remember my asking you not to go alone?"

"Yes, I do. Don't worry, I've learned my lesson. By the way, how did it happen that you were in the neighborhood?"

"I didn't trust you to wait for me so we could go together tomorrow."

"Lucky for me, huh?"

"So, what did the grandfather say to you? Was he receptive to your plan? My guess is no."

Reaching for a piece of the huge fried onion, she replied, "No. In fact, he practically threw me out. This thing has become an obsession. It breaks my heart to think some punks can dictate someone's life with such cruelty. And the more I think about it, the madder I get. I'm just angry and frustrated."

Drinking from his glass of water, Farley advised, "Alex, sometimes you have to let go for the sake of your own sanity. You can't go around trying to save the world. Someday this Masked Marvel we have running around town will realize that and hopefully it'll be before he's caught and put behind bars like a common criminal. Inside, I cheer for him every time I read or hear about his latest heroics. If he were a woman, I'd ask her to marry me."

Smiling out the side of her mouth, Alex answered, "Really. That's interesting. Would you clean your guns together?"

"I'd just hope I could get to her before the law locks her up. Now that sounds stupid. We're not talking about a girl anyway. We're talking about some magnificent male folk hero running out of his nine lives."

Laughing out loud, Alex offered, "Better marry him before the law does."

"You're real funny. Does this mean some of that electronic force field surrounding you is losing some of its wallop?"

"Maybe," she responded, taking a sip from her tall glass of water while maintaining eye contact. "What kind of car is that you're driving? God, it just shook the ground when you pulled into the parking lot. I just love that sound."

Chest all pumped up, Farley replied, "It's a 1970 Boss 429 Mustang. They only made five hundred of those things. The motor was developed for Ford's NASCAR race team. In order to use it for that purpose, the rules required five hundred had to make their way into a street machine. Ford chose to put it in the Mustang."

"I'm impressed, and that doesn't happen too often when it comes to cars. It just looks fast sitting there."

"Maybe I could take you for a real ride sometime."

"You're winning me over an inch at a time."

Chapter 8

Tuesday morning Alex arose thirty minutes earlier than customary to take a shower and shampoo her hair; a move affording enough time for the preparation of a breakfast with a greater nutritional punch. Oatmeal, half a grapefruit, along with an omelet consisting of four whole eggs, lean pork, cheddar cheese, green peppers, and milled flaxseed provided the extra go-power punch to support her ramped up anti-Grimm Reapers workout regimen. Afterward, she blended her customary protein shake to carry with her to school, a food offering to her muscles for a mid-morning feeding frenzy.

With her new morning ritual complete, she grabbed the keys to the Jeep and proceeded to steer the vehicle through the streets on the path to school. Her mood was especially upbeat, as Scot Barton was scheduled to entertain her first period history class, revealing some of the research findings supporting his cult following's contention our Founding Fathers would have preferred prayer in school

Addressing the class in an amusing fashion, Alex informed, "We seem to have a dynamic leader of a student uprising in our presence; a champion of God and a crusader for payer in school. Would such a hero please stand and be recognized?"

Beaming with pride and playing along on queue, Scot Barton stood tall in the saddle. "I want to thank you for your testimony, Ms. McCord. I'm honored to be held in such high esteem."

Shuffling his way amongst the class, Scot gave each student a short summary of the famous Supreme Court case: *Engle v. Vitale* (1962). "It was the first of many such cases that started the ball rolling on the separation of church and state, removing prayer from school. The Engle family, members of the Unitarian Church, challenged the Board of Education of New Hyde Park, New York because it adopted a non-denominational prayer to be recited each morning before class began. By the way, our U.S. Congress does something similar when they convene. Arguments were made before the Court on April 3, 1962 and on June 25, 1962. The Supreme Court ruled 7-1 that it was unconstitutional for a government agency like a school, etc. to require students to recite prayers.

"I shall read the prayer in question: 'Almighty God, we acknowledge our dependence upon Thee, and we beg Thy blessings upon us, our parents, our teachers, and our country.' So, where's the harm acknowledging the very maker our Founding Fathers credited with the success of the Union? Can anyone please tell me, how this one sentence prayer offends any religion? Does this infer the Unitarian Church does not believe in God? Actually, some Unitarian churches, do not. They are the ones looking for answers."

Before Scot could continue, Alex asked, "Do you mind sharing with the rest of us some of your findings which indicate our Founding Fathers did not intend for prayer in school or any other government agency be abolished? Anything to show separation of church and state was misinterpreted?" Alex had done her own research.

"Be glad to. Exhibit A is a quote from the famous Alexis de Tocqueville, the French statesman and theorist who came to America in the 1830s. He was asked, and I quote, 'What makes America great?' His answer spanned hundreds of pages and was published in two separate volumes. His response: 'There is no country in the world where the Christian religion retains a greater influence over the souls of men than in America, and there can be no greater proof of its utility and of its conformity to human nature than that its influence is powerfully felt over the most enlightened and free nation of the earth. Not until I went into the churches of America and heard the pulpits flame with righteousness did, I understand the secret of her genius and power.' You want to hear some more?"

"What do you say class? Shall we let him keep the floor?"

The resounding answer was unanimously in favor of Scot continuing.

Scot appeased. "This is part of a prayer George Washington wrote down:

'Bless, O Lord, all the people of this land, from the highest to the lowest, particularly those whom thou have appointed to rule over us in church and state.'

Let me add from his farewell address:

'Reason and experience both forbid us to expect that national morality can exist apart from religious principle.'

"In 1789, Congress approved a measure directing President George Washington to declare a day of Thanksgiving and prayer for the specific purpose of allowing the public to reflect on the many favors of God, especially by affording them an opportunity peaceably to establish a constitution of government. Congress also mandated and approved our currency to have the phrase 'In God We Trust' engraved on every bill and coin.

"I won't read the extremely long Thanksgiving Prayer. Instead, I'll just pass it around. Also, I give you a copy of a prayer he wrote asking God for wisdom enough to govern the nation. Jesus Christ was mentioned, so we're talking a Christian belief here, not some Scientology or higher nature. Specifically, God as spelled out in the Christian Bible."

The class had several minutes to discuss Scot's findings, and they were unanimous in their support for his delegation's cause. Just prior to the class bell ending first period, Scot added, "Let me read one of John Adams' prayers:

'It must be felt that there is no national security but, in the nation's humble acknowledged dependence upon God and His overruling providence.'

Smiling approvingly while clapping her hands, Alex praised, "Scot, we all thank you for your presentation. I've been asked to inform you of Principal Long's request you see him after school today. I would love to have you share some more tomorrow. Go home tonight and read about Ben Franklin's request for prayer asking God's guidance as the framers were not making any progress after four weeks. Class dismissed."

Scot immediately ambled up the aisle to Alex's desk. "Ms. McCord, is Dr. Long upset with my organizing this prayer movement?"

Looking up from stuffing the roll call book in her satchel, she replied, "Not the least, Scot. He's wanting to turn this into something positive for the school to rally behind. He really thinks this can create school unity. Personally, I think it's a great idea."

"This could get bigger than I ever dreamed, huh?"

Smiling while looking him in the eye, she said, "Well, I don't know just how big you wanted this crusade to catch on to start with. Did you initially want it to grow school wide?"

Pausing a moment, he replied, "I wanted it school wide but thought it would not have a chance to launch like this. I guess I thought Dr. Long would squelch it. I have some more preparation ahead of me now that this thing is going beyond my wildest vision."

Closing her satchel, Alex concurred, "You better have your arguments tight. Study the Engel case transcripts and start punching holes in it. Use the dissenting opinion of Justice Stewart as your launching pad. The argument for *Engel* was pitifully weak and a liberal Court ignored the real intentions of the framers in favor of their own agenda. To me, this shows their lack of character and integrity. It was a combination of Engels wanting to impose their will on an entire nation and the Court pre-disposed to the idea. Kind of like a kangaroo court during the great movement West with towns building quickly and dispersing justice even quicker."

Emotion running high, Scot blurted out, "What we need is another Amendment that can't be so loosely or liberally twisted to allow this to ever happen again."

Alexandria, informed, "I have to run, but I'll be glad to help you in any way I can. The real need is to find a devout Christian with the money and national notoriety to reopen the case for prayer anywhere people so choose. Unfortunately, the Supreme Court has the authority to choose the cases it hears. That's the real problem. Research the possibility of Congress getting into the act. But right now, I must get to my next class. I think the possibilities are exciting. The climate might be right. You could become quite famous. Get some of the more astute history students to help you research." Smiling while placing her arm around his waist and guiding him toward the door, she added, "For a star football player, you have more academic and social conviction than I anticipated. You may change my opinion of your kind."

"Was that a compliment or a put down?" He responded while laughing.

"Take it as a compliment; one I seldom give. An admiring testimony of your convictions. Convictions that could render truly wonderful social resurrections. But remember, this is a crusade that will test your resilience, your resolve, and sincerity of conviction. This is not just some game. You better be prepared to meet the challenge and determination of the opponent. Think of it as a running back believing in your ability to open a hole for him that he blindly thrusts his body toward. Can you reach down deep enough to not let his faith in you wane? Is that a good analogy Mr. Barton? Is that enough of a challenge to cause you to rise to the occasion? Oh, by the way, research the Unitarian Church. They are a collection of congregations, each with their own emphasis, hence the word 'Unitarian'. Few if any are Christian in belief, as you inferred in class today."

"Wow, Ms. McCord, have you ever thought about becoming coach Salley's speech writer? I'm now ready to run through fire."

"That's exactly what Christians must be prepared to do in today's environment. We're not the same nation that rose to the occasion back in 1787, where our leaders recruited wisdom from the Greatest Thinker of all time. See you tomorrow Scot Barton. Make us proud," she commanded, closing the door and proceeding down the hall.

Alexandria spent her lunch period in the teachers' lounge with Principal Long discussing Johnnie Wimbush, and Scot Barton's prayer crusade.

"Tell me Alex, has Barton put all the pieces together? Is this a sincere all-out effort with research and all?" asked Dr. Long, while putting a plate of food in the microwave.

Uncapping a canister filled with her protein shake, Alex answered, "You'll be surprised. We were exposed to some awesome information this morning. He plans to exhibit some more tomorrow morning."

Standing beside the microwave waiting for the timer to ring, Principal Long said, "I can't wait to see him after school today. If he's legit, I'm going to try to get him on Good Morning Houston. This could really boost school morale and inspire academic effort."

Looking at Dr. Long, Alex asked, "What about Johnnie? Thought anymore about his situation?"

"I talked to Detective Kinstley late last night. Evidently our own Farley Fontenot convinced Buddy Hodges at the Post to urge Defective Kinstley to consider putting forth an effort to rid Houston of its number one gang. Kinstley acquiesced, coming up with a brilliant plan. We'll have to pay an unwanted visit or two each to the grocery and Johnnie's job. The plan is to bait the Reapers without the grandfather or Johnnie knowing it. Kinstley insists he can keep a constant tail on the two until the gang actually assaults either one." Pulling his plate from the microwave, Dr. Long continued, "But they really need to nail Willie Buchanan. If they don't get the ring leader, the effort failed. I wish somehow for whatever reason, the Masked Marvel would take him out."

Pausing a moment, Alex softly replied, "I never thought of that. I mean, yeah, that'd be great, but it's unlikely he even knows about their existence."

Taking a seat beside Alex, he replied, "You scared me for a moment there. That far away expression on your face coupled with the response, gave me the impression you are the guy in question.

Ha! Just kidding."

"So, what you're suggesting is, we make a nuisance of ourselves until the Reapers retaliate against Johnnie or his grandfather. I can't believe Kinstley went for the idea, seeing he has pressure out the 'wazoo' to catch the Masked Marvel, as you call him."

"Yes, we need to make a nuisance of ourselves. We have to be persistent enough to cause Willie himself to take part in an attack on our boys. If not, Willie Boy will know we set a trap, and he'll bide his time knowing the police can't watch them forever. I think they'll kill both if this plan fails even once. Better still, what if a local police officer finds out about the entrapment plan and warns Willie. The possibilities of this plan failing miserably are growing by the day the more I think about it. A little scary when you stand back and think about all the variables. The solution might just have to be found outside the law, if you know what I mean."

Pushing her chair away from the table overwhelmed by the principal's bleak revelation, Alex announced, "Well, lunch is over. When do you think we'll begin making nuisances of ourselves?"

"A week or two. Whenever Kinstley contacts me. Hopefully his plan entails protecting us too. We'll need to square that away. Who knows, they may have to rescue us and that'll be disastrous if Willie isn't there. I hate to say it, but this plan is a long shot at best. I've been told Willie Buchanan is no fool. He's likely to wonder why we haven't heeded his warning. That might tip him off. In that case, the Reapers may attack minus their leader."

Launching herself to a standing position, she mused, "Well, thanks for the pep talk, Dr. Long, but I gotta run teach some WWII history. By the way, how does your wife feel about your involvement in stuff like this?"

"She divorced me three years ago and died of Leukemia two years ago."

Visibly shaken, Alex begged, "I'm sorry. I had no idea. You're still wearing a ring."

"When we discovered Carolyn had the disease, she wanted a divorce so she could die alone. Didn't want the pain of the last bedside scene. We were really in love, so quite naturally it tore my guts up and broke my heart beyond repair. She was the personal legal assistant to the senior partner at a rather large law firm, so he took care of her finances, expenses and all up to the end. Sharla and I never had kids because we enjoyed each other so much."

Overtaken with sudden grief, Alex offered, "I know what it's like to lose someone you love. Did you go to the funeral?"

Laying down his fork, Dr. Long gazed aimlessly across the room, saying, "No. I guess by staying away I'm able to pretend we're still just divorced. I don't have to face the fact she's really dead. You better go. By the way, what are you doing this weekend?"

"Going to Victoria Friday night."

Continuing to focus nowhere, he eked out, "See ya."

Wednesday morning Alex took roll and asked Scot Barton to continue offering his group's research concerning the Founding Fathers and prayer.

"Ms. McCord, I would like to pass out the Declaration of Independence, written by Thomas Jefferson and John Adams on July 4, 1776. I'll read key parts while all of you look on. After the initial paragraph that justifies the declaration of independence, the document says:

'We hold these Truths to be self-evident, that all Men are created equal, that they are endowed by their Creator with certain unalienable Rights, that among them are Life, Liberty, and the pursuit of happiness.'

Scot explained, "Notice the word Creator and the fact it's capitalized. We all come from the Creator. Some argue that Creator is ambiguous; that it doesn't necessarily mean the Christian God. So, we must go to another document written by Jefferson to see how he means for Creator to be held. Here's a copy of a prayer delivered by Jefferson on March 4, 1805. I'll read the last sentence:

'…In time of prosperity fill our hearts with thankfulness, and in the day of trouble, suffer not our trust in Thee to fail; all of which we ask through Jesus Christ our Lord, amen.'

"Is there any doubt as to his meaning of Creator? Now go to the final paragraph, first sentence. It says:

'We therefore, the Representatives of the United States of America, in General Congress, Assembled, appealing to the Supreme Judge of the World for the Rectitude of our Intentions, do, in the Name, and by the Authority of the good People of these colonies… And for the support of this Declaration with a firm Reliance on the Protection of the divine Providence, we mutually pledge to each other our Lives, our Fortunes, and our sacred Honor.'

"Jefferson saw the violation of God's laws by the Mother country as justification for the colonies to declare independence. Not only did our Founding Fathers see a direct correlation between religion and state, but they also saw the two as inseparable. That's my basic argument. I've only presented the tip of the iceberg."

Alex gave Scot applause and the class followed. "You're definitely on the right track, Scot. Dig deeper and tighten your arguments even more. It's out there, but show writings by the others like James Madison where they indicate the Christian God is the omnipotent one. Nice job so far. So, let's open it up for discussion and constructive criticism."

The discussion that followed was laced with conviction and intensity. After class, Scot approached Alex. "The meeting I had with Principal Long went really good. Can you believe he's going to try to get me on Good Morning Houston? Wouldn't that be something? Would you have time to help me this weekend?"

"I'd love to Scot, but there's something I must do in Victoria. I will lend you a hand any time after that," she promised while closing her satchel.

"Thanks, Ms. McCord. You are the inspiration for my crusade. You have truly inspired me."

Tossing the satchel over her shoulder, Alex said, "Thank you, Scot. You're so sweet. Don't worry, I won't let on to a soul. It'll be our secret."

"Thanks. I'll return the favor somehow," he replied, gathering his books under his right arm.

Guiding Scot toward the door, Alex advised, "Just protect the quarterback and help us win some games."

"You gotta promise to come to some of the games next fall."

"I may just do that. I want to see what a high school superstar looks like."

After her final class, Alex walked swiftly to the teacher parking lot. She wanted to visit Richard and plan the next car she would use, this time to stalk and attack the Reapers. Her secret plan was to flush out Willie Boy and deliver him to the police.

As she approached the Jeep, much to her surprise was Farley sitting in his awesome Boss 429 Mustang, waiting for her arrival.

"Hey, Alex, I need to talk to you. Let's go for a ride."

Somewhat puzzled, she agreed and took a seat in the ground-pounding hulk of a car. "Why do I have this feeling you're about to lay some bad news on me?"

Working the clutch and guiding the muscle car out of the parking lot, he came clean. "One of my sources just informed me the Reapers have been tipped off about the plan Kinstley intends to implement. I just called Mike and the scheme is officially aborted.

So, tell Dr. Long. I didn't want either of you jumping the gun. You both could have been hurt along with Silas and Johnnie. The Reapers now know you have zero police protection. I'm sorry, Alex, this was the best I could do."

Staring out the windshield from the passenger seat, she mumbled, "I know what I must do now. Thank you so much Farley for taking time from your teaching schedule."

"Wanna stop for an A&W Root Beer in a frosted mug and just talk?"

"No thanks. I'd appreciate it if you take me back. I have some things to take care of. I also need time to think. This news is a tremendous let down. A life is wasted because no one can stop the senseless actions of a destructive gang. So much for 'Protect and Serve.' So why try to stop the only guy who can effectively serve justice? Can you tell me that?"

"No, but I'll take you back to your car…What guy are you talking about?"

Driving home, Alex suddenly realized a promise she had made to her friend, Laura Reynolds. Four guys were terrorizing girls going to the Community Center and badly beat two boys attempting to shield them. She quickly changed lanes and flicked on her left blinker to turn down Lockwood Drive where she drove under I-10 on the way to the Youth Center on Canal Street.

As Alex approached to within a block of her friend's activity center, she spotted the blue four-door Mercedes Benz with four guys inside. Sure enough, they were harassing girls walking along the sidewalk. Alex steered the Jeep toward the curb and stopped to grab a pen and piece of paper from her satchel so she could write down the license plate number. Mumbling to herself, she said, "Come on boys, get out of the car so I can get a good look at you."

No sooner had she sounded out the last syllable, two of them climbed out of the car and grabbed a girl, tossing her in the back seat. A boy from the Center intervened, but he met with the barrel of an aluminum baseball bat across the face, knocking him to the ground unconscious.

The Mercedes then sped off, causing Alex to prod the Jeep Cherokee in pursuit. The driver of the Benz wheeled his car through back streets taking turns at high speeds while increasing the distance between the two vehicles. Then suddenly, the right-side back door swung open and the girl was hurled out of the car, bouncing along the pavement; an ugly sight. Alex gave up the chase to render help, not knowing if she'd find the victim alive.

Halting a few feet from the girl, Alex exited the Jeep and sprinted toward her. She was breathing, but barely conscious. Visible injuries were simply lacerations and small bruises all along both arms and legs. The obvious question would be the extent of head injuries. An old man outside checking the mail hollered, "I'll go call the police!"

Holding the young girl's head off the pavement, she attempted to sooth and comfort her while waiting for the police and ambulance. Under her breath Alex threatened, "I caught your license plate number, you low life scum. I will make you pay soon, real soon. You'll never bother anyone again. I promise."

The ambulance was the first emergency vehicle to arrive at the scene, so Alex exited, avoiding having to give a statement for the police. She was in a hurry to see what Richard had rigged up for her new ride, alerting him of an unexpected visit. On the way she would stop and tell Laura what happened and phone her ever faithful uncle.

The internationally respected scholar lived in a modest home on five acres in Lomax, a country type community southeast of Houston, bordering Pasadena, Deer Park and LaPorte. He purchased the property because it was somewhat secluded and had a huge barn at the far end from the road; perfect for some of his fabrication activities for Alex.

Turning off Highway 225 East, Alex drove about seven miles before approaching her uncle's place. Maneuvering her Jeep to the front door of the barn, she climbed out only to be met by Richard coming through the double door.

"I'm almost finished. I hope you like what I've prepared. Come on in and take a look."

Following him into the barn, she gasped, "My god, it's awesome looking! A '69 Road Runner 440 Six-Pack. Look at the armor! I can't believe it!"

Richard proceeded to explain, "Both front and rear windshields, along with the front seat passenger glass, are bullet-proof. Radiator has bullet-proof sheet metal up front with breathing holes to guard against overheating. The doors have armor plate inside the door panels. The fuel tank is wrapped in armor plate. You can see the back tires are armor protected from the side and rear."

Continuing he explained, "The engine has been balanced and blueprinted with a very streetable cam. For added power and ease of tuning, I added a Paxton supercharger. Turbos are tricky and have a spool up delay. You have about 900 horsepower and huge torque. Not real nimble, but it'll take the hole shot and pull away in an all-out straight-away chase."

"I see you chose flat black for night time advantage…I can't believe what I'm seeing. You've outdone any expectation I could have had."

Beaming with pride, Richard instructed, "You better take care of her. She's my interpretation of a magnificent B-17 on four wheels. Let's go up to the house and tell me what is your reason or the need of this creation."

Once inside the house, they took a seat at the kitchen table. Richard poured Alex a glass of mango juice and he a glass of red wine.

"I get mango juice and you indulge in some wine. What's up?"

Smiling while amused, he fired back, "You have to drive home. So, what's your big mission or need for that rocket tank?"

Looking at him in earnest, Alex explained, "Someone tipped off Willie Boy that the police were planning a trap. Dr. Long and I were supposed to pay a visit to Johnnie and his grandfather to provoke the Reapers to attempt violence on the two of them. Both would have undercover teams within reach. The plan has been scrapped, and that detective, Mike Kinstley, expects to redirect his efforts at bringing in the Masked Marvel. Johnnie's doomed."

"That doesn't explain why you need that monster in the barn. Come clean, Alex."

"I'm going to flush them out and that neighborhood will think Armageddon has arrived. I'm going all out; gonna let it all hang out. Might be my last ride. I'm so depressed about the decision I must make about Mike and all the cruelty happening around me. I'll just go down in flames, but the Reapers and Willie Boy will go down with me. I have one last good deed in me. God can have me after this last hard ride."

Tears in his eyes, Richard understood. Words escaped his grasp, forcing him to sit motionless. Maybe a final conflict was appropriate. In the end, it's all about God's plan for everyone's life.

"Everything works out for the best, Richard. You've been the most wonderful person in my life. I gotta run; things to do." Heading toward the front door she turned to say, "I'll let you know when it's time. I need to make a plan…Bye, bye, Unc."

Thursday morning, Alex arrived in the teachers' parking lot thirty minutes early. She wanted to inform Dr. Long the mission to rescue Silas and Johnnie had been scrapped.

Knocking on the open door, Alex addressed the principal as he turned in his chair, "Dr. Long, the rescue plan for Silas and

Johnnie has been called off. There must have been a leak somewhere, because Willie Boy was tipped off."

Pointing to a chair, the principal instructed, "Please sit down. This is the first I've heard this. When did you find out?"

"Farley told me yesterday afternoon. That guy Hodges, the renowned investigative reporter for the Post, got the word from Detective Kinstley. We're dead in the water."

"If you remember our conversation, this was one of my fears. Now our only hope is to pull a rabbit out of the hat," he offered while removing his spectacles to clean them with a handkerchief. "And that's not likely to happen. There's a roadblock at every turn. Alex, this may be one of those times we have to finally put the situation behind us and concentrate on what we can affect. The police know the situation, and that's about all we can do. There are fifteen hundred other students who need our very best effort. As far as I'm concerned, this case is over. There are hundreds of students who drop out of school every year in HISD. They all have sad stories. Alex, anymore effort on our part could get Silas and Johnnie killed. Remember that, and just go teach."

"Yes sir, you're quite correct. It won't be that easy to put this behind me. But I must pick myself up and attend to a bunch of enthusiastic first period students, looking to put prayer back in school where it belongs."

Arms crossed at his chest, the principal reflected, "We did everything we possibly could. We're not equipped to take matters into our own hands; as much as I would like to."

Exiting the office, Alex channeled her motion toward the first period classroom. Students were beginning their charge through the halls to beat the tardy bell. A mood change quickly was in order, as she skirted down the hallway desperately seeking some motivation for a mood change. As she passed by the admission office, a secretary flagged her down, saying, "Ms. McCord, I have a note for you handed to me moments ago. Some man came in and insisted I give this to you personally."

Alex took the envelope and thanked her. Breaking the seal, she pulled out a small handwritten note that said:

I took the picture of you the night you rescued the old-folks money;

the picture on the front page of the Post. I know who you are.

Come see me today at Luster's Mopar Restoration at 2623 Harrisburg.

Mumbling to herself, she said, "My God, how can this be? Better go immediately after school."

Chapter 9

Leaving the faculty parking lot, Alex entered Lyons Avenue, just a few blocks north of I-10, carrying with her a truckload of butterflies and anxiety at the thought of meeting the guy who could possibly send her to prison or execute unlimited blackmail. Four blocks later, she made a right-hand turn onto Hirsch Road, which changed to York Street after crossing Clinton Drive and the Buffalo Bayou. From there, she passed Navigation Boulevard and Canal Street before finally turning left onto Harrisburg Boulevard traveling in a southeasterly direction. Harrisburg was an old commercially zoned area, as she passed Maxwell House Coffee, Medel's Ice House, American Legion Post, and Thunderbolt Products, before setting eyes on a blue and red sign on the right-hand side of the road designating Luster's Mopar Restoration Garage.

It was an old red brick building spanning one entire block. The structure was dotted with numerous pane glass windows surrounding a double wide opening into the shop itself. Alex wheeled her Jeep through the opening and stopped in front of the office, another large area to the right side, almost immediately after entering the garage. In the background were a dozen or so Dodge and Plymouth automobiles from the muscle car era of the 60s and 70s, all at different stages of restoration. This was definitely an extremely high-end shop, ultimately requiring many thousands of dollars from the vehicle owners. As she was admiring the layout, there was a loud tapping on the passenger side window, where a stocky built white-haired man was motioning her to climb out of the car. That had to be Johnny Luster himself.

Alex exited the Jeep and walked around to the front of the vehicle where the apparent Mr. Luster was waiting, strangely sporting a wide grin. She was about to come face to face with the guy who somehow knew not only who she was, but actually caught on camera one of her unlawful exploits at night. This was surely to be a most defining encounter. Reaching out to her with the offering of a handshake, she returned the greeting somewhat reluctantly, while he said, "I'm Johnny Luster. Come inside so we can talk without having to shout over all this noise."

He held the office door open for her, and then she followed his lead past the customer service counter and down the hall to the very back, where Luster's office was laid out. There were two other offices, and a rather large lunch room with 50s diner décor, including tables, booths, and soda fountain with bar and stools. The man motioned Alex to take a seat at the front of his desk while closing the door before plopping down on a high back leather chair.

Before Alex could manage to say a word, Johnny instructed, "Please let me explain before you open with a barrage of questions or accusations. First off, I'm on your side; have been applauding your every move

"I'm not one to beat-around-the-bush or attempt to say the right words in a manner the listener wants to hear. Hurt feelings have their legitimate place in this world, as much as wonderful feelings. Without both, life is just one big lie. Absent the raw truth, societies crumble from denial that there is something wrong but don't want to face."

Continuing, he dropped a bombshell on her, stating, "I am your real father – your biological father. I can prove it, and you have to face this fact, as I have had to live with it all these years. Also, Richard is not your real uncle; he's a true friend of mine and a partner with me in this business."

Overcome with disbelief and anger at what must surely be lies, Alex screamed, "You're lying! The next thing you're going to tell me is that my mother is really not my mother! Why did you ask me here? Let's get on with the reason we're having this ridiculous meeting. I don't want to hear your filthy lies – just get to the point, Mister Luster!"

"Alexandria," Johnny informed, leaning back in his chair, "Marie Stewart and I were high school sweethearts at Victoria High School, graduating in 1943. I played left halfback for the mighty Stingarees, and your mother was head cheerleader. I received a scholarship offer to play football for several colleges, one being Texas. Tensions in America were high, as Hitler's war machine was ravaging Europe and quite nearly bombed England into submission. After much crying in each other's arms and counseling from my father and Marie's dad, I joined Uncle Sam in the fight. It was my duty to help keep the world a safe place for

Marie, even if it entailed sacrificing my life. My final night before pushing out, we made love like there was no tomorrow. Little did we know; there would be no tomorrow.

"From December, sixteenth, nineteen forty-four until January twenty-fifth, nineteen forty-five, I was trapped in the Ardennes Forest, along with the rest of the Ninety-ninth Infantry Division during the Battle of the Bulge. It was a sixty-mile-long area where Germany executed its final assault in a desperate attempt to win the war. It was the bloodiest group of battles for Americans in history.

"I never figured out what happened, while I was gone, but Marie married a guy named Frank McCord, a second-year student at Victoria Junior College. Just before myself and the rest of the Ninety-ninth were sent to Ardennes, Marie's father wrote me saying she was pregnant with my child. Said I should never have anymore contact with her for the sake of the kid, because she was going to marry Frank. He thought it was his.

"You have no idea how heartbroken and lonely I have been since that moment in nineteen forty-four. You only truly fall in love one time. That was my one time. After the war, I went back to Victoria to see my parents and old friends. On a couple occasions, Marie and I, from a distance, laid eyes upon each other but never spoke. I know she saw the tears in my eyes and the hurt in my heart.

"Frank got his two-year degree from the college and went to work as an assistant general manager for some big Chevrolet dealership. Later became the general manager and eventually bought the damn thing. I moved to Houston and went to work as an apprentice mechanic right here, for a guy named Eddie Yariger. I'm not going to bore you with details, but right before he died, I bought this place. Two weeks before they buried him, he said, "Johnny, give me five-hundred dollars and a promise not to sell the place, and I'll sign it over to you right now. I had about seven hundred dollars to my name, so I slept here till I could afford to rent a room. Today, I live in a place I made home; just through that door behind me."

Confused and yet moved by the most unbelievable story she's ever heard, Alex asked, while Luster paused, "Who, then, is Richard?"

"Your grandmother, Jeane, raised him. He said she found him abandoned on a street corner during a visit to Houston. I met him in high school during our sophomore year. We were in the same metal shop class and became friends while working on a project together. I didn't realize it at first, but he was an academic genius, who of all things, liked working with his hands. Next thing I know, we're in auto mechanics together; don't figure. We've been friends ever since. About two years after he retired from being a big-time college professor, he walks in here and hands me a chunk of money to be my partner. So, I decided, why not? In case you haven't figured out just yet, that's how I found out about your midnight adventures in crime stopping."

Solemnly, she asked, "Supposing that I recover from this bombshell revelation and believe you, why am I here?"

"I killed Paul Getty last week in his own office parking

garage, right in front of his scumbag associates. I promised to kill the CFO next." Chuckling, he added, "Got good results, don't you think?"

"That was your work?"

"You bet, and it felt redeeming. Kinda like I was born again. Got rid of an evil guy and restored the hopes and dreams of those, who he walked on. Someday, I'll have to stand before God and answer for that. But I'll have to be who I am and say unashamedly, Sir, there are no regrets."

In total awe, Alexandria said, "That's why Craig Longnecker, the CFO, announced the reinstatement of all the pensions, bonuses, and jobs. That was you, and I'm blown away."

"I wanted to save you the trouble and consequences. Alex, they're starting to put things together. Anyway, I wore a different uniform in hopes of making the authorities think another nut case was loose. Actually, I am a certified, bonafied nut case. I'm a lot larger than you, so they'll really be confused, because you have never killed anyone. He had a lot of enemies. I also used a Pontiac GTO Judge. You use a Mopar. Detective Mike Kinstley and I have extensive conversations all the time. That's what's so funny, don't you think? He picks my brain now and then, because he knows I am familiar with what goes on in the streets around here. Quite a quagmire, huh?"

He leaned forward, placing his elbows on the desk top and stared directly at Alex without saying a word. Seemed like minutes passed by while Alex remained seated, staring at the floor, almost oblivious to Johnny's presence. Fingers tapping on the desk, his patience expired.

"What part of all this could possibly leave Alexandria McCord, Mistress of the Darkness, speechless?" he asked while smirking.

Raising her head, she asked in all sincerity, "How could you just kill Getty gangland style? I mean, you didn't even try to do it without witnesses."

"If you continue down this path, sooner or later you are going to feel righteous enough to kill someone. Actually, you'll execute them and have no remorse. It becomes contagious. And what is so convincing is, you are going to do what law enforcement can't do because of our legal system, where the bad guys are entitled to a trial. Proving to a jury you know what the accused has done is almost impossible due to what evidence is accepted or unaccepted in a court of law. I promise you, you will kill someone and enjoy it."

"Are you not afraid of prison?"

Never turning his head from that laser-like stare directly at her, he answered rather gruffly, "Don't give a shit; I did it for your mother, the woman I never stopped loving. A day didn't go by that I didn't think of her. Don't want our daughter going to prison. Knew you were going to have to make good on your promise soon. Besides, do you really think I felt bad about killing a bunch of Germans hell-bent on destroying the lives of the innocent of this world? They took from me the love of my life just like Getty took the life savings and hopes of the innocent; the ones whose sweat got him his millions."

Alex continued staring at the floor, but offered, "I still have work to do that'll jeopardize my future outside of prison."

"Silas Wimbush is a customer of mine. Get the drift? I know about their unfortunate situation. By the way, Kinstley knows too, but can't do a thing. The Reaper boys have great attorneys, who turn back the law at every corner. Kinstley told me in private he would love for someone to kill them that can afford to go to jail. I might just oblige him…Your world is a lot smaller than you thought, huh?"

Continuing, Johnny added, "I do the maintenance and repair work on Silas' seventy-two Chevy pickup; the only non-Mopar I'll work on. That GTO I used to blow away Getty was given to me by an old Ninety-ninth Infantry Division buddy. He died of prostate cancer four years ago. Never changed the title, so when the cops read the plates, they'll be looking for Ron Lange – a dead man. Hell, I ain't got long myself, so what are they going to do if they catch me? Give me the death penalty? Ha! The joke will be on them. In fact, wouldn't it be fitting for Kinstley to bring me in?"

"There is just one thing that makes no sense, especially if you are afraid I'll get caught. Why did you take that picture and give it to the Post? They put it on the front page," Alex inquired rather perplexed.

Without flinching, Johnny confessed, "I was hoping it would strike the fear of God in you. Maybe then you'd quit. When it didn't work out that way, I decided to meet with you, face-to-face. Believe me, I thought long and hard. I even prayed about it, and this was my answer."

Still unable to process the overwhelming substance of this meeting, Alex requested somberly, “Would you mind if I excused myself. This discussion has totally destroyed the way I have viewed my entire life. I just can’t believe it’s been one huge lie. Somehow, I think I’m even feeling so much hurt for you; for all you’ve been through. If this is true, God cheated you so bad. How could I have been so deceived and cheated out of knowing my real father? I have to go before I start crying. I’ll see you some other time.”

Not saying a word, he just watched her walk out the door crying.

It didn’t take long for Alex to call Uncle Richard once she arrived home, dialing his phone number while sitting at the kitchen table. When Richard answered, Alex immediately demanded, “Why didn’t you tell me Johnny Luster was my real father?”

Silence pervaded on his end of the line, as she waited patiently for an answer, not wanting to believe Luster’s story. The silence from Richard was quickly turning the story’s verdict apparently in favor of it being true after all.

“Alexandria, give me thirty minutes, and I’ll be at your place to explain.”

“I need to know right now if Johnny Luster is my real father,” she demanded impatiently.

“Yes, he is your biological father. Let me go, so I can get ready to come see you.”

"Bye," and she hung up the receiver. Alex began pacing the floor, overcome with the gamut of emotions encircling her thoughts like a war party of American Indians in a movie circling the wagon train. She wanted to cry; should she attempt to get to know Johnny; why did Richard deceive her; and most of all, why this, God? But no matter what, nothing Richard could possibly say would ease the pain of this grand deception. And the tragedy her real father endured was having a haunting effect. Should she even resent the man she thought was her father? After what seemed like hours, a sudden banging at the backdoor snapped her out of the trance.

Opening the door, she saw Richard standing before her with a worried expression covering his face. He knew Armageddon was approaching. In fact, he was downright on the 'bound-for-the-sewer' list.

"Come in and start explaining, please. I'm not even sure what to call you; uncle or just Mister Kim."

Richard entered the kitchen and they took a seat on opposite sides of the kitchen table, Alex's favorite place to discuss any subject matter. Overcome with embarrassment and shame, Richard placed both elbows on the table and clasped his hands together. Taking a deep breath, he began the long painful explanation.

"Your grandmother, on your mom's side, found me abandoned on a street corner in Houston, sitting on a suitcase crying. Jeane took me back to Victoria with her and enrolled me in school. This was before a birth certificate was needed. All I knew was my name, Richard Kim; written on a tag pinned to my shirt along with my age.

"Went to Juan Lynn Elementary, Pattie Welder Junior High, and graduated number two in my class from Victoria High School. I knew of Frank McCord, but he was a year ahead of me and a star tennis player who went on to Victoria College with a scholarship to play for the Pirates. I liked working with my hands, so I took auto mechanics and metal shop to fulfill elective courses needed for high school graduation. It was in those two classes that I met Johnny Luster, the school hero on Friday nights during football season. Hell, the whole state knew of him. We hit it off immediately. In fact, he was the only one who would befriend me. South Koreans were not cool back then.

"I cried the day I went off to SMU for my freshman year in college. Johnny promised to write me weekly, and I promised the same. He kept his word, and so did I, even after he went off to war for Uncle Sam. Got lonesome after receiving my BA in Political Science, so I moved here and attended the University of Houston, where I received both my Masters degree and Doctorate in Political Science. By this time, Johnny was home from the war and working at Yariger's Garage, so it would enable us to have our friendship renewed on a daily basis. In fact, I worked there part-time to help finance my education. In case you haven't figured out yet, your grandmother supported me financially and in just about every other way."

Pausing to take note of her reaction to the deluge of unsettling information that must have seemed like a science fiction tale, allowed Alex an opportunity to interject; to no avail. Alex just sat staring right past Richard, seemingly as though suspended in another dimension. Sensing it was time to bring her up-to-date, he continued.

"I took a job as an instructor at Stephen F. Austin in Nacogdoches, just about a hundred and fifty miles from here. Eventually, I became a professor with full tenure, and I busied myself writing books and essays for magazines and professional journals. By this time, Johnny owned the garage and renamed it. Meanwhile, I made a lot of money, retired in this area and invested in Johnny's shop. That's how I learned to do the things you want me to do to your cars."

Seemingly from out of nowhere, Alex yelled, "Why did you keep passing yourself off as my uncle and being my mentor? I feel so violated for some reason! I feel like such a fool. What did you get out of all of this? Can you please tell me that?"

Exasperated, Richard shouted, "Because I grew really fond of you. I had lived the lie so long, I'd forgotten I really was not an uncle. It should have occurred to me; how did you buy into it since I'm South Korean and your grandmother obviously was not. At any rate, I felt obligated to be your mentor, because I cared and it was God's will. Now find something immoral about that. Lord knows I could have saved myself from brown-eyed agony had my conscience allowed me to walk away."

Alex explained, "My grandmother had been married so many times I just assumed one husband had been Korean. My father was mentor enough, when he was alive. I didn't need you."

"Alexandria, may God forgive me, but your father was no good. He treated your mother badly, but she hid it from you. He was into a few shady undertakings on top of that. He was a fraud! Johnny Luster helped pay your way through college. He's the one who gave Sam Houston State the money to offer you that scholarship. He paid the rent on your apartment you lived in, not Frank McCord. Frank used your mom as a way to help his rise in local politics, where he was able to make underhanded real estate deals. He was hoping to get you married off to Mike Koehl so you'd leave the house and stay gone. That way there were no witnesses to how he eventually treated your mom. I cared! Frank McCord did not!"

"My father treated my mom just fine as far as I could see! I never once detected anything wrong!"

Frustration and anger mounted, causing Richard to reveal, "When you were two years old, your mom got pregnant, but Frank did not want another child. He forced her to get an abortion. Until the day your mom was murdered, she had to see a shrink in an attempt to overcome the burden of guilt. She was a magnificent woman, who hid all this from you, so you would think Frank McCord was wonderful!"

Richard slid his chair from the table and quickly waltzed to the backdoor and left, slamming it behind him.

Alexandria remained seated and speechless, while beginning the difficult process of digesting all she had just heard. To help sort things out, she called Laura at the Community Center and asked that she come by the house after closing the center at six o'clock.

Laura answered, "I can leave now. Sarah will close for me. This sounds urgent. Is it?"

"Yes."

Sitting across the kitchen table from Alex, Laura said, "Well, the suspense is killing me, so get on with it and don't worry about where to start. It'll all get sorted out."

Alex wasted no time, revealing Johnny's entire story of his love affair with her mother, including the war and why he had to promise never to talk to her mother ever again. "My whole life has been one big lie, so I just found out. My real biological father is some grease-monkey named Johnny Luster; Richard is not my real uncle, and mom's husband, a pillar in the community, mentally abused her. In fact, he made her have an abortion. What should I think about all of that? I feel violated in some strange sort of way. You're my best friend, so what now?"

All Laura could manage to do was look up at the ceiling in hopes of finding some consoling words to convey. She finally offered, "Alex, let's both rest on this disconcerting development. This is not what I was prepared to hear. I do know Johnny Luster, and you need to know he channels funds to the center to help keep it open and offer some extras. The city cuts back a little every year as their controller advises. Johnny more than makes up the difference without them knowing. If they knew how much he contributed, that controller, Walter Pyle, would make larger cuts. In fact, they know nothing of Johnny. The mayor has to keep the Community Center open to receive the votes to stay in office. That should at least ease your mind a bit as to the fiber of Mr. Luster's character. But wow, I'm at a loss for words. How and when did you find out about this?"

As Laura paused, looking directly at her life-long friend, Alexandria further unveiled the tangled mess of her family. "Johnny Luster left me a note at school to come visit him at his car restoration shop. Said he was the one who took that picture of me which made the front page of the Post. Naturally, I complied thinking it was some guy who wanted blackmail money or something. He told me everything. I didn't want to believe it, but Richard corroborated Mr. Luster's story. In fact, Richard left here a little while ago."

"Why did Johnny give the Post that picture of you - the one on the front page?" Laura asked while thinking how out-of-character that seemed of Johnny.

"Said he was hoping that would strike the fear of God in me, causing my retirement from all this vigilante work. When it did not, he prayed about what to do next. His answer was to summon me, using that terrifying note."

Shaking her head, Laura finally responded, "Oh my God, girl, I feel so sorry for you, but I hardly know what to say. Seems to me, you need to develop some sort of relationship with Johnny and be grateful he's such a good man, who loved your mother deeply. Whatever you do, restate to Richard how wonderful you think he is for all he's done. He owed you nothing."

For the next fifteen minutes, neither spoke a word. Finally, Laura confessed, "I'm at a loss is the understatement, but I must go home and feed the dogs. I can say with confidence, Alexandria, pray for God's guidance."

As Laura opened the backdoor, Alex asked, "Why have you never married, if I may ask? We've never explored that subject in all these years."

Heart pounding and the look of panic spread across Laura's face. She confessed like someone admitting guilt to committing an atrocious crime. "I was once…Spent five years in prison for murdering the bastard. Mister charming swept me off my feet. Two years into our marriage, I got pregnant. He did not want children, so one night he got drunk and punched me in the belly with the butt of a rifle he was cleaning. I got in the car and drove myself to the hospital emergency room and crawled on my hands and knees to the desk. An hour later, I lost the baby. They cut the baby out. The doctors kept me in the hospital two days. No one came to visit me. Seven months pregnant and the baby died in my womb.

"When I got home from the hospital, Phil was on his way home from work. I sat in a chair facing the front door, holding his shotgun. The moment that asshole walked in the door, I let him have it with both barrels. Now, you can decide if we will continue to be friends. You have a lot to think about, Alexandria. Don't feel like talking anymore. I'll never allow myself to fall in love again. Wish I had been a lesbian. Bye."

Chapter 10

After school Friday, Alex drove home to change clothes in preparation for her second trip to Victoria. The unexpected revelations about her real father, Richard not really being an uncle, and the fraudulent persona of the man she was made to believe was her father has turned this trip into a real downer of sorts. One big problem would be how to react with her parents on this trip. How does she hide the truth she knows? Just as she was about to leave, the phone rang. It was Farley.

Quickly jerking the receiver off its cradle, she answered, "Hello, Farley, how are you?"

"How'd you know it was me?" Fingers crossed, he cautiously inquired, "Would you like to go to a movie? I could sure use some company tonight."

"Oh, Farley, I'm sorry. I would if I wasn't already about to leave for Victoria. Gonna see my aunt."

Puzzled, he replied, "Didn't you go last week?"

"Yes, I did. But I need to see her again. It's family business."

"If I didn't know better, I'd say you have some guy down there. But that'd be none of my business…Well, I'll give you a rain check…Like you'd really want one."

"I would really like that. I need to run, though. Call you when I get back. I promise."

"Well, have a safe trip. Please don't pick up any hitchhikers, you hear?"

"I promise. Bye, Farley."

Hanging up the telephone in frustration, Farley mumbled, "She probably has some guy down there she's beginning to like a lot. If I had any brains, I'd give up this lost cause."

As soon as Alex pulled onto Highway 59 South, she popped in one of her old 50s and 60s rock' n roll cassettes in an effort to set the mood for the weekend with Mike. Her love for him and his for her was now the only real thing in her childhood. Otherwise, her whole life has been a lie. Adrenaline was no longer pumping with each mile, as before. Anticipating the moment, she would see the little boy wearing only Jockey underwear and oversized cowboy boots, was now scary. In fact, she was having second thoughts about continuing with this visit. Maybe the meeting with Johnny Luster, with all his revelations, was a sign to give up on seeing Mike ever again. Maybe it was even a sign to give up the vigilante work while she was still unknown to law enforcement. And maybe it was time to settle down with Farley. Why did God send a toddler in cowboy boots as a messenger? This whole other dimension thing with Mike, coupled with having her head pulled out of the sand, was beginning to seem ridiculous. Maybe this was

God's only way to make her come to these conclusions on her own. All these questions were rattling around in her brain like a pinball machine.

The sun went down just as she drove through El Campo, and her anticipation heightened; this time for a different reason. The mind sometimes plays cruel tricks on a person at night, and Alex could not help but wonder what would happen if the little boy did not make an appearance. Could she still continue on to Victoria and find herself back at the Optimist Club dance in the year 1962? Would the clicker still work? Was last weekend a cruel trick by some ungodly force? Mumbling, she said, "I'll never recover if this dream is bogus." Looking up toward the stars, she pleaded, "Lord, I'm not getting your message. I need a bigger, better clue."

Alex motored on past the last grain silo in El Campo before leaving the city limits with Edna the next town before Victoria. Nothing but farmland dotted the landscape and dark was serious dark. Once in Edna, there was only 26 miles left to Victoria's outskirts and the exit for Business 59. Anxiety was choking off her air supply, so she pulled into a small all-night grocery and gasoline stop. There she purchased a small tin of six Bayer aspirin and a cherry coke. After downing two aspirin, she re-entered the highway and headed further south.

Thirty minutes later, she saw the magical exit for Business 59, but there was no sign of the little cowboy. Apparently, there would be no Victoria weekend with Mike. She has obviously again been deceived. Pulling over onto the shoulder about ten yards from the exit, she put the Jeep in parking gear and waited with the headlights on and the engine idling. Several minutes came and went with no sign of the messenger. Her spirits caved in as it was more and more obvious the night would be a washout; the whole scheme was some ultra force with a sick sense of humor.

Just when she was preparing to turn the Jeep around and go back to Houston, the headlights shone on the little guy. Euphoria, coupled with unexplained fear, blanketed her emotions immediately. God had answered her prayer, but in what way?

Opening the passenger side door, the little half-naked cowboy, seemingly perturbed, said, "You're a little earlier than last week. I almost didn't get here in time. Do you still have that clicker?"

"It's in the glove box."

"Next time click the clicker three times when you get to Wharton. It'll give me time to drop whatever I'm doing and get here. If I'm not here, the exit will do you no good. Do you understand?"

"Yes." Giving a deep sigh, Alex mumbled, "Thank you, Lord."

"What are you waiting for? Let's go," the boy commanded, while turning to look out the rear window.

Alex pulled the gearshift lever down from 'park' to 'drive' and maneuvered the vehicle back onto the highway and up to speed in a matter of seconds.

Looking at Alex, the boy asked, "Have you made up your mind yet? Are you going to ride out the three and a half years or what?"

"No. I'm too mixed up right now," she answered, looking into the rearview mirror.

Showing some empathy, he tenderly reminded her, "You have one more free trip after this. A fourth trip will require you to stay the entire 3 ½ years. I'm sorry, but He did not agree to any extensions. Believe me, I tried...Hey, here's where I get out. You know what to do from here." Staring into her eyes he said, "Alex, I truly feel for you. I wish I could have known you. Just so you can know the final piece of your real family history, I am the aborted child. Don't have time to explain, but that's why God sent me instead of someone else."

Before she could react, the little guy was gone. Confused was the understatement to express the way she felt. As reluctant as she was to continue what now seemed like an exercise in futility, Alexandria still pushed on to see how the weekend would play out.

Soon after the Jeep headlights began to dim, I pulled the SUV into the parking lot. Taking a deep breath, I opened the door and began that short walk to the Optimist Club. I still couldn't help wondering how it was the little boy was the child my mom aborted. Suddenly, I was not liking all of this. Unexplainably, I wanted to just go back to Houston, where life was real. As I reached the entrance door to the dance hall, my legs were just as shaky as that first night. Johnny Dee and the Rocket 88s were rockin' the place. The sounds grew louder and louder with each step. Oh, Lord, that is the place I want to be forever. I just feel it.

Immediately upon passing through the door, I saw Mike standing and looking right at me with that captivating grin. You'd never know by looking at him, he was a mere mortal. How could he have not survived that night? He proceeded to walk briskly in my direction. Those long self-confident strides quickly brought him in front of me. Like a mesmerized school girl, I just stood there trembling.

He reached out with his big strong hand and said, "I'm going to have to start bringing you myself so we can dance the first dance. I've got a request in for when you arrive. Come on – as soon as we embrace they're going to play *You Belong To Me*. That's going to be our song."

I couldn't think of a better song. It was recorded by the Dupree's. I followed Mike to the dance floor and as we embraced, Johnny Dee began singing our song. In my mind every song was ours. *Talk To Me* was my favorite song, but when the '88s T-Bone Holly sang *Earth Angel* by the Penguins, I began to cry. Mike pulled me in closer and like always, never said a word.

Song after song kept Mike and I on the dance floor. Before we knew it, Johnny Dee announced he and his Rocket 88s were going to take a short break. That's when we all gathered around the snack tables and attacked the punch bowls. Thirst quenching was a must as we were all covered in perspiration. The guys gathered together and rehashed the basketball game played Thursday night against Travis Junior High from Port Lavaca. Mike was the team's second leading scorer with 16 points behind John Synnot's 19 points. Our unbeaten Comets handed Travis their first loss, 60-54. Johnny Dee, standing beside his beautiful wife, Marilyn, smiled and winked at me as he headed back toward the stage for another set.

Johnny approached the microphone and to my utter surprise announced, "I'm gonna dedicate this next song to a couple of special friends of mine you all know: Mike Koehl and Alexandria McCord. Someday, they'll probably be Mike and Alexandria Koehl. So, hold each other tight as we play *Talk to Me."* He stepped back and began picking his guitar while the rest of the band kicked in. That gesture made the night so very special.

Lee and Diane danced their way close to us and poked fun with Diane saying, "You two need to just go ahead and elope. You were made for each other. I wish we all could marry and go off together to some 'Neverland.' That'd be so great."

I began to sink, wishing that would have happened. It was as if Johnny Dee saw me sinking, because as soon as he finished *Talk to Me* the band broke into *Sea Cruise* by Frankie Ford, followed by Bobby Rydell's *'Kissin Time;'* all fast upbeat songs. Just like last week, he had taken me from melancholy to happy in a matter of minutes. I can't imagine the drugs of the 70's being this good.

After the dance, Mike drove me home and we sat in the big swing on the front porch, our simple tradition. The only light on in the house was the one Mr. McCord read by while waiting for us to come home. I can't imagine having to refer to the man in such a manner. It was taking all the gloss away from what should be euphoria. Seconds later, my fake dad turned on the porch light, stuck his head out the door and said, "I'll be up a while reading, so if you two want to sit out here for a while longer, feel free."

Leaning my head on Mike's shoulder, I said, "Mike, I love you so much."

He kissed me on the forehead and said, "I love you too. I can't imagine a day without you, let alone a life without you. God made you for me."

"Do you still think you'll be a baseball player after high school?" I knew the answer; I just wanted to hear it again.

"You know I'm going to be a Major League Baseball pitcher. You're going to be the best-looking baseball wife, and I'm going to be the Yankees' ace pitcher."

"I wish you'd never leave me." Wow was that an understatement. I'm sure it confused him. What was I thinking? My new family dynamics had me messed up.

Somewhat stunned, Mike replied, "What are you talking about? Leave you? Never. You're stuck with me for as long as I live. When I do die, I want that moment to take place in your arms. You hear?"

That's when I began sobbing. I just couldn't hold back the tears. I know Mike couldn't help feeling me shake. I slurped out a very weak, "Yes, sir."

"You sure have been weepy lately. Are you…you know, in that time? I'm beginning to worry about you."

That's when the porch light flicked on and off, a sign to kiss goodnight and come in. We kissed so tenderly and Mike grinned, saying, "Pick you up tomorrow for the YMCA dance. We might just never grow up, and I'll always pick you up and take you somewhere our music is playing. Whatta' you say we just spend our whole life in each other's arms?"

"I can't think of anything I'd rather do. I wish I could be the one to die in your arms."

Ambling down the sidewalk to his car, he hollered, "Neither one of us will ever die. Bye!"

To myself, I said, "One more free trip. Then I have to make the most important decision of my life. Why does this have to hurt so much?"

Saturday was the exact same as the previous blissful weekend. I helped mom with the chores and Mr. McCord took care of the yard and changed the oil in mom's car.

While mom and I were folding clothes in the laundry room, she said, "You and Mike are just meant for each other. I just hope nothing ever comes between you two. I may sound selfish, but I just love that boy."

Smiling proudly, I answered back, "I don't know how I could possibly love someone more than I do Mike. We just go together like bacon and eggs; toast and jam; or better still, love and marriage."

Mom continued. "Everyone says he'll be the next great Yankee pitcher. That Yankee scout must have watched him pitch seven or eight games last summer. He's certain Mike is a sure thing. You'll be the prettiest baseball wife the Yankees ever saw, that's for sure."

I added, "They label him 'a can't miss.' The only drawback is having to live in New York, away from you and daddy and our friends." Boy was it hard to choke out that 'daddy' word.

Mom consoled, "Honey, after high school, there'll be a lot of separations between friends. Some will go far away to college; some couples will split up and go separate ways…"

If that piece of wisdom wasn't depressing enough, her next remark brought me back to reality like an arrow to the heart.

"…and others will be separated by death. You and Mike must therefore make each day count. Tomorrow is not promised to any of us. Any differences you have now, you better work them out fast."

I really didn't pay much attention to what she was saying once that "death" word floated from her lips. At that point, my heart was racing, and it was if everything around me was a blurred spin.

Mom put her arm on my shoulder and asked, "Sweetheart, are you feeling OK? You look like you're about to pass out."

Shaking my head side-to-side to clear out the cobwebs, I weakly replied, "I'm OK. I was caught in a daydream thinking about what you were saying. I'll be OK."

"You looked like you had just seen something horrible or tragic. You scared me for a minute."

She was correct; I was imagining Mike's '57 Chevy roll over and over. It was if I was there and saw his lifeless body once the car came to a rest upside down. Some accounts claimed he was thrown from the car right before it rolled over on top of him, crushing him to death.

I went to the fridge and poured myself a glass of Hawaiian Punch. Mom and I then began the task of ironing dress pants, skirts, blouses and shirts. The conversation lightened up, and my mood improved with every minute, anticipating Mike's arrival for a night at the YMCA. We were going to arrive early tonight so we could shoot some buckets and play ping pong before the music started.

After the ironing was done, I helped mom prepare that fraud's favorite dish: chicken and dumplings. That was also one of Mike's favorites, so he'd be by to share in the feast. He and Frank enjoyed that time together. That's what I just could not wrap my mind around; he was not my dad, and besides that, my mother's magnificent performance hiding the truth about that bastard. Now I had to convincingly hide, from my mom, my ill feelings toward Frank; not to mention hide them from the creep himself. This was not going to be easy.

As the chicken was placed in the pot to boil, I asked, barely able to keep from gagging, "What do you suppose it is that makes dad like Mike so much?" I knew the answer, but wanted to hear what lie mom would tell. That made me a partial member of the deception group. We were all just lying now.

Wiping her hands on a cup towel, she answered, with the biggest lie I have ever heard in my life, "He's the son your daddy never had."

She told me that story without flinching. Mother had protected me in spectacular fashion. So spectacular, I hated Frank McCord more than ever. Surely, Marie Stewart must have secretly wished she had waited for Johnny Luster to come home from the war. What must that have been like all these years?

Mike came by just in time for supper before our usual night at the YMCA. Johnny Dee and the Rocket 88s again played rockin' songs, and I had the most wonderful night. Johnny made sure I got caught up in those great old tunes that were so upbeat. We even played some ping pong, pool and shot some buckets. All in all, it was another typically wonderful Saturday night.

Mike took me home like always and we kissed until the porch light flashed on and off. But unlike last week, Mike said, as he walked down the sidewalk, "Officer Gordon Brown's going to extend the time the drag strip at Foster Field stays open tonight. Some hot shot from Cuero is in town looking for me. Going to have to shut him down too, I guess. Seems like everyone, lately, thinks they can take me. Cousin Lee told me to stop by his dad's Gulf Station tonight and we'll put the car on the hoist so I can uncap my headers. I'll call you tomorrow. Goodnight."

I stood there while he climbed in his car and drove out of sight. Fear struck my heart, but I reminded myself this fantasy would play out exactly as before. He wouldn't die tonight.

Sunday morning I awoke and ran downstairs to wait for Mike's call. Girls didn't call guys in 1962. Couldn't check the paper for car accidents, because you know who was sitting on the couch reading the *Victoria Advocate*.

I decided to wonder into the kitchen to see if mom could use some help with breakfast. It'd be a way to keep busy. As I passed through the swinging doors, mom said, "Mike called, while you were in the bathroom. He apologized for not being able to call you later. He and his parents were attending early church, and from there, heading to Refugio to eat with his grandparents. They wouldn't be getting home till late, so he said he'd see you Monday."

"Did he say anything else?"

"Said he won the race last night by a full car length."

"God answered my prayers."

"What, dear?"

"Nothing, nothing at all. I'm just glad he won and there wasn't an accident. Want me to scramble the eggs?"

"No, but you might pull the biscuits out of the oven and start buttering them. You know how much your father likes the butter melted on a fresh biscuit."

"Boy, how I know that. And it has to be real butter. No margarine for that man."

After breakfast, I ran upstairs and pressed the clicker. I could not stomach being around Frank McCord anymore than I had to. The little boy appeared beside my car again. We both climbed in the Jeep, and I put the vehicle through the usual maneuvers to enter the highway and zoom up to traffic speed. It wasn't long before he asked, "Just curious, how are things going? I feel it's not quite the blessing you had imagined."

"I've been living on the edge for three days. I cry for happy; I cry for sadness; and I've had the greatest time in my otherwise uninspiring life. And then Saturday night's race scared me beyond anything I ever felt since the night he died. But you knew all this from the start didn't you? In fact, you've known all along my life growing up was a fraud. Mike was the only thing real. And I can't begin to understand anything about you. If you were aborted, how are you like this?"

"All I can say about me is that I am a work in progress. Yes, I did know all about your childhood being a lie. But would that have changed your wish?"

"No. Of course not. You knew that too. I've never been so mixed up in my life. I'm all tied up in knots. There's no part of my life where there's peace, except certain moments when I'm in Mike's arms. But the longer I'm here, the more reality sets in about Mike dying again in that wreck, and I'm once again alone. I'm also alone in my real adult life. Maybe I could change things. Maybe I could go with Mike on that fateful night and die with him. That'd solve everything."

After several miles and conversation waning, the little cowboy said, "This is where I get out, Alex. Consider this: Maybe you should have asked Him to reveal his plan for your life without Mike instead of asking to be in his arms again. Just a thought. Bye, and see you next time?"

I nodded my head affirmatively and directed the Jeep back onto the highway toward Houston. I was emotionally drained, yet had so much to think about on the way home. Mr. Kim, or shall I say Richard, was quite correct. I feel like I'm betraying Mike when I so much as meet Farley for lunch. I want so bad to play this out to that final night and die in that crash beside Mike. That's my solution, my final wish. But God doesn't change history.

That bed is sure going to feel good. Right now, I just want to hurry and get home so I can escape for a few hours into a much needed deep sleep. Johnny Dee, how are you going to sing me out of this mess?

Chapter 11

Monday morning, just prior to Alex checking roll and calling the class to order, Karen Austin approached her informing, "Ms. McCord, I think you should know Johnnie Wimbush's grandfather is in the hospital. They think he was beaten up by the Grimm Reapers."

Fear written across her face, Alex asked, "How bad Karen?"

"He's in ICU at Taub, but no one knows the details."

"Thank you for telling me. Please find your seat." Alex then moved around to the front of her desk to address the class.

"Listen up, folks. I've just heard the disturbing news about Johnnie's grandfather. I need to make a quick trip to Principal Long's office. Scot, I want you to continue reading the research you and your group have uncovered. Class, please give him your utmost attention." Looking directly at Scot, she continued, "If I'm not back when you finish relating the material, open it up to questions or discussion. You're in charge." She then exited the classroom and scurried down the hall to the principal's office.

Just before reaching the office door, she spotted the principal drinking from a water fountain across the hall. Swiftly changing her course, she approached, asking, "Dr. Long, have you heard about Johnnie's grandfather?"

Looking up at Alex, Principal Long wiped the water dripping from his chin. "Detective Kinstley told me early this morning. He said the grandfather is conscious and will not say who beat him up. There was a warning note attached to his shirt, and it left no claim to the deed."

"I suppose the police are not going to do a thing? Who else do they think would commit such an act?"

Dr. Long pointed out, "Alex, Kinstley said with sincere regret, there's not even enough evidence to bring the Reapers in for questioning. Any chance of convincing Johnnie to cooperate just flew out the window. He's probably scared to death. Kinstley is certain the attack on Silas was a direct result of the gang being tipped-off about the stakeouts."

Bending over to pick up a broken pencil lying near the fountain, Dr. Long confessed, "It's too late. Johnnie won't let you get close now. He won't dare anger Willie Boy any more than he already is. The Reapers can now lay low indefinitely as long as Johnnie continues working and making protection payments...Shouldn't you be in class?"

"Believe me, it's in good hands. Nothing to worry about."

Staring down at Alex and placing a hand on each of her shoulders, Dr. Long earnestly pleaded in a fatherly tone, "Alex, we have to walk away from this for the sake of our sanity and the other students. You can't lose focus on why you are here. Your effectiveness as a teacher could wane, and that's not fair to the students taking your classes. I can't lose focus on my job. We have to look at the big picture. It's also not our job to become law enforcement officers. We have no training or experience. We'd be a danger to ourselves and Johnnie. Believe me when I say, this is just as hard for me to swallow as it is for you."

Disappointment taking a stranglehold, Alex crossed her arms and promised, "I'm not letting those creeps get away with this. I'll find that masked marvel. He'll hold his own trial and execute sentencing. My kind of man." Dejected, she turned and headed back toward her classroom.

Watching her walk away, Dr. Long left the water cooler and marched across the hall to his office, all the while puzzled about Alex's last statement. He grabbed the phone as he sat behind his desk, and made a call to Detective Kinstley. There was no answer, so he left a message conveying concern for Alexandria's attitude.

After school, Alex rushed home to contemplate her next move. Flopping down in a recliner and kicking back, she realized her precarious position after that angry outburst toward Richard. Without him, there was no one to service the war wagons, and she had no idea if the man had finished the armored vehicle they had discussed. It became obvious, the only option entailed making amends with Richard, who had served her so faithfully with impeccable results.

Nervously tapping her fingernails on both arms of the chair, Alex sighed, while deciding to just bite the bullet and ask Richard for his continued help, despite her previous tirade of screaming insults. A heaping spoonful of humility might serve her best. Bringing the recliner to a sudden upright position, she marched toward the kitchen where the phone hung on the wall in its familiar spot, next to the so-named conference table.

Upon reaching the kitchen, she quickly pulled the receiver off the cradle and immediately began dialing Richard's number, while still maintaining the courage to do so. She slid a chair away from the table and sat down, waiting for a response on the other end of the line. Never in her entire life had she been this nervous about anything.

"Hello…Hello…Anybody there?...Alex is this you?"

"Yes," she answered rather meekly and embarrassed; more like ashamed.

"I was wondering when you might call. You have a problem, don't you?"

"Yes," was all she could choke out.

"You want to talk about it?" he asked, calmly and sincerely. He was no stranger to being sympathetic.

"Silas has been beaten up. He's in ICU at Ben Taub. It was the Reapers. They even pinned a note to his bloody shirt."

Compassionately he asked, "What do you need from me, Alex?"

"I need you to be my wonderful uncle and mentor again. I've come to realize you're all I have; all I've ever had for that matter."

"Now, that's what I was hoping you'd finally conclude. You don't know how relieved I am. Now let's address the reason you called, shall we?"

"I need that new car you built. Is it ready yet?"

"Yes."

"Is it at the hangar?"

"Yes. Do you need it tonight?"

"Yes."

"What time do you want me to meet you there?"

"How about six o'clock; it's four-thirty now."

"I'll leave right away. You can tell me what you have in mind when we get there."

Alex hung up the phone and collapsed in a sigh of relief. The first huge hurdle was over. Shame elbowed its way into her emotions, knowing the last hurdle was still ahead; coming face-to-face with Richard again.

It was a long drive from the entrance gate on 59 South, down the roadway to the hangar door, where Richard would be waiting. She felt a certain uneasiness anticipating the manner Richard would receive her. Strangely, there was uncertainty how she was going to feel facing the one who deceived her so convincingly. But her self-appointed mission in life luckily was beginning to take precedence over the other. The commando mentality had kicked in.

Just as her vehicle was within 50 yards of the hangar, the large 30-foot door began sliding open; a sign Richard had been monitoring Alex's path of approach like all the other times. As the

Jeep came to a halt just inside, Richard hit the close button and approached the vehicle.

"Let's just take this like we used to. What's the emergency, and what are your plans? While you tell me, let's go inspect your new armored car. Need to make sure it will fit your needs. Come on, it's over here."

Far away from the hangar door and living quarters sat the car she ordered, sporting a magnificent aggressive stance. It was a 1969 ½ Plymouth Road Runner with a 440-six-pack engine. But not your typical factory production model. It was unlike anything she had driven to date.

Admiring the craftsmanship while making a close visual tour around the car, Alex felt like she was having a religious experience of some sort. "I can't believe what I'm seeing. It's majesty takes your breath away. God, I love these Road Runners. This fella could hold off an army."

"You've got a fortress on wheels. It's my best work. You're ready to absorb a pretty heavy attack. I hope you won't need it, but I have a really bad feeling about this outing you're about to undertake."

Deflecting concern, she said, "I'll slip into my Kevlar suit and get started. My shotgun and .45 automatic on the front seat?"

"And the ammo boxes are in the center console I built especially for that. I threw in an extra 870."

"Moving swiftly through the door to the living quarters, she instructed, "Get my helmet. I'll be in the bedroom buttoning up."

Minutes later, she made her appearance in full body armor.

Grabbing the helmet from atop the war wagon, she opened the driver's side door and climbed in behind the wheel. "It's time to go hunting, so open the hangar door." Sliding up the face shield, she smiled at Richard, ordering, "Stay by the phone and say a prayer, cause when I get through bombarding their hangout, the place will look like the Battle for Iwo Jima."

Pushing the button controlling the hangar door operation, Richard crossed his fingers declaring, "God willing, I'll see you back here unhurt."

Alex winked at him and fired up the big block 440.Giving it gas, the powerful Road Runner propelled through the opening, pipes echoing that magnificent sound.

It took less than an hour to reach the front of Silas Wimbush's corner grocery store. Inside there appeared to be a light shining. Cruising around the corner, she spotted two low-slung unoccupied cars in the parking lot. As she scanned the lot with her hand-held spotlight, she saw Johnnie's bicycle leaning against the store wall.

Dialing the phone number at the hangar, she mumbled to herself, "You boys have gift wrapped this mission for me."

Seconds later, Richard answered the phone, "Alex, surely you're not in trouble already."

"Richard, the action is about to begin. I'm circling the block in front of the grocery store. It appears the Reapers are inside with Johnnie. His bike is up against the wall in the parking lot, along with two unoccupied cars. They look like an '84 Grand

National hugging the ground and a Cadillac also sitting low."

"What's your plan?"

"I'm gonna shoot up their cars and hope they come running out. When they do, I'll nail them. I'll be specifically looking for Willie boy. There's also some extremely loud action in Tess's Lounge across the street. I could blow up these cars here and they probably would not hear it. If Willie isn't in the first wave coming out of the grocery, I'll wait to see who runs out of the lounge after I light up the vehicles over there. I'll call you back when it's over."

Placing the phone down on the seat beside her, Alex guided the beastly Road Runner into the grocery store parking lot. She proceeded to step out of the car and pump shots into the rear of both cars in hopes of igniting the gas tanks. Halfway through the second round of shots, the Grand National exploded and the Cadillac followed with another wild detonation. Quickly reloading her cannon, she prepared for an onslaught of gang members by sliding behind the open driver's side door. Her car was also positioned for an easy exit from the parking lot after engaging the first wave from inside.

Within seconds, five gentlemen came sprinting around the corner into the lot with plenty of high caliber handguns waving. Stopping in their tracks, the boys looked in panic at the cars engulfed in flames. The raging fire offered just enough light for one guy to spot the Masked Marvel staring at them in the distance from behind the car door.

"Who's that guy over there?"

The others immediately turned their attention from the burning cars, as one youngster so astutely proclaimed, "He's probably the one who destroyed our cars. Let's get him."

Prudently, another advised, "Man, you know he's got a gun or he wouldn't just stand there, looking all scary in that weird suit. We better spread out so he can't get a shot at us all close together. So, make some separation and we'll see what he has."

Taking several steps toward the dark intruder, they spread out and opened fire, pelting the Road Runner's driver door and several windows. To their surprise, nothing penetrated.

Alex then displayed her pump shotgun and then opened fire, taking down all five. She quickly loaded several more shells and moved with cat-like quickness toward the wounded gang members all sprawled on the ground in pain. She caught a glimpse of one to her left roll over and raise his gun, but she pumped one into his upper torso sending him back down for good. As she approached another reaching for his gun, she kicked it out of his reach and slammed the side of his face with the stock of the shotgun. Inspecting the other three, disappointment draped over her; Willie Buchanan was not in attendance.

She then darted toward the grocery store and cautiously maneuvered inside, where she spotted Johnnie tied up in a chair with his face covered in blood. He was conscious, so she used the electronic voice to say, "I'll call 911. I'm going across the street to the bar and finish this. Then I'll stay until the police arrive. I'm going to leave you tied up, so there is no doubt what happened here."

She then exited the store and ran to her car, grabbing the other short stock short barrel Remington 870, tossing it over her shoulder by the strap. From there, she walked toward the bar across the street. Standing in the roadway, she pumped shells through the windows and proceeded to discharge shots in all three cars parked at the curb until they burst into flames.

Two youths charged out the door with guns blazing, but she took them down quickly and pulled the backup Remington off her shoulder as they fell face-first along the curb. Neither was Buchanan. She then returned to the grocery store parking lot and yelled through the electronic device, "Tell Willie boy I'm going to kill him when I find him! I will find him!"

One youth bleeding profusely from his leg asked, "Who are you, man? What'd we do?"

Looking down, the nightrider explained, "I don't like what you are doing to this neighborhood. I only kept you alive to deliver a message to Willie. I'm going to enjoy killing him. He won't see me until he takes his last breath. I let you boys see me. You won't see me next time. If you're still with him, you'll die too."

Sirens screaming, and lights flashing on the roofs of several police cars fast approaching in the distance, interrupted the discussion with the wounded Reaper. Within moments black and whites would be converging on the Wimbush grocery store. It was safe to leave Johnnie, and prudent to do so.

Sprinting to her car, she reloaded both weapons and roared out of the parking lot and entered the boulevard. Four blocks down the road, two more cars loaded with Reapers pulled out from a cross street and commenced firing. The shots were sprinkling all over the Road Runner as she stomped on the accelerator and hit third gear putting some distance between her and the attacking cars, still giving chase.

Just as she was pulling away, Alex slammed on the brakes, downshifted into second gear and turned the wheel hard left, reversing the direction of her black beast. She grabbed one of the shotguns on the front seat and swung open the car door, standing behind it for protection. Just as she was thinking a miracle would be appreciated, a black 1970 GTO Judge came roaring out of nowhere, shots firing from the driver's side window, sending one of the cars crashing through the glass of a storefront and moments later exploding into flames.

The second car continued its direct path, and Alex unloaded her weapon of destruction on the oncoming vehicle, sending it to a skidding halt up against a street light. Reloading, she approached the car from behind and blasted the gas tank area, igniting a huge fire.

Skipping around to the driver's side, she opened the door and pulled the unconscious youth away from the car. Running to the other side, she pulled the wounded front seat passenger from the car. There was another in the back seat still conscious, but he had shot wounds in the shoulder and neck, offering no resistance while she extracted his battered body from the car and tossed him to the ground with the others. As he looked up at her, she instructed, "Tell Willie I'm going to kill him when I find him. I'll kill anyone still with him. You hear me?"

Groaning, the kid asked, "Who are you? What'd we do to you?"

"Keep guessing." And she raced back to her car, shifting it through the gears as the monster fishtailed before straightening out and disappearing.

Meanwhile, the black and whites were pulling up in front of the Wimbush store. Among the attendees was Detective Mike Kinstley. As he rushed inside along with several officers following, Johnnie was still sitting all tied up, tape over his mouth facing them. One of the officers pulled the tape off the youngster's mouth and commenced untying him.

Kinstley asked, "Who did this to you, son?"

Gasping for breath, he blurted out in disgust, "You know who did it. So, what does it matter? You're not going to do anything."

The detective then asked, "Who shot all those gang members outside?"

"I don't know. I don't know. He was all covered up in a blue suit and wore a motorcycle helmet. It had an electronic voice."

"What did he say?"

"Just said he'd call 911 and wait till the police get here. Said he'd leave me tied up so it'd be obvious what happened."

"Nothing that'd make him identifiable? Did you see the car?"

"No. But there was something about him that left me thinking we've met before; like I know him and he knew who I was. It doesn't make sense how he knew to be here. Now I'm in real trouble."

Scratching his head, Kinstley instructed the officers to haul every one of the wounded gang members downtown who don't leave in an ambulance. Turning to Johnnie, he said, "I'll have one of the EMTs check you out and you're free to go. I'll have a squad car pick you up later on in the week so you can press charges."

"I'm not going anywhere to press charges, so forget it. I'll be dead before you guys do anything; not that you care. So just go away and leave me alone. God has a plan for me, and it ain't on this earth."

Back on the freeway and driving the speed limit in order not to attract attention, Alex called Richard. "Man, you should see the mess I left behind tonight! Wow, it felt great! I really put it to them…But I didn't get that Buchanan creep. I don't know where he was, but I left a message for his boys to repeat to him. I'll kill him when I find him. Told 'em they'll die too if they're with him…Richard, they beat Johnnie while he was tied to a chair in the grocery. I got there before they hurt him too bad. Called 911. Wanted the police to see him tied up so maybe they'll lock up the ones I left behind in the parking lot."

Plopping down in a chair inside the hangar's living quarters' kitchen, Richard was relieved Alex was not hurt. "Lord, I can't believe you got away with all that."

"The grandfather was right, the police don't patrol near the neighborhood, so it takes them a long time to respond. Yes, I was lucky in that respect, but I was also counting on it."

"Did you kill anyone?"

"Pretty certain. Not that I give a shit at this point. Tonight's action should make the paper tomorrow. We'll find out then, I guess."

"What about the car? How'd it do?"

"Richard, it was magnificent! It took a bunch of hits, but nothing penetrated. The driver's door took the majority of them, but it didn't give way. I've never felt so invigorated! The feeling of redemption is awesome! I feel alive! … Mr. Luster saved my ass tonight. He came out of nowhere, while I was cornered by two carloads of Reapers, and literally blew one up. I got the other and looked around, but he was gone. He was driving a black GTO."

Leaning forward with both elbows on his knees, Richard demanded, "Come on in so I can begin the repair process. I have a plan for a dual radiator set up in the event someone punctures your radiator. That fear ran across my thoughts tonight. You're like Bonnie without Clyde."

Far from smiling, Alex replied, "Story of my life, Richard. I only hope this will allow Johnnie to re-enter school. Maybe there will be enough fear in their hearts to let go of Johnnie; maybe a compromise. If only I knew what Willie boy is going to do after tonight. I honestly believe I could have assassinated him tonight. There will be no peace for me until he's under the ground. See you in a few minutes." She put the phone back on its cradle beside the seat and placed both hands on the wheel at the 10 o'clock and two o'clock position, while shoving the accelerator closer to the floorboard.

Chapter 12

Pressing the 'liquify' button on her blender while stirring a pot of oatmeal, the telephone rang. Alex picked up the receiver answering, "Hello."

On the other end of the line, Farley Fontenot could hardly contain his excitement at relating the events which took place in the neighborhood where the Silas Wimbush grocery stood. "Alex, you will never guess what happened last night!"

Lodging the receiver between her shoulder and ear, while hitting the 'off' button on the blender and turning down the gas burner under her pot of oatmeal, Alex rolled her eyes answering, "They caught the Masked Marvel?"

"Not quite. Someone reenacted the invasion of Normandy on the Grimm Reapers. Wounded seven or eight, blew up their cars, and shot up their hangout. He actually killed three of our boys. He's never killed before. Unfortunately for all his fans, that puts him in real peril."

"Did he get Willie Boy?" she asked, feigning surprise upon hearing Farley's news.

"No, but he told the ones he wounded to tell Willie Boy he will find him and kill him. Can you imagine? Wow!"

"That's really good news, Farley. But until Willie Buchanan is under the turf, Johnnie will never be completely free. I only hope this marauder can find and kill that son-of-a-bitch soon."

Puzzled, Farley asks, "Is there something wrong? You don't sound all that happy. Personally, I thought the news was uplifting."

"I'm sorry, Farley, I'm tired and frustrated. I want Buchanan dead for Johnnie and Silas's sake. That would be news worth celebrating."

"Well, girl, I'm with you. See you at school. Just thought you might need a 'lift-me-up'. Hope to do better next time," he said hanging up the receiver, shaking his head in disappointment. Mumbling under his breath, while grabbing his sport coat from the hanger on his way out the door, he muttered, "Never seen someone who just refuses to be happy."

Slamming the receiver down on the cradle, Alex sat at the table and commenced devouring the oatmeal and gulping down the protein shake. She was out of the coveted grapefruit, further aggravating her already negative mood. So much so, she had no idea it totally frustrated a well-meaning Farley.

Alexandria steered the Jeep Cherokee into the teacher parking lot and quickly exited the vehicle with slightly under seven minutes before the warning bell. Out of nowhere, a voice echoed loudly across her path.

"Hey, teach!"

Stopping in her tracks, Alex quickly turned to see who was addressing her. That voice was all too familiar. Unable to spot the one stalking her, she reached in her satchel to click off the safety on her .45 automatic. Taking long deep breaths while scanning between vehicles, she knew it was imperative to keep control of her heart rate in case a chance to get a clean shot at the one and only Willie Buchanan presented itself. How dare he pleasure at thinking his presence would terrify her. Whispering under her breath, and dropping to one knee while peering under the cars, she smirked, "Come on show yourself, you sorry coward. Come to momma. Let me have one shot at ending your worthless life."

Again, the all too familiar voice pierced the air. "You won't spot me teach! Listen good! If that unruly masked friend of yours dare comes back to my turf, I'll kill Johnnie. I have Johnnie right now. I know you somehow have connections to that masked guy. Better call him off."

Calling his bluff, Alex challenged, "I don't think you have Johnnie. Show me. Come out in the open and show me."

Still on one knee, she anxiously awaited Willie Boy's response. Silence was not golden. Staying low, she maneuvered to a position between two vehicles in the row closest to the school, her back to the school sidewalk across the street. She guessed Willie Buchanan was probably hold up behind the trash dumpster at the end of the parking lot with the open field behind it. If he made a move toward her, he'd be in her line of fire.

Silence was finally broken. Another familiar voice rang out. "Ms. McCord, he really does have me! I'm in hand cuffs with a knife at my throat! Please don't cause me anymore trouble!"

Then came Willie Boy's last message. "It's Johnnie's birthday in two weeks. I'm gonna break both his legs that day to wish him a happy birthday. That's his punishment for your stupidity. I'll send you a tape of his begging and screaming. You can play it over and over again as a reminder to do as you've been told."

Unable to control her anger Alex shouted, "Why don't you come after me? This is between you and me – not you and Johnnie. Come on, be a real man, Willie Boy! Are you scared? Are you so afraid of a woman, you have to pick on a boy?"

The next sound she heard was a car screeching its back tires as it scurried away.

Taking a deep breath while wiping sweat beads from her forehead, Alex stood up and placed the .45 automatic back in her satchel while clicking on the safety. The tardy bell had already sounded, so she hurried toward the school.

Quickstepping down the hallway amongst some students also late for class, Dr. Long crossed her path, commenting, "Running a little bit late? You look frazzled."

"I'll tell you during my third period conference. Willie Boy and I just had words in the parking lot." Continuing down the hall to her first period class, she yelled, "We're in trouble."

Opening the door, she did not know what to expect. But then she wasn't really surprised to find Scot Barton standing at the front of the class delivering some more information on our

Forefathers and their emphasis on prayer, especially for those in governing or leadership positions. It was heartwarming to see such leadership on his part and cooperation from the rest of the class. This was a Kodak moment reward for her efforts.

After closing the door, she waltzed behind Scot to her desk and laid down her satchel. In a nonchalant manner, Alex offered, "Sorry I'm late folks. Just made poor use of my time this morning. However, I'm really proud of the way you all handled my brief absence. Please continue sharing your information, Scot." Alex proceeded to sit in her chair and pulled the roll book out to quietly check who was in attendance. Scot was long winded enough to continue right up to the class bell, announcing, "I would like to hand each of you a list indicating the religious affiliations of the thirty-nine signers of our Constitution. In all, there were 55 delegates, 16 of whom for various reasons did not sign. If you'll remain seated just a minute, it won't take long."

The list read: 31 Episcopalian Christians; 16 Presbyterian Christians; 8 Congregationalist Christians; 2 Lutheran Christians; 2 Dutch Reformed Christians; 2 Methodist Christians, 3 Quaker Christians; and 2 Roman Catholic Christians.

Scot further explained, "You'll see the number of Christian religions will total sixty-six; kinda puzzling. Some of the signers at some point changed affiliations, so that's the reason for the discrepancy between the number of signers and number of Christian religions."

Sliding the attendance notebook into her satchel, Alex said, "See you people tomorrow. I'll try my best to be on time...Oh, by the way, thank Scot for such eye-opening information."

At the beginning of her third period conference, Alex wandered into Principal Long's office as promised. She took a seat in a chair off to his left side near the coffee maker.

Dr. Long was conversing with someone on the phone but hung up shortly after Alex took a seat. Turning his attention to her, he asked, "You had a confrontation with Willie Buchanan in our parking lot? My God, what happened? Tell me, I've suffered anxiety having to wait these two long hours wondering why he made such a bold yet desperate move?"

Rising from her chair and ambling over to the water cooler to get a drink, she informed, "I never saw him. He yelled at me from some hidden place. He's got Johnnie alright, because Willie Boy had Johnnie tell me to lay off. Plans on breaking both his legs in two weeks on his birthday. That's my punishment for supposedly knowing something about that Captain America guy and last night's shootout with some of his Reapers. Said he was going to send me a tape of Johnnie begging and screaming."

Stunned at her information, Dr. Long revealed, "I was about to ask if you heard about last night. That was Detective Kinstley on the phone as you walked in. They're not sure if it was the Masked Marvel or not. If it was him, he's finally killed someone. The car was unrecognizable, and he wore a full-face helmet instead of a mask. Told the wounded gang members to deliver a message to Willie Boy that he was going to find their leader and kill him. It could have been someone else who has a beef with Willie, and he was trying to make it look like the Masked Marvel. Get this, an eye witness said another car was involved in the shootout. Apparently, whoever he was shot up one of the gang's cars, sending it through the front of some liquor store. The car caught fire, but the four guys managed to get out before burning up. So that further complicates things from Kinstley's perspective."

Tossing the paper cup in a nearby trash can, Alex leaned against the wall, arms crossed, saying, "We gotta find Willie Boy before he hurts Johnnie. I'll spend every spare waking second hunting down that creep."

Alex remained upright against the wall next to the water cooler while Principal Long leaned back in his high back leather chair, hands behind his head. No one spoke for several seconds. The principal could not help focusing on Alex's remark about 'hunting down that creep.' It was an extreme aggressive side of her that had not shown itself until now. Though he felt ridiculous for entertaining the idea she was the masked man, there were some strange coincidences. Her intense aggression however was not of his imagination.

"We have to tell Kinstley what happened this morning. It's all we can do, but we have to at least do that," declared Dr. Long, breaking the silence.

Reaching down for another cup and filling it with water, Alex remarked, "You can do what you want, but I'm going to find Willie Buchanan. Justice will be swift if he harms that boy, I promise you." Squeezing the drinking cup and tossing it in the trash can beside her, she exited his office and headed toward the teacher's lounge.

Dr. Long immediately grabbed the phone and dialed up Detective Kinstley. The principal was now concerned he had two people in danger; Johnnie and Alexandria. The situation had decomposed radically, something way outside his job description and qualifications.

Detective Kinstley picked up the receiver, answering, "Homicide, Detective Kinstley."

Dr. Long proceeded to explain the circumstances, requesting the detective counseling Alex. "I'm hoping you can convince Alexandria from doing anything foolish. At the same time, maybe she can give you some helpful information on the whereabouts of both Johnnie and Willie Buchanan, should she have such a clue or two."

"How about I come by after school? Can you have her there?"

"I was hoping you'd contact her on your own. Right now, she is a bomb with a short fuse. Might get real angry if I approach her, because she'll know I am trying to stop her quest. It's my opinion, she will not agree to a meeting. But I'll request she come see me and by surprise you could be here. What the hell."

Kinstley said, "I'll be there before school lets out."

Alexandria made her way to the teacher's lounge for lunch. At one table near the door, quite on cue, was Jerry Walker, Jack Klam, and Ed Hughes; the jocks. It was an unfair assessment and wrong to take out her intense hatred for Willie Buchanan on three of the school's finest. On the other side of the room was her faculty friend and mentor, Farley Fontenot. She decided to take a seat across from where Farley sat before a crowd gathered around the most popular teacher in school; one who coached the academic decathlon team.

"Mind if sit here, Mr. Fontenot?" She inquired playfully. "That is if they are not all reserved for your fan club."

"You're certainly not a member of my fan base, but you are free to sit where you like," he replied never looking up from the newspaper he was reading.

Taking a seat, she admitted, "I have not been appreciative enough of your efforts to be a friend and mentor. You have taken it upon yourself to make my first year at Centennial a smooth landing. Not to mention how you saved me from harm that day in Silas's parking lot."

He continued reading a newspaper story, replying, "Apology accepted."

Attempting to strike up a conversation to relieve the tension, she asked, "What are you reading?"

Looking up, he answered, "Captain America's rampage last night directed at the Grimm Reapers. Rather surprising the police didn't get there in time to so much as catch a glimpse of him. Bystanders gave a description of the car so different from the one he normally uses; they're wondering if there may be a copycat out there. Guess what else?'

"What?"

"A rogue GTO Judge managed to enter the melee on the side of the masked marvel. That guy shot up a car with four Reapers in it, sending their vehicle through the front of a liquor store."

"Well, good for him," replied Alex, pulling her protein shake from a bag and removed the lid. Taking a sip, she exclaimed, "What else does it say?"

"Detective Kinstley thinks he, the vigilante, is somehow connected to Johnnie and his grandfather. Claims this was not a random act against the Reapers. The guy was specifically targeting Willie Boy for his treatment of Silas and Johnnie. Currently, Johnnie and Willie Boy are not to be found, and Willie Boy's associates are not talking. Silas is no where to be found."

"You might as well know. Willie Boy yelled at me in the teacher parking lot this morning. He has kidnapped Johnnie. He's going to break both legs and send me a video. Claims I put the masked marvel up to last night's wholesale attack on his gang."

"Wow! Why does he think it was you?"

"Who knows?"

Farley stared into Alex's eyes, asking, "Are you the guy?"

"What have you been smoking? Are you crazy?"

"Just asking in case you need help."

"My watch says our half hour lunch is up. Hate to leave a conversation that links me with such a wonderful folk hero. But I have class to teach. We must get together some time," she remarked with a wink. Then suddenly she snapped, "You say Silas is nowhere to be found?"

"That's what Kinstley said in the article."

After school, Alex hustled to Dr. Long's office after receiving a message during fifth period. He urgently wanted her to drop by when school was out.

The door to his office was closed, so she sheepishly knocked. Seldom is his door closed. His secretary Amanda Blinn had already left.

"Come in."

Alex opened the door and entered. Detective Mike Kinstley had already arrived and was seated. Caught by surprise at the detective's attendance, Alexandria acknowledged his presence, "Detective Kinstley, what a pleasant surprise. Good afternoon, Dr. Long. You wanted me to see me?"

"Yes, Alexandria, please find yourself a seat. I invited Detective Kinstley here to inform us on the status of the Wimbush situation and what we could do to help. I also informed him what you told me about your run-in with Willie Boy." Glancing at Kinstley, he motioned, "You may take the floor detective."

Staring at Alex, he remarked, "You know, I knew there was something peculiar about you the first time we met. Know what it is?"

Finding it hard to swallow, she played along, "No Detective Kinstley, tell me."

"You have heterochromia iridum," he replied, studying Alex's facial response.

"Two different colored eyes. I have one blue and one green. You are very observant. Most people don't look into the eyes intensely enough to notice. It's very rare."

Detective Kinstley smiled, "In my business, being observant could be the difference between life and death. Having just been informed Johnny has been grabbed by our illustrious suspect, we will call in the FBI since the crime is apparently kidnapping. You must stay out of the way or you could screw up their operation. I'll be assisting them, and out of the compassion I have for your unbelievable concern for the boy, I will keep you posted with the up-to-the-minute developments. Do you understand? Do nothing!"

Obviously unhappy with Kinstley's instructions, she stood up and marched out of the office saying, "You made your point... By the way, where's your sidekick, Sharon Murphy? Did you chase her off? Most importantly, is it true Silas is not to be found?"

"To answer your first question, Murphy quit law enforcement. Not that I see any reason you should know. And yes, we cannot find Silas," he replied as Alexandria left the office, closing the door behind her.

Kinstley looked toward Dr. Long, asking, "Do you trust she'll comply?"

Sighing the principal remarked, "Yes, but she won't like it."

The detective differed, "I don't trust her as far as I can throw her."

Alex drove out Highway 59 south to the hangar. Richard was there attaching a fitted piece of plate steel to the front grill of the armored Road Runner to protect the two radiators mounted side-by-side.

Climbing out of the Jeep, she approached Richard from behind, but he never looked up. Before she could say a word, he spoke, "There's trouble on the horizon. I can just feel it off your aura. Plus, there's only one reason you came this far to visit with me. Am I right?"

Sighing, Alex admitted begrudgingly, "Yes you are most correct."

"Alex, it took me several hours to drill the holes in this quarter-inch steel plate so these two radiators could breathe."

"Richard, Willie Buchanan has Johnnie. He's gonna break both his legs in two weeks on the boy's birthday, because of what I did last night. Now get this: Silas is missing."

"And?"

"How did Johnny Luster know where I'd be last night? As if I didn't know."

Ignoring her question and answer, Richard continued tending to the small details of his radiator protection plate.

"I need this car to hunt down that mound of horse manure named Willie Buchanan before he harms them both. Today's Tuesday; I'm beginning the hunt Friday night and all day and night Saturday and Sunday. Every second of my spare time."

"I'll try to finish this thing by Friday. Right now, I don't have anything to say about your uncontrolled behavior. My focus is on the details of this job here. Besides praying for God to intervene, the next best thing I can do for you is make this car impregnable. You're going to ignore any advice, so I'll just save my breath. I'll take my own advice and let God deal with you."

"I understand your feelings. If the roles were reversed, I'd be telling you the same thing. However, you are not in my skin. I can't explain this obsession in a way you could understand or accept. This fills the void in my life concerning the need for justice on this earth be dealt to those who steal lives. I don't have anyone to go home to. So, there you have it in a nut shell."

Unable to hold back his empathy, Richard just shook his head. "Actually, for the first time, I understand your need to make things right in this world. I'd feel the same way, if I had caused someone to be harmed. It'd also teach me to stay away from those sorts of situations, however. That was not as simple as saving old people from being robbed. Do you think?"

"Johnnie is being robbed of his education every day and any possibility of living out his dreams. Don't you think he was also being robbed of God's plan for him?"

Pausing a moment to gather his thoughts, Richard answered, "You don't think God is capable, without your help, of carrying out His perfect will for someone?"

"All throughout history, Richard, He has used people to see to it His will manifested itself. Just maybe He has chosen a willing soul like myself to carry out His plan for Johnnie."

"Touché."

"I would like to recruit your prayers for both Johnnie and myself. Excuse me, now we must add Silas."

Looking her straight in the eyes, he warned, "You better

hope Farley doesn't start asking questions."

Puzzled, she asked, "What do you mean?"

"There will be even less time for him now than in the past, and he's bound to wonder why? I wouldn't put it past him to follow you at some point."

Taking a seat on a five-gallon bucket turned upside down next to the battered Road Runner, she placed a worried face in her cupped hands. "Oh my goodness, I haven't given that a thought. You're one hundred percent correct. I know he'll follow me, because he did that day he rescued me in the parking lot of the Wimbush Grocery Store." Pausing a few seconds, she finally concluded, "I need to come up with something to keep him from being suspicious."

Richard halted work on the radiator protective plate and declared, "You better alert him ahead of time rather than make excuses after your manhunt begins. Maybe tell him you have a lot of papers to grade before report cards come out. Also, you are helping Scot Barton's crew do that research on school prayer."

"You're on to something there. You always seem to know the answers."

"Except the ones to convince you to halt your self-appointed missionary work for God, who does not need it in the first place."

Rising to her feet and ambling toward the Jeep, she replied, "No one's perfect, but you're close. I gotta run. Promise me one thing: Never think I take you for granted. I thank God everyday for you being my compass, even though you deceived me somewhat. I listen more than you think. May we go back to Uncle Richard?"

Touched by her testimony, Richard returned his attention to the work at hand saying, "Go on, get out of here so your uncle can get you saddled up by Friday."

Amused at Richard's attempt to cover up both his gratitude and embarrassment, Alex said, "See you Friday night." She slid into the driver's seat, guiding the Jeep out the hangar door, down the path to the highway.

Placing the vehicle on cruise control, Alex began to search for some way to explain to Farley, why she would be unavailable for social activities between them outside of school hours during the coming two weeks. Suddenly a novel idea surfaced. Tell him the truth; she's hunting for Willie Boy. She wouldn't have to let him know she was using an armored muscle car stocked with enough munitions to arm up for an invasion at Normandy; just trying to help the police.

As the miles passed, Alex muttered to herself, "You idiot, what if you have another lead throwing incident like last night? Then Farley will know you're the whatever; Masked Marvel or vigilante. Your cover's blown. Well, back to square one…Maybe I could tell him I have to go out of town the next few weekends. Maybe helping my aunt line up her estate affairs. That's better than grading papers or helping Scot research his project, because Farley would call and wonder, why I didn't answer the phone. Looks like out of town is the winner by default. Why did I have to get involved with Farley at this point in my life?"

Finally, she steered the Jeep up the driveway and into the garage. There would be just enough time to down some Bomber Blend protein and workout before climbing into bed. Exiting the car, Alex entered the kitchen and locked the door.

Placing her satchel on the table, she pulled the Bomber Blend from the cabinet and proceeded to concoct her pre-workout nutritional enrichment of protein, banana, honey, and strawberries swimming in Borden's hormone free milk. For a machismo effect, she drank it straight from the blender – no glass for this woman about to undertake the cast iron symphony.

After rinsing out the blender, she made her way to the bedroom and dressed in the proper attire for attacking the huge weight room her fake father had added on to the back of the house just before his death. It was the place that soothed the savage beast inside, healed wounds, and built character. Here she was in a throwback world, a woman of the iron, an architect of strength and determination.

First on the agenda would be the most revered lift in all the weightlifting kingdom – the squat using the Olympic Bar. It is the ultimate strength builder. If a powerlifter wants to increase his bench press, he first ups the poundage of his squat workout. Loading the 45-pound bar with a 45-pound plate on each side gave Alex an opening warm-up set a total of 135 pounds for 15 reps. The move from a standing position to one where the quads were slightly below parallel to the floor required a tremendous amount of oxygen to go along with muscular effort. The quads orchestrated the downward motion, and the hamstrings contracted while the glutes puckered in an effort to hoist one back to the upright position. It was truly a religious experience to repeat the process for five sets while increasing the load with each set.

From there, the Masked Marvel performed leg presses on the incline leg press machine, lying leg curls, knee extensions, stationary lunges, and calf raises. All in all, the labor of love took an hour and a half, leaving her exhausted, exhilarated, and renewed. She was ready for a post workout meal followed by a night's rest, in preparation for the next day.

Just as she was about to settle in for a long night in sugar plum land, the phone rang. It was Farley.

"Hello, Farley."

"Haven't heard from you in a couple of days. Thought I'd call and set something up for the weekend. Vince Vance and the Valiants are playing in Kemah. What do you say we shake it up? Your kind of, I mean, our kind of music."

"I'd love to, but I'll be in Victoria the next two or three weekends helping my aunt get her affairs in order. She's not doing too well with that colon cancer."

Heartbroken, frustrated, and finally disgusted, he reached down inside himself for enough manhood to declare his independence. "Alexandria McCord, I hereby declare you a free woman. I'm cutting you loose from the shackles of my attempt to form a meaningful relationship. You may now consider yourself to no longer be in any shape or form obligated to appease my wishes for continued companionship. I am checking out of your life. So, good luck and good-bye."

Farley hung up the receiver before she could say a word. Stunned, Wonder Woman laid her head back on the pillow and replaced the receiver on the cradle. Staring at the ceiling in disbelief, disappointment, and relief, she now needed not to worry about Farley possibly being suspicious of her activities and a threat to follow her – stake her out. Those were the last thoughts before she fell into the temporary night-time coma.

Chapter 13

Tuesday morning, after first period, Alex was trucking down the hallway toward the history department office to check her mail when a female student intercepted her flight. "Ms. McCord, can I have a quick word with you? It's really important."

Halting her march, Alex asked, "You're George Ann Patterson, are you not?"

"Yes ma'am. I'm in your third period class…Ricky McWhorter is in big trouble. His mom and dad are nowhere to be found and he's alone taking care of his ten-year-old sister and four-year-old brother."

"Ricky is in my first period class. How do you know this about Ricky?"

"We have biology together and he's my lab partner. I went to his house to study for our biology test. I suspected something wrong, because not one of his parents was there. I asked him where they were and that's when he revealed they were gone. I was there past seven o'clock and there was no mother or father."

"Who baby sits the little boy while he and his sister go to school?"

"They leave Cole in the parents' bedroom with the door

locked. The bedroom has a small bathroom. They leave snacks in the room for him to eat while they're gone."

"Where does he get money to pay the rent and stuff like that?"

"He sells drugs. That's why I said he is in trouble."

"Nobody can find his mom or dad? I mean, did they leave together or separately; or does he even know?"

"Your guess is as good as mine. All I know is somebody has to help them. I don't know anyone else like you. You just seem like someone who helps people."

Pausing a moment to process this incomprehensible circumstance, Alex promised, "I'll have a chat with Ricky and see if I can get to the bottom of this. Trust this with me, George Ann, so don't carry this burden any longer. If you do, it'll just affect your schoolwork. Now run along to your next class. If you are late, tell your teacher to see me about it."

"Ms. McCord, I'm scared for him. He's liable to get in too deep with the wrong guys. A guy named Ronnie, some friend of my cousin Joel, found his entire family executed gangland style. Ronnie was withholding money from the man to support his mom and dad's efforts to pay for his older brother's college. Two days later he shot himself in the temple."

"I promise Ricky won't end up like your cousin's friend. Come on, I'll walk with you to class in case you don't beat the tardy bell. I can explain why you should be excused."

The remainder of the school day was uneventful until Alex received word to see Dr. Long after her last period class. Hopefully it'd be some good news concerning Johnnie.

Knocking on his door, the principal hollered, "Come in."

Alex peeked in saying, "You wanted to see me?"

"Yes, Alex, come in and have a seat. I don't know why Amanda closed the door. I apologize."

She took a seat in front of his desk, she said, "No need to apologize."

"Alex, I'll be brief and to the point. Max Wedge has ordered the school prayer project cancelled. It's already caused trouble with seven or eight parents of other religions and of course, our resident atheists." He leaned back in his reclining high-back chair and said not another word, waiting for her response. It was not a long wait.

Slamming her fist on the desk, Alex shouted, "The project is student driven with a forum planned that is student directed! Are we this gutless? Where's the democracy in that decision? What kind of democracy allows the overwhelming majority to be ruled by the wishes of the minority? A small one at that. Don't they call this 'minority tyranny' in most academic circles? Can you answer that one? Can anybody make sense of that? It's prayer in school today, but what else will it be tomorrow or any other day? If they can, I'd love to hear their explanation. Believe me, I would."

Not surprised with the intensity of her convictions, the principal expounded on his frustration. "Alex, I too am at my wit's end. We already as Christians don't have any rights. I don't know how you can separate prayer from our history when it was that very fabric this nation was founded. All you have to do is read the letters and the numerous speeches. There's no gray there. As the history books, school boards, and ACLU erase prayer, they are in effect erasing America. Soon we'll be nothing but a huge piece of real estate where people make money and live in fear of each other and are told what to believe. Of course, if the EPA continues to ignore some realities, we might all be out of work hugging trees, breathing more than perfect air while starving to death. At least then we would not have to worry about illegal immigration, because nobody in their right mind would want to come here ... I better quit before I go off the deep end. The real tragedy here is the young people of this country are crying out for something or someone to believe in. In my humble opinion, I believe that's one of the biggest reasons we have gangs."

Alex slumped in her chair. "I guess I'll have the unenviable job of telling Scot. He'll be devastated. But he will also let his temper runaway with him. How does a young person have faith in their leaders if they allow this to happen? Oh well, that's life in the no longer Christian America."

"I plan to schedule a school assembly to break the news to the rest of the school."

"An all school assembly? Wow, isn't that a little dramatic?"

"You'll understand after I make the announcement. Believe me, you will. And I'll be getting something off my chest."

"If you want to leave Centennial, why don't you just hand

write your resignation? Seems like it'd be a lot easier than going down in flames from ground fire of the opposition."

Sitting on the front edge of his chair, Principal Long related, "My father once said, 'If you get cornered by your adversary, look him in the eye without blinking and spit. Then let him have your best shot.' I'm simply tired of evil out witting good. Yes, my address to the student body could be my last act. Probably will, actually. I have inadvertently missed on some defining moments in my life – I won't miss this one."

Momentarily at a loss for the words to express her swirling collage of emotions, she finally blurted out, "When do you plan to deliver this certain-to-be farewell address?"

The principal rose from his chair and wandered over to the window looking out at the atrium between his office and the cafeteria. "Probably Thursday or Friday; when I've had time to talk this over with Jerry Walker. I use him as a barometer. Know what I mean?"

"Yes, I do. Richard is mine, but I don't heed his advice as much as he'd like. For that matter, as much as I should."

The stress from caring about the young victims of a societal system sinking from its own courtship with evil and lethargy had escorted the principal to the crossroads of his life for the final showdown. Staring out to the courtyard he revealed, "Since my wife died, I don't give 'two-shits' about what is expected of me, when that expectation is substantially wrong."

Reeling in despair at the thought of his leaving, Alexandria responded, "Wow! That's not quite what I expected, even though I didn't know what to expect, if that makes any sense? There's way more to you than I ever dreamed. If you'll excuse me, I have to run. You've given me much to digest. You've caused me to rethink some things. All I can say is – right now I feel so sorry things have turned out this way for you."

"Follow your heart, Alexandria, because that's where God talks to you. See ya tomorrow," he answered never turning to look at her.

Wednesday morning during first period class, Alex very discreetly approached Ricky McWhorter. "Ricky, I need to see you after school right here."

With a puzzled look on his face, Ricky asked, "Am I in some kind of trouble, Ms. McCord?"

"No, Ricky. I need your help with a project. I'll drive you home and we'll talk about it."

"OK, Ms. McCord. I'll see you after school."

"Thank you, Ricky."

While having lunch with Dr. Long in the teacher lounge, Alex related the Ricky McWhorter story.

Taking a bite out of a tuna sandwich, the principal advised, "When the state finds out, they'll place each one of them in a separate foster home. There's no need for you to get involved unless you're going to let them live with you. I'm not suggesting that - just letting you know that it's really out of your hands otherwise. Lord knows how many others face a similar situation.

Think carefully how you plan to handle this, and I'll help any way I can. Not to change the subject, but have you told Scot Barton the bad news?"

"My God! I had forgotten! Can you believe it? I guess Ricky's situation just caused me to have a lapse of some sort. I'll tell Scot first thing tomorrow."

Laying down his sandwich, Dr. Long replied, "Gets kinda complicated around here doesn't it? The entanglements, I mean. Those outside this building have no idea nor do they want to know. We're like a ship at sea in a storm trying to work with a half-broken rudder and nowhere to call for help. But those who own the ship want it in port on time and without any loss of cargo or any details regarding structural problems. No one wants to hear about the difficulties…or shall I say, they don't want to be made aware of the truth."

"Dr. Long, my problem is I care too much. It'll probably be my downfall."

"Jerry Walker is just like you. He somehow managed to get Jack Klam and Ed Hughes involved. For the sake of a lighter load to carry, try to get one or two others to help. You can support each other. Who knows, maybe you'll start a good epidemic."

Ambling toward the sink to wash out her protein shake container, Alex remarked, "Wonder what it'd be like to teach at some suburban school, or better still, some rich private Christian Academy?"

"Fortunately, or unfortunately, you're here for a reason. There's work to be done in the inner city. Those of us that grow weary and leave must pass the torch. Can you imagine what would happen if there were no teachers to staff the inner-city schools? Talk about ugly. There'd be mass hysteria with all these kids running the streets without direction. Not to mention massive illiteracy. Think about it – how many thousands of youngsters would not be able to read and write. Churches talk about the mission work they do – especially overseas. Tell me why we don't perform our own mission work here. America without a public school system would not be the great country it is right now. Actually, illiteracy is exactly what the liberals want so they can install a dictator to draw footprints on the ground, directing our steps. We'll have our tongues cut out so we can't communicate with each other or say the wrong thing. It's hard to have a revolution if we are unable to speak or read and write."

Laughing, she asked, "Can a girl buy your last couple of speeches? You accomplished your objective. I feel guilty for just wondering what it'd be like to have it easy."

"I'm not so sure the suburban schools have it that easy," he said, gathering up his trash. "The private schools might, because they can refuse to allow a student to attend should he or she be a big enough problem. The business world doesn't realize yet how much they should be doing to help us. The anarchy could get ugly. This next time will be worse than Watts, Newark, and Detroit combined."

"I'm going to make it my business to make a difference with Johnnie Wimbush and Ricky McWhorter. I guess any other inclination would be an indication I am in the wrong business, huh?"

Smiling while tossing his lunch sack in the trash, the principal observed, "Lunch always seems to be the fastest forty minutes of the day."

After school, Ricky met Alex in the classroom. She greeted, "Hi, Ricky. Let me give you a ride home and we can talk about this project. Soon as I finish gathering up all my things, we'll head on out of here."

Panicking, the youngster replied, "Why can't we do it here?'

"They'll be in to clean the room and close the school soon," she answered, fending off his efforts to avoid her discovering his dismal situation.

In a further attempt to stall, he came back, "My parents won't be home and we'd be interrupted by my ten-year-old sister. She's a real pest."

Nudging him toward the door, she assured, "Come on, I can deal with her."

Unable to initiate another stall tactic, he dejectedly followed Alex to her Jeep and climbed in the front passenger seat. Looking at her, he suspected there was some other motive for her making a trip to his place.

It was about a mile drive to the neighborhood in which Ricky resided. To her surprise, he did not live in one of the many housing projects that dotted the Centennial school boundaries. As she pulled up to the apartment complex, Ricky directed her into the driveway leading to a coded entry gate. This definitely was not what she had envisioned. Ricky was supposed to be living in a HUD housing project within a depressed neighborhood. Once inside the complex, he pointed to a visitor parking area.

Exiting the car, Alex followed the young boy upstairs to a spacious three-bedroom apartment. Sitting on the floor with her legs crossed was ten-year-old Sierra sharing a coloring book with three-year-old brother, Cole. Both youngsters looked up as Ricky entered and announced, "Hey kids, meet my teacher, Ms. McCord. We're gonna be working on a class project, so ya'll just keep busy doing what you're doing."

Ricky ushered Alex to a large glass table in the dining area and took a seat. He looked at her questioning, "We're not here to work on a project, are we?"

Taking a deep breath, she admitted, "I came here to see for myself. How long have you had this responsibility?"

The boy stared at the floor for several seconds, uttering not a single word. Ms. McCord's presence made him realize the magnitude of his responsibility and their surmounting loneliness. Also embarrassed concerning the situation in which their parents left them, Ricky answered, "I came home from school one day about two months ago, and by suppertime, I suspected we were alone."

"You're pushing drugs to keep the lights on and pay the rent, aren't you?"

"I tried an afternoon job, but it didn't pay enough. Even selling drugs, I can only keep the lights on and feed us. If the rent isn't paid next month, we're out on the streets. The man wants me to step up my sales. Then I could afford to pay the rent also. But I'm scared. I guess I'll have to get an apartment in a bad place and hope I can support us then. We're in trouble, Ms. McCord. Another lady here knows our situation, and she said we'll each, sooner or later, be placed in foster homes and may never see each other again." He broke down and began sobbing softly enough to keep Sierra and Cole from noticing. Through his tears and sniffles, he added, "I told Sierra and Cole, mom and dad went on a little trip. It breaks my heart every day."

Placing her hand on his arm, she offered assurance, "I am going to do all I can to keep you three together. You hear me? You won't be alone."

He grabbed some Kleenex from a box on the table and added, "About seven o'clock tonight, these three guys are going to meet me outside in the parking lot to give me some more drugs to sell. I'm getting in too deep with the wrong crowd, but what can I do?"

She stared right into his eyes intently and said, "You're going to tell them you can't do it anymore. You hear me?"

Wiping his eyes and then blowing his nose, the boy explained, "These are real mean guys. This will be my first time to actually meet them, and I'm really scared. I heard they've murdered two others from this apartment complex. All I've ever met is a courier who gives me the drugs."

"When they call, go down there and tell them you're done dealing drugs. I'll be out of sight in the background. Believe in me, Ricky. Just believe."

"They said they would call when they get here. Boy, am I glad the phone still works. They'd really be mad then."

"Exactly where downstairs are you meeting them?"

"Behind the dumpster next to the maintenance building."

"I have something I must do at home, but I will come back and pick a spot near the dumpster to hide."

"But what can you do? You're just a woman."

"Trust me. You won't regret it. And don't worry, I'll be on time." She walked through the living room toward the front door, telling the little ones, "Be back in a little while." Ricky opened the front door, and Alex began skipping down the stairs toward the Jeep.

Once at the vehicle she climbed inside and called Richard. "Richard, bring the Challenger to my place, please."

"Alex, what's up?"

"I'll tell you later. We have no time to spare. Can you be there in less than an hour?"

"Give me forty-five minutes."

"Please don't be late. A young boy's life could hinge on my being on time. I'll use the artillery I have here in my safe so you won't, for some reason, get stopped with all in the car. Probably take you to jail on suspicion you mean to do some real damage yourself. I'll drive you home in the Jeep when I get back from my mission."

Back at home, Alex hurried inside to the bedroom and began changing into her bullet proof Kevlar/leather bodysuit. After adjusting the suit to fit, she grabbed her helmet and kneeled at the foot of the bed. She began to pray: "Heavenly Father, please guide my steps for which I'm about to undertake. Please let your will preside over the outcome. If necessary, let my aim be true and carry me to safety. In Jesus' name, I pray. Amen." Climbing to her feet, she sped from the bedroom to the kitchen, out the back door and into the garage. While grabbing her two 870 Remingtons and a .45 automatic from the gun safe, she opened the garage door to await Richard's arrival.

Sure enough, Richard came rolling in right on time. Bringing the car to a halt inside the garage, he stepped out saying, "You sure know how to give me writer's block. I was just about to give direction to my paper on Judas Iscariot. It's going to set the Christian community on their backsides. You'll love it. That is if I can get a chance to finish."

"Thanks so much. You're my hero. Stand by the phone, because I think I'll come back here since you've painted the car white." Turning to look over her shoulder, Alex remarked, "But you're Christian. What's with a paper on Judas?"

"They need a little shaking up. Something to bite on. Awaken them from lethargy. Ha!"

Shaking her head in disbelief, Alex commenced to climb into the driver's seat and start the engine. She put the beast in reverse and steered it down the driveway with the throaty exhaust bouncing off the houses in the neighborhood.

Roaring through the streets putting the Hemi through the gears, she was on her way to Ricky's and a destiny with some more predators. A sense of urgency dominated her emotions as adrenaline coursed through her veins. Being late could be fatal for Ricky. Her big fear was the drug dealers showing up early. She would be too late to save Ricky and his siblings.

Back at the apartment, Ricky's phone rang. He nervously picked up the receiver. "Hello."

"We'll be there by the dumpster in fifteen minutes. Don't keep us waiting. We expect you to pick up the pace."

Before Ricky could reply, the caller hung up. The youngster was frantic. Where was Ms. McCord? She had promised to be here. They were asking for a bigger commitment on a night he was to inform them he was quitting.

Taking two deep breaths, he informed his little sister and brother, "I'm going downstairs, kids. Be right back. Stay here and keep the door locked. I have my key."

He proceeded out the door and locked it behind him. Big brother then hopped down the stairs and around the back to the parking lot. Nerves firing off the chart, he mumbled to himself, "I hope you know what you're doing Ms. McCord. Here goes. Please God, be with me."

Making his way around the back of the dumpster, he was confronted by three of his suppliers. They were all dressed in short sleeved Polo shirts and slacks with gold dangling from their neck, ears and wrists. A tall, well-built man stepped forward and identified himself as DiAngelo. Like the two men in the background, he wielded a large .44 nickel-plated revolver.

"You kept us waiting, man. If you like the way you look, don't be late again. Now, your package is double what we've been giving you. You better have it all sold and our money this time next week. Would hate to hurt your little brother and sister. Understand?"

Barely able to choke out the words, he said, "Uh, huh…I'm gonna have to quit. I can't afford to go to jail and leave my brother and sister alone. I have to find another way to make money, Mr. DiAngelo."

Mr. DiAngelo pulled the hammer back on the .44 and pointed it at Ricky. "You've got about sixty seconds to figure out if you want to change your mind. If not, we'll have to hurt you real bad and then pay a visit to your sister and brother."

Knees trembling and near tears, he wondered if Alex was anywhere close. Where was she? She promised she'd be here. His heart was pounding through his chest, and he was almost too frightened to speak.

Then, out of nowhere, the roar of the white Dodge Challenger engulfed the early evening, echoing off the apartment buildings and the tall wood fence behind the dumpster. In a flash, Alex propelled the monster car across the parking lot and halted broadside between Ricky and the drug lords. With the passenger side facing the assailants, she climbed out and placed the shotgun over the top of the car and immediately discharged all seven slugs in their direction just as DiAngelo fired at her. With the intent and conviction of an assassin, Alex reached in the back seat and grabbed the other cannon and sent seven more in their direction to assure there would be no survivors. All three gentlemen lay sprawled out on the ground motionless in a huge pool of blood.

Using the electronic voice device in the helmet, Alex instructed, "Ricky, Alex sent me. Run upstairs and stay put. Wait for her. Now get."

Awe-stricken by what he had just witnessed, Ricky needed no further instruction. He heeded the advice and took off running for all he was worth toward the stairs.

A .45 automatic in her hands, Alex looked over the bodies and none showed any signs of life. She had apparently killed for just the second time. But for good measure, she placed one shot into each of their foreheads. Hurrying back to the car, she drove to the other end of the parking area and punched in the code to open the gate. As the Dodge roared down the street, she could hear police sirens. Somebody had already reported the gunfire, but hopefully there were no witnesses. Her only concern now was to get home, change clothes and get back to Ricky's apartment.

Nearing her neighborhood, she called Richard to put him on alert. "I'm three blocks away, so open the garage so I can pull in, please."

"I'm headed that way. Are you OK? Everything turned out all right?"

"It did."

Moments later she was pulling into the driveway and coasting to a halt inside the garage. Exiting the vehicle, she pulled off her helmet and notified Richard, "Those gentlemen just quit the drug business for good."

Sporting a solemn expression, Richard inquired, "You killed them?"

Nodding affirmatively, she explained, "I meant to. They would have never stopped hunting for Ricky. Richard, I've crossed that line you talked about. I am now an assassin. Regrettably, it felt good."

"Sooner or later, it had to happen. Now you are in for real trouble, Alexandria. You're a full-fledged felon wanted for murder. God help us."

"We'll talk later, but I need to go get Ricky and his sister and brother."

An hour later, Alex knocked on Ricky's door and hollered, "Ricky, it's me, Alex. Open up."

The door opened slowly and Ricky was standing there with Sierra and Cole beside him. "Ms. McCord, am I glad to see you! You won't believe what happened!"

Interrupting she asked, "May I come in?"

Sliding out of the way, he said, "Yeah, sure. Man, what a night! This guy dressed in dark blue with a black helmet drove up and started shooting! The three guys I had met were going to kill me! He saved my life!"

Trying to calm him down, Alex instructed, "OK, slow

down, slow down. Do you have any suitcases?"

"In my parents' closet."

"Get three of them if there are that many. We're going to pack clothes for all three of you, and you're coming to my house. So, let's get started. The police I'm sure will find the drugs on those boys downstairs and will assume it was a drug deal gone bad."

"Man, that guy in blue was awesome. Did you know he said you sent him?..."

"Tell me about it when we get to my place. Right now, we need to leave before the police come around asking questions. You're so nervous they'll know you saw something. Get your toothbrushes also."

Chapter 14

The morning sun had just risen above the eastern horizon, radiating its magnificent color against a crowded sky of low-lying stratus clouds when Alex guided her Jeep into the dimly lit faculty parking lot. Tossing the keys into her purse and grabbing a leather satchel, she rushed toward the front entrance to the school, passing Principal Long's pickup, the only other vehicle in sight. The urgency in her step was to reach Dr. Long's office before his day became too busy to afford hearing the long-involved circumstances surrounding Ricky McWhorter and his sister and brother.

The principal was standing behind his desk while pulling two breakfast burritos and a cup of coffee from a red and white Whataburger bag as Alex marched into his office.

"I'm sorry, Dr. Long, for interrupting your breakfast. I know you get here early to set yourself mentally for each taxing day, but I have some disturbing news."

Pointing to a chair in front of the desk, he replied, "Have a seat, Alex. You'll have to excuse my eating while you explain. This stuff's not much good unless eaten while it's warm."

She proceeded to relive the previous day's events involving Ricky McWhorter and his siblings, while he listened intently without interrupting. She ended saying, “So, I took them home with me.”

He scratched his head and leaned back in his chair, overwhelmed with what he just heard. “You mean you just happened to arrive at their apartment moments after the shootout?”

“Yes, sir, it was scary to say the least,” she answered, feeling as though she was betraying his trust and their developing friendship.

“How do you suppose the stranger who rescued Ricky knew of the meeting with the drug bosses? How was it, his timing was so perfect? Doesn’t that seem strange to you?”

“I agree, it’s baffling…”

The perplexed principal took a bite of his burrito and stared directly at Alex, commenting, “This guy, if we’re just talking about one guy, seems to be following you around. How did he know about Johnnie’s connection with Willie Buchanan? It’s almost like he’s listening in on our conversations. Uncanny don’t you think?... But the real issue now is what you’re going to do with those kids.”

“For the lack of a plan yet, keep them until the school year’s over and go from there.”

“Who’s taking care of the little brother right now?”

“Until I find a housekeeper, Richard has agreed to babysit Cole and pick up Sierra after school. In case you haven’t figured it out, we’ve come together just like before.”

“I would love to meet this guy sometime. We might have some similar intellectual interests. Might possibly share some ideas and philosophies. But before I forget, need I remind you about what Defective Kinstley's instructions concerning Johnnie? I worry that somehow you will push your involvement to greater heights. There's just something about you that's a little mysterious."

Sliding her chair away from the desk and standing, Alex thanked the principal for his time. "I haven't forgotten. Meanwhile, I'll be keeping you posted. Have faith, Dr. Long."

"Alex, I can't express enough my appreciation for your work and involvement in your students. Keeping this school a viable place for learning is overwhelming with all the forces out there trying to destroy our efforts. However, since you're here, I have some more news. When Superintendent Wedge informed me the school wide forum to bring back prayer will not be allowed, I gave the asshole my resignation, taking effect at the end of the school year."

Saddened of the reality she hoped would not have materialized, she uttered, "Well, that's just what our poor kids needed. What are you going to do?"

"Probably get me a bungalow on some Caribbean Island and drink pina coladas while listening to island music and watching half-naked local girls frolic on the beach. The turquoise water isn't bad either. Life's got to be good away from stress and the PC bullshit. Anyway, enough of that – get to class."

"Maybe you should take your secretary, Amanda, with you."

"Don't think I wouldn't like to."

She nodded and grabbed the doorknob behind her while saying, "Now I have to tell Scot Barton his beloved principal stood up for him up to and including his resignation. Just when the kids had someone to believe in, the liberals snatch him away and plan to replace him with a misled phony of some sort who wouldn't know how to help anyone, nor care to."

Navigating her way through the hallway amongst the maze of students shuffling to their various classes, Alex stopped at a water fountain where Scot Barton was bent over gulping down some water. "Scot, we need to talk briefly prior to class time. We still have about seven or eight minutes."

The big guy raised up with drops of water dripping from his chin. "Sure, what's up?"

"I don't know how to tell you any other way than to be straight forward. Principal Long just informed me he is resigning effective at the year's end. It's over Max Wedge cancelling the school forum on prayer. I wanted to let you be the first to know, so you can pull yourself together before I explain this to the rest of the class."

Head down, Scot stood erect and spoke not a word for several seconds before exhibiting his frustration and anger. "Damn it! We can't keep good principals! We've had three since I've been here. All left over stuff like this. Who do you believe in anymore?"

Most definitely feeling his pain, Alex placed her arms around his waist and unashamedly hugged the hulk of a young man. "Stay here and take a few minutes to compose yourself."

"Thank you, Ms. McCord. You're truly a wonderful person. You're also a great teacher. But I'll walk into class with you. Would you mind if I told them, myself? I feel they could take it better if the bad news came from me, instead of you. They need an example of taking bad news like a man."

Releasing her grip around him, she stepped back and looked up saying, "I'm so proud of you. Of course, you may. You're their leader, and what could be more fitting than to hear it from you. Come on, let's go deliver the bullshit bad news."

Looking down at Alex, in shock at her profane language, he said smiling, "Ms. McCord, I'm surprised you just used that language in the presence of a student."

Never breaking stride nor looking at Scot, Alex replied with conviction, "I call it what it is when the circumstances beg for the truth. Ironically, the 'Bible Thumpers' can shove it if they take offense. Believe me, God doesn't care either in this case."

Together they walked through the door of Room 207 and settled in their respective places. After taking roll, Alexandria called Scot to the front of the room to deliver a sure-to-be knockout punch; a morale destroying message.

The class could sense something was amiss as Scot ambled toward the front, displaying an untypical somber expression and no handouts from his research. Alex displayed a detached look on her face, far from her usual animated demeanor. A strange hush came over Scot's disciples as they braced for some inevitable sort of bad news.

Clearing his throat, the school's colossal All-State offensive left tackle announced, "It's my wish to be the one to inform you all of a decision made by our beloved principal. Dr. Long has turned in his resignation, effective at the end of the year. It's over the district's decision to disallow our school wide forum to bring prayer back into school. Truthfully and regrettably, my morale is in the tank. Seven or eight kids and their parents are determining what we're allowed to talk about. This project took me through some of the most interesting pieces of the Revolutionary War and the framing of our Constitution. The average person has no idea the impact prayer had, not only in shaping the Constitution, but holding the colonies together through impossible challenges, not to mention how Lincoln went to God for guidance during the Civil War. Now we're not allowed to even reveal these realities. To me, it makes our education system a hoax. We're being taken over by a lie; a bunch of liars with no concern for what's best for the whole. I'm going to leave it at that before I get ugly." With that last remark, Scot walked back to his assigned desk.

Not a single classmate could manage a response. Glancing around the room for a hint of discussion, Alex stood up from behind her desk and announced the latest news revolving around Johnnie Wimbush and his grandfather, Silas. "In closing, I cannot add to Scot's so encompassing speech. I will ask that you say a prayer for Johnnie and Silas. You may quietly sit at your desk until the bell rings or maybe exchange with each other what you are feeling at this moment. To help heal our disappointment, let's come up with a subject forum that will be acceptable. We need to get back in the saddle immediately, so choose a topic. That's an order, troopers. We must rise to the occasion. After all, our mission is to seek the truth and share that knowledge."

After school Alexandria hurried home with Ricky to check on Sierra and Cole. As the two walked through the backdoor to the kitchen, Richard was there to greet them, but he was not alone.

"Hey, Alexandria," greeted Richard, "meet half of the new housekeeper team. Please say, 'hello' to Lian Wok. She'll be taking the day watch so she can attend nursing school at night. Her mother, Hua, will be the live in. You'll meet her later."

Alexandria reached out to shake hands with Lian, saying, "It's so nice to meet you, Lian. I'm sure if Richard chose you, caring for young kids will be something you do really well."

"Yes, ma'am, I love kids. That's why I am studying to be a maternal-child nurse. It's a holistic approach to the family. The commonly used name is that of a Parent-Child Nurse."

"Wow. I have no idea how my uncle found you, but I feel very fortunate."

Richard interrupted the exchange of dialogue, explaining, "Excuse me ladies, I must attend a meeting with one of my publishers. Alexandria, may I see you in the garage for a moment? Lian meet Ricky; you two get acquainted."

Alexandria followed Richard into the garage where the Dodge Challenger sat. He raised the hood of the car, exclaiming, "For once you had a mission that didn't damage the car. I replaced the thermostat housing gasket. It had a small leak." Wiping grease off his hands, he further informed, "I put in a 160-degree thermostat, replacing the 180 degree one. It'll give you a little more horsepower."

"That's why I leave everything up to you," she said approaching the vehicle for inspection.

"Speaking of that, what are your long-range plans here with the kids? You know you can't keep them forever."

Smiling, she replied, "Who said so?"

"Alex, they need a full-time mom, not a part time mom and part time vigilante. Now that you have taken six lives, you might consider retiring in place of facing jail. Because they will conduct an all-out manhunt once they figure the Masked Marvel is responsible."

Crossing her arms, she argued, "Richard, did you ever see the television series called *The Courtship of Eddie's Father* with Bill Bixby? He was a single father. Why can't I be a single mother? You've already provided two perfect caregivers slash housekeepers."

"It's your night work that throws a wrench into things. Bill Bixby didn't do that. Then comes the big question: What happens when you go to Victoria for that extended stay?"

Finally, she conceded, "I haven't worked out all the details. I'll have to take this a day or a week at a time. All I know is, those kids don't need to be alone in that apartment, and they need to be together."

"I'm not arguing that fact. I'm arguing about their need for a fulltime mother. We must look for their paternal parents first, since they are the legal guardians, as silly as that sounds. There's a lot to do and I don't feel you are embracing this fact. And by the way, when is your next Victoria saga?"

"I'm going back this weekend. The next time I go, it'll be for the duration. I'll have to think long and hard on that one. But that's down the road."

"That's tomorrow. What about Farley? Have you seen him lately?"

"Why'd you ask about that?"

"Just curious."

"Still hope I'll marry someone, huh?"

"Not just someone. The right someone."

Hesitating, Alex admitted, "I may have blown it with Farley."

Richard closed the Challenger's hood and wiped off the front edge while suggesting, "Better think twice about letting him go. I think your friend, Laura, has a crush on him. There are probably others."

"Laura for sure does."

"I gotta run. Better try to figure out if you don't mind losing him. Call me when you get back. You have a lot of heavy thinking ahead of you. Better seek the guidance of the Lord. Look what the rest of our society has become since it turned away from Him."

Alex was motoring along Highway 59 south toward Victoria. Passing through Wharton and El Campo, the realization she must make this her last trip, permeated her thoughts. Saying good-bye to Mike without saying a word will be far more heartbreaking than she anticipated.

Right outside Victoria she picked up her little brother. He reminded her this was trip number three. "Alex, you better enjoy this weekend if you don't plan on coming back."

Glancing in the little cowboy's direction, she managed to eke out, "No matter what happens, the only certainty is, my heart will be broken again. But that just coincides with the rest of my pathetic life."

Silence pervaded for several miles before the little messenger informed, "Here's where I get out, Alex."

She pulled the car to the shoulder of the highway while bringing it to a halt. As the boy opened the door, he said, "I sincerely hope you make peace with this. Make sure you have my clicker."

"It's in the glove box. See ya Sunday afternoon. Oh, by the way, do you have a name I can call you, since we're sister and brother?"

"God calls me 'Child.' You don't get a name when you're aborted. But He loves me like a father. If He was married, I'd have a mother. You have to admit, having Jesus as your uncle ain't bad. Must make Mary and Joseph my grandparents. Whatever, everyone where I live knows they're equally loved. Can't say that down here. I guess I was lucky enough to get a head start. See ya."

I brought the Jeep to a halt as usual, in the Jet Drive-In restaurant. I sat there a few moments to gather some composure. After wiping tears from under my eyes, I exited the vehicle and started the seemingly long two-block walk to the Optimist Club dance hall.

It was all I could do to keep from crying. It was just that time of the month also. I didn't want Mike to always have to ask what was bothering me. The closer I came to the dance hall, the more I was able to compose myself. Entering the door, Johnny Dee and the Rocket 88s were playing, quite naturally. The dance floor was packed as they ripped out Buddy Holly's *Oh Boy* and followed with the Penguins' *Earth Angel*, a great slow dance. I nervously searched for Mike, because I wanted to be in his arms for that song.

Then out of nowhere, a hand touched my shoulder and a voice whispered in my ear, "Want to dance?" I knew it was Mike.

As I turned saying, "You know I do," he wrapped his arms around me and we danced at that spot near the snack table. It had been two weeks; two weeks too long since we last embraced. But to Mike, no time had passed. Life was as usual to him in this dimension. Wish I could say that.

As the song ended, he asked, "I'm pitching tomorrow afternoon at 3:30. Can you come watch the game if I pick you up? I'm going against Jimmy Cataan for the Alkek Oilers. We're the two top teams right now. What do you say?"

Without hesitation, I answered, "I wouldn't miss it for the world. You shouldn't even have to ask."

"Well," he said looking at me with that handsome big smile, "I don't want to take anything for granted. Plus, I didn't know if you had plans with your parents. Thought we'd go to the YMCA dance right afterward. I'd still be in my baseball uniform."

"That'd be great."

"Let's get on the dance floor," he said pulling me by the arm.

Johnny Dee went into a medley of Elvis songs. He was so good, he was Elvis. He sang: *Don't Be Cruel, Loving You, Love Me,* and *Jailhouse Rock*. Just plain awesome.

Like always, at the first break Mike went to the men's room, and I stood by the punch bowl. Johnny Dee and Marylyn made their way to my side. She said, "This is your final free visit, huh? I don't envy your dilemma. I can't imagine if it were Johnny and me."

Looking at Johnny, I said, "I'm not exactly thrilled with the situation. I don't understand why He can't let us just go on in this dimension; us being fourteen. I mean, He's created this miracle, why can't He just let it go on and on?"

Johnny thoughtfully asked, "Could you stand being fourteen forever?"

"I can't go through the wreck again. God's not going to change history. And to answer your question about being fourteen forever, the answer is 'no.' I've suddenly come to realize I don't want to be lonely in old age. My whole damn life is one big cluster of problems and heartache."

"Have you ever asked God to reveal his will for your life

and wait for the answer? He knows when you need immediate answers because of time constraints you did not bring on yourself. He also knows when you did bring the time constraints on yourself, and for those answers you must wait. You'll have to sit quietly without the TV, radio, and any other distraction."

Marylyn gently explained, "Your wish was for a few more moments with Mike. That much has been more than granted. I wouldn't go through the accident again. There's nothing to gain by watching him die again. Knowing it will happen again should be your closure."

"I can't imagine this being our last weekend together. The last time I'll ever see him again."

Johnny added, "People make wishes everyday and they never come true. You have to ask, why your wish was granted? That's what you must look for baby girl. Ultimately, you need to know the reason He granted what essentially amounts to a miracle. The long shot of a lifetime. I better get back, here comes Mike. Do you have a song request?"

"I keep coming back to *Talk to Me* and *We Belong Together*."

"What if I throw in *Queen of the Hop* and *Sea Cruise*? Two upbeat songs from Bobby Darin and Frankie Ford. How about that?"

"Sure, that'd be great."

As Mike approached her, he said, "That Johnny Dee's great ain't he? Don't blame him for hanging around the punch bowl when you're here. This is where we met. Remember?"

"How can I forget? It was the after-game dance the same night you ran 76 yards for a touchdown to beat Port Lavaca Travis with seconds left in the game. Then you carried some little grade school boy on your shoulders clear to the locker room. You were his hero. That made you my hero too."

Mike confessed, "I've wanted to meet you since the eighth grade. Never had the nerve to ask you to dance, let alone go out with me. Besides, you and Mike Fulton had exchanged discs."

"He turned out to be so pompous. I didn't know how to break up with him. Thank goodness his folks moved at the beginning of summer."

Johnny Dee took the microphone and announced, "I want to dedicate this next song to my good friends Alexandria McCord and Mike Koehl. It's called *We Belong Together*. So, all you guys grab your sweethearts and let's polish those belt buckles. Here we go."

I wanted this night to go on forever. So, what's new? I wanted all the others to go on forever. Dancing with my cheek against Mike's was the perfect way to spend life. I was on my tip toes while he bent way over. All was again right with the world. Johnny Dee kept his word and finished out the dance with upbeat songs, making the night end on a high note like the old days.

Saturday afternoon Mike's team, the red and white York Oilers, were playing the green and white Alkek Oilers. Mike was pitching against 15-year-old Jimmy Cataan. Jimmy's dad owned a big grocery store and was a huge supporter of teen-age baseball in Victoria. As a sophomore, Jimmy was the number-two pitcher on the varsity for the Victoria High School Stingarees. It was spring break and they allowed him to pitch this big game for Alkek. Normally, he couldn't join the teen-age league until the high school season was over. The stands were full, and people were standing all along the fence lines. I had my fingers crossed as the game got underway.

Alkek was designated the home team, so Jimmy Cataan went to the mound first. He was really dominating, striking out two and getting Mike to fly out to right field.

Mike then did the same thing to Alkek, striking out two and forcing Jimmy to ground out to the short stop.

In the fifth inning, with the score 0-0, Mike hit one over the left field fence after Ronnie Meyer singled to center. My guy then proceeded to strike out the last six batters and York won 2-0. Jimmy had the only hit off Mike, a double in the fourth inning.

Every game that Mike pitched, dozens of youngsters would run on the field and ask him to sign their baseballs, baseball caps, or just a plain piece of paper. One kid didn't have anything, so Mike signed his tee-shirt. It seemed like everyone loved Mike Koehl.

Instead of going to Ferguson's Drugstore with everyone else, we went to Whataburger. Mike bought me a hamburger, French fries and we shared a chocolate shake. It was symbolic of how we were going to spend our life together.

"Why didn't we go to Ferguson's?" I asked.

"Sometimes I'd like to just spend some time alone with you. Are you disappointed?"

"No, No, I'm just surprised, that's all." If he only knew how trilled it made me.

"Lately you always seem to have something on your mind. You seem to cry more. I know something's bothering you, but I can't begin to guess what. It's almost like we're going to part company or something. Like you know something I don't."

I was hard pressed to come up with a lie that was convincing. "I guess I'm just ready to start high school, so we can hurry and graduate and get married. I'll just be glad when we can make a life together. Sometimes I think something will come between us and it won't happen. Nothing really complicated."

"Nothing really complicated, huh? Sounds impossible to me for something to come between us. Three years is a long time to me. Let's just enjoy not having any real responsibilities. Outside of having to keep up with our schoolwork, we're care free."

I didn't know how to turn off thinking about this being my last moments with him - ever. All I could say was, "You're probably right."

Still puzzled, Mike inquired, "Do you still want to go to the YMCA dance tonight? Maybe we can go to a movie? You know I can't bowl during baseball season. It's too hard on the arm. Your choice. Could play some pool and dance if you want."

I used to like to go watch the drag races on Saturday night when it warmed up in late spring. Mike said the cold dense air in winter and early spring was better for the engines. Something about the ETs was always lower. I was trying to think of something just the two of us could do. Especially considering the limited time we'd have together. So I blurted out, "'That Touch of Mink' is showing at the Uptown."

There were two indoor movie theaters in Victoria. The Uptown was quite the exquisite one. The bright marquee spanned across the top of the building and the carpet inside the lobby was two inches thick with multiple chandeliers hanging from the ceiling. The ushers and snack bar hosts were all dressed in tailored uniforms. Inside the auditorium were plush seats, brightly colored carpet, private balconies and gorgeous forest green drapes covering the giant screen. On the other side of the town square, was the El Rancho Theater. It ran mostly B western movies and was more functional. There was no carpet, the ushers and snack bar hosts were dressed less formal and the auditorium seats were vinyl. Instead of individual balconies, there was one large balcony. The marquee in the front of the theater was smaller, but adorned with many bright flashing lights, much like the Uptown.

Mike looked at me with that irresistible grin saying, "The movie it is. Better call your parents and tell them where we will be. Otherwise, they'll think we're at the dance. I don't want to do anything to lose your dad's trust. I don't want him to say no when I ask his permission to marry you."

It was all I could do to keep from breaking down and crying an ocean of tears. Suddenly this fantastic fantasy was going sour; I got what I asked for, but the pain was almost too much to bear.

***

The little boy was once again waiting by the Jeep. I was more depressed than usual, as I opened the driver-side door and unlocked the passenger side.

"You haven't made up your mind have you?"

Wiping tears from my eyes, I managed to say, "I'm not coming back."

"It wasn't an easy decision, I'm certain. Johnnie Wimbush and Ricky McWhorter and his sister and brother would be lost without you for the next 3 ½ years."

"I can't believe how complicated this simple wish has become."

"The Lord is amazing in his methodology. I guess that's a word.... Here, let me out."

I brought the Jeep to a halt on the shoulder of the lonely highway.

As the little guy exited the vehicle, he said, "Good luck to you, Alex. You made the right decision. This was all about closure, so you could get on with your life. You'll always be in my thoughts. But remember, should you change your mind, I'm only one final 'click' away." No sooner had the last syllable left his tongue, he disappeared.

I was so startled, I could hardly keep my hands from shaking enough to guide the Jeep back onto the highway and head home. Now I had more on my mind than before. Never have I been so mixed up. What could all of this mean? I was very distraught and covered with doubt; doubt about my ability to make any decision. Because of being headstrong, I had not waited long enough for God's answer on anything. Need to get home and back to reality. I need God's guidance in facing the challenges and entanglements with being in serious trouble with the law, to say the least.

Chapter 15

Alex steered the Jeep up the driveway while opening the garage door with the remote controller, and guided it inside, closing the door behind her. Climbing out from behind the steering wheel, she shut the driver's door and leaned face first against it. Emotionally drained and physically exhausted, she managed to pull herself together and exit the side door to the garage.

Once through the back door to the kitchen, she quietly shuffled past the living room to her bedroom. It was slightly after midnight, and there was no one stirring, not even the new live-in housekeeper who admitted being a night owl. Slithering down the hallway and peeking into the largest guest room where the children were sleeping, a warm feeling came over her while observing the innocence of children at sleep. More apparent than ever before, Richard's plea to solely concentrate on teaching and mentoring students rather than surrendering to inner demons made sense. Being solely responsible for the daily lives of three other people, made the potential consequences of her actions far more reaching and impacting. Life's game had changed.

Monday morning Ms. Wok awoke early, preparing a delicious breakfast. Alex entered the kitchen and saw Ricky, Sierra and Cole scarfing up some eggs, bacon, and biscuits covered in gravy. The self-appointed surrogate mom proceeded to inform Ricky she would take the lad to school and bring him straight home, by-passing his part-time after school job for fear friends of the deceased drug suppliers would be looking for him. Ms. Wok assumed the task of caring for Cole during the day and escorting Sierra to and from Parkwood Elementary School.

With much apprehension, Ricky asked, “How long are we gonna live here Ms. McCord?”

“As long as it takes to come up with a plan. And right now, I don’t have the slightest idea about a plan. Just make sure you keep this under your hat. Know what I mean?”

“Yes ma’am. I can’t tell you enough how grateful we are. I had no idea how we were gonna make it. I’d have been in trouble selling drugs sooner or later. I prayed every night God would help us. He answered my prayers by sending you. I promise we’ll try to not be much trouble. We’ll pick up after ourselves and even help Ms. Wok with the chores.”

Sierra chimed in, “Yeah, I can help do the dishes, wash the clothes and clean the bathroom. Ricky can help me with my schoolwork. We won’t be any trouble.”

Hugging the young girl, Alex reassured, “I’m glad to have you stay with me. I always wanted a family. We’ll all pull together and help with the chores and homework. It’ll be fun.”

Meanwhile, Detective Kinstley made a trip to the Houston Post for the purpose of discussing with Buddy Hodges the episodes surrounding the Masked Marvel. Farley too was invited, because of his previous experience as a San Antonio police detective. The three had collaborated many times over the years. Kinstley was especially appreciative of Hodges' work as a private investigator after leaving the Oklahoma City detective's job.

Sitting in Buddy's office, feet propped up on the front edge of his counterpart's desk, Kinstley wondered out loud, "What if the guy who killed those three drug dealers was also the one who shot up the Reapers' hangout, killing three? And suppose he's also the one who has been rescuing the old folks from losing their social security checks? Is he and our Masked Marvel the same guy?"

Hodges answered, "The guy who rescues the old folks hasn't killed anyone. He inflicts wounds and leaves them for you. Went out of his way not to kill. That'd be way out of character. But it is an intriguing thought."

Farley questioned, "How do you suppose he even knew about the Wimbush kid fixing to get pummeled? What alerted him to be at the scene where that drug exchange was to take place at that apartment complex the other day if indeed he was involved there? Maybe he's got some crystal ball?" Shaking his head, Farley added, "We must be missing something fellas."

"We can't ignore the shell casings found at the scene of each crime are from a shotgun. That seems to indicate we are talking about the same person who has self-appointed himself to by-pass all the legal work necessary to get the bad guys off the street permanently," reckoned Kinstley.

"We're forgetting one thing; the rogue GTO that murdered Getty and participated in this last episode against the Reapers," chimed in Hodges. "Maybe that guy killed the drug dealers, making it two different gentlemen we need to look for, not just one. Or, are they working together? It's getting kinda complicated, huh?"

Looking at Kinstley, Farley countered, "Years ago, we thought the same thing in a similar case, remember? Turned out to be a 'copycat.' I'm a little puzzled why you're looking for this guy or these guys, whichever the case may be, with such immediacy? Some mighty handy police work is getting done without the interference of lawyers and the rest of the judicial system."

Kinstley pointed out, "His stunts are too overwhelmingly spectacular now to ignore. He's showing us up, and the Chief's taking heat from the mayor, who in turn is taking his share of pressure from the political machinery. The public may like his deeds but the political pressure is overwhelming. The mayor does want to be re-elected."

"Mike," offered Hodges, "I must confess, I've been racking my brain trying to find that common denominator; a clue to how he seems to be Johnny-on-the-spot, so consistently. That common denominator seems to be the McCord lady. It's just a gut feeling I have. Nothing based upon any evidence. I've had this on my mind for some time now."

Kinstley came clean, "I did a background check this morning on Alexandria McCord. Her parents were murdered ten years ago by a gang during a robbery. I was not involved in the investigation, but coincidently the police reports identified the gang to be the Grimm Reapers. A couple of mornings ago before school had opened, Willie Boy contacted her in the teacher parking lot. As we speak, our gang leader now has Johnnie in his possession. Kidnapping brings the FBI into the picture."

"Well, there's some developments that support my gut feeling Ms. McCord is somehow connected. Can you imagine she being the one dishing out all this carnage? Wow!" exclaimed Hodges. "She's my kind of girl."

After looking at Buddy rather perplexed, Farley asked, "If Alex is connected in some way, where do we go from here? Follow her everywhere she goes? I just don't believe she's capable of all this. I had to rescue her myself when she went to visit Silas not long ago. She was genuinely scared."

Reluctantly, Mike declared, "I have no choice but to put a tail on her twenty-four hours, and hope she makes a move to either rescue the kid or, God help her, in some way try to confront the gang. The worst that can happen is she leads us to some answers."

After several minutes of silence, the much-stressed detective asked Farley, "Are you good friends with the McCord woman? If so, see what you can get from her in casual conversation. Any kind of clue will do."

"Not to change the subject, but whatever happened to your shadow, Detective Murphy?" asked Hodges. "I kinda liked her. Had some spunk."

"She quit the force, to become a private investigator; another Buddy Hodges."

Puzzled, Hodges pleaded, "OK, you threw me there. What does that mean, or is it classified?"

"She's decided her chances of fighting crime as a private detective would yield faster results. She wouldn't have her hands tied behind her back like myself. Sharon wants very badly to nab our city's deadliest criminal, the Masked Marvel ... It's a long story, Buddy."

"I'll take your word for it, but the life of a private detective is hardly without its drawbacks. It's also a very lonely one," Hodges added. "Back then there were days I wished I had remained with the Oklahoma City Police Department."

Sliding his feet off Hodges' desk, Kinstley stood stretching. "I better prepare to initiate that tail on one Ms. McCord. Then I'll pay a visit to my friend, Johnny Luster. His auto restoration shop is in the same vicinity as the Wimbush grocery. He happens to know a lot of stuff going on in the streets. Should have gone to him in the beginning." Tapping his hand on Buddy's desk, Mike added, "Let's keep in touch. Something tells me this all will come to a head real soon."

It was a typical Monday morning first period class weekend hangover atmosphere which Alex had to face. With enthusiasm being almost non-existent, the youngsters could not agree on a class project to replace the prayer in a school forum setting. As a last resort to ignite some interest, she instructed the kids to divide into groups of five with each submitting one topic. This would narrow the choices down to five; a more workable number.

As the class split up into groups and began lawyering for their ideas, Alex launched into deep thought, planning her strategy to hunt down Willie Buchanan and save Johnnie. Her concentration, however, was broken, as Scot Barton approached with a bombshell announcement.

Leaning over her desk and whispering so none of the others could hear, Scot informed, "Ms. McCord, can I talk to you in private? I have to quit school."

Snapping back into the reality of his announcement, she stood up saying, "Sure Scot, let's go out in the hall. I'm...I'm at a loss for words here."

Alex followed Scot into the hallway and closed the door. "I can't believe what you just told me. I'm so flabbergasted. Why, is my question? Why are you quitting?"

"Ms. McCord, my dad lost his job at the refinery. He's had a drinking problem for a long time, and he got caught drinking at work. He had been hiding his Jack Daniels in one of the toilet tanks in the locker room. The company had no regard for the 30 years he was a good hand, so they severely cut his retirement. This happened last Thursday and he's not been sober since. So, I'm going to have to get a job to support us. He's getting real mean. Told me Saturday he's happy I can't play football next year and go to college to be a big shot," he explained, bowing his head with embarrassment as tears began to trickle down his cheeks.

Taking a deep breath to control her disappointment, she

thought for a moment before answering, "Look at me Scot. Look at me now."

The hulking teen-ager raised his head looking into her eyes with a pleading look of desperation.

Offering much needed hope, she consoled, "Somehow we'll figure this out. Give me some time to think about this. There's always a solution. You hear me?"

"Yes, ma'am. But we're gonna need some money for the house note pretty soon. He refuses to use his retirement money.

Things got really bad after mom died. She was the love of his life. In fact, he was a great college football player himself at SMU, but quit so he could go to work full-time and marry her."

Although moved by such a touching story, Alex forced herself to regroup and direct Scot. "Your father can get unemployment. That'll help. Do you think you can get him down to the unemployment office? It's the Texas State Unemployment Office on the corner of Harrisburg and Lockwood. Eastwood Park is just down from there on the same side of the street."

"I don't know, it won't be easy. My dad has a lot of pride. But just in case, what does he have to do?"

"He files an application with one of the agents there. I'll get you the exact address. Having been fired, he will be eligible for benefits. From the time he applies to the time he receives a check takes approximately two weeks."

"I don't know how to face everyone. I'll be letting my teammates down. We had unfinished business to take care of next year, and now I won't be around to finish it. It just breaks my heart. I had such high hopes of playing football for the University of Texas." Fighting back the tears, he continued, "I saw this coming when he kept missing work, but just kept hoping some miracle would happen. I go to bed praying every night. That's all I had to cling to Ms. McCord. I must be doing something wrong."

Struggling to come up with the right words, Alexandria managed to offer, "I'll ask God, myself, what you can do to get Him to answer your prayers. Meantime, go wash your face so you can return to your seat while I give the homework assignment. Class is almost over."

"Yes, ma'am."

As Scot lumbered toward the restroom, Alex returned to her desk and just sat, observing the interactions inside each group. Surprisingly, the exchange of ideas was materializing in a respectful demeanor. The sincerity driving the discussions proved to reinforce her conviction these kids are for the most part earnest in their intentions; a stance without much community acknowledgement or support.

Big Scot returned to class and promptly received an invitation from Lee Zimmerli to join his group. Zimmerli was a move-in from a suburban school where he was honorable mention all-state as a sophomore baseball shortstop. His father transferred the youngster to Centennial, feeling there was an advantage playing baseball for the soon-to-be Hall of Famer, Jerry Walker.

Barton immediately pulled up a chair and joined in the discussion. He had such a rare quality as a natural leader, the kids were drawn to him. Alex was beginning to feel an immense obligation toward both Scot and the school to find a solution for their dilemma. Student leadership was a huge factor in the success of any high school's ability to offer an atmosphere friendly to both learning and unity, especially those in the inner-city.

As the class bell sounded, she commanded, "Have your ideas ready for discussion on Wednesday. That'll give you a chance to work in groups tomorrow during class and possibly the library or cafeteria after school. See you tomorrow."

While the kids proceeded to evacuate the class room, Alex grabbed Scot by the arm instructing, "I'm going to see Dr. Long concerning your predicament. The two of us will put our heads together and figure something out. Do not quit school. You're such a natural leader, I'm certain the Lord does not have that in mind. Through prayer, He is able to use people as instruments to accomplish His will. Keep the faith, Big Guy."

Upon finishing her second period class, Alex hustled to Principal Long's office, all the while, thinking about how she always runs to him when trouble rears its ugly face. It was probably due to the fact the two of them share a compassion for these kids few others do, or comprehend. Secretary Amanda Blinn had stepped out, so she tapped on the door and entered. The underappreciated principal was pouring a cup of coffee and greeted her, "Hi Alex, what brings you in here so early? Trouble I assume?"

"I should sit down to lay this on you: Scot Barton appears to be on his way to quitting school. His father lost his job due to having an alcohol problem. Can't stay sober and has ordered Scot to quit school and find a job to pay the bills. Can you believe this? I'm about ready to check myself into the 'nut ward'… soon."

Frustrated, Dr. Long replied, "This place is the nut ward, I'm afraid. And I ask myself why I should be shocked at what you just informed me of." Sarcastically he added, "By the way, you are not supposed to end a sentence with a preposition."

"I've only got a moment because I'm meeting with a student and her mom at the end of my conference period. I just wanted you to know so maybe we can somehow save this boy. Honestly, I never dreamed these inner-city schools had so many problems. The dysfunctional families are producing so many lost kids, no wonder our society is strapped with drugs and crime. And the parents that do try hard have to battle the gazillions of piss-poor role models in the entertainment, sports, and music industries they absorb. It never stops. Pretty soon, I won't be doing any teaching at all – just counseling and losing that battle."

Just after Alex left her seat and headed for the door, Detective Kinstley made a surprise appearance. "Sorry Principal Long, your secretary must have stepped out. I took the liberty of coming back here unannounced due to the nature of my visit. May I sit down?"

Standing up, Dr. Long pointed to a chair saying, "Yes, of course, Detective. Do you mind if Ms. McCord stays? We both could use some more bad news. Neither one of us has had the recommended daily dose yet. I assume that's why you're here."

"By all means. This involves Ms. McCord also," he explained, glancing in her direction and a bit confused by the principal's response.

Somewhat fearful, Alex retraced her steps and sat down in the chair she had just vacated, saying, "I only have a minute, but it's about Johnnie, isn't it Detective Kinstley?"

Looking her straight in the eyes, the veteran detective somberly replied, "Yes ma'am." Mike turned his attention to the already distraught principal and relayed the shocking news. "Johnnie and his grandfather, Silas, have been murdered. I just came from the crime scene and wanted to relate to you both the news and my concerns. We have more than enough reason to believe it was the Reapers."

The principal leaned back in his chair, hands clenched, mumbling, "My God. Oh, my God."

Leaping to her feet and shoving the chair aside, Alex marched over to the window and glared out over the courtyard next to the cafeteria, demanding, "Don't spare me the details Mr. Kinstley. How did they kill them?"

Mike paused for a moment before reluctantly revealing, "They were hung inside Silas' grocery store."

"Is that all? Just hanging?" she asked while continuing to stare out the window with a laser-like focus.

"I'm not at liberty to hand out any more information than that. The rest would be pointless."

"They'll pay, Mr. Kinstley. They'll pay dearly," Alex promised, continuing her focus toward the courtyard where some students were passing through to their next classes.

Fighting back the tears, Principal Long finally remarked, "This will be a major blow to the school. Johnnie was such a tremendous leader with a big heart and a cheerful outlook on life. We'll all miss him dearly… Hands cupping his face, the beaten school principal squeaked out, "It just never seems to end."

Detective Kinstley pushed his chair away from the principal's desk and stood asking, "Ms. McCord, I don't know what you meant by what you said a moment ago, but it's in your best interest to let it go, please. We will get them, I assure you. I don't know what background you could possibly have to tackle this on your own. You'll only get yourself hurt. On the way over here, my major concern was how you would react. I fear you'll not heed my direct order and something will severely go wrong."

Alexandria never said a word nor acknowledged his statement in any way.

Moving toward the door, the detective added, "I'll see my way out. I'll also keep you posted on anything significant."

Several minutes had elapsed following Detective Kinstley's exit when Dr. Long confessed, "I think we are responsible for their deaths. We didn't take the warnings serious enough. I'll never forgive myself. When I call it quits at the end of the year, this will hang over me the rest of my life. I haven't accomplished a single thing here except get two wonderful people killed."

Alex fired back with extreme bitterness, "I'm the one responsible; me alone! Don't take blame you don't have coming. I harassed them, and both Johnnie and Silas paid for it with their lives. Now I must make them pay with their lives."

Cautioning, the principal pleaded, "Alexandria, you're talking crazy here. That gang of murderers is way out of your league. You have to leave this kind of stuff to those trained for these circumstances. There's too many of those thugs for a sole inexperienced civilian like yourself to tackle."

Speaking with impregnable conviction, she replied, "Not for Captain America." Turning from the window, she marched out of the principal's office saying, "Good day, Dr. Long. Good day, sir."

Standing, he shouted, "What about your students? Don't you owe them something?"

Never looking back, Alex continued her march past Amanda's desk toward the main door, yelling back, "I'll tell them about Johnnie and Silas tomorrow! That's all I owe them aside from killing every single Reaper!"

With a sense of urgency, Alex exited the faculty parking lot after school with intentions of paying a visit to Johnny Luster after delivering Ricky to the house. She wasn't quite sure what her new-found real father could offer besides some words of wisdom. Maybe by chance, Johnny knew where Willie Buchanan might be holding up. At any rate, it just felt right to get the man's input.

Traveling south on Harrisburg, she pulled into the Toyland of car restoration. Johnny just happened to be helping one of his body men level a rear bumper on a 1969 Dodge Charger. Looking up, he saw Alexandria exit the Jeep, so he proceeded to walk briskly toward her.

"Well, well, what brings Alexandria McCord to my humble place of business?"

"I need to pick your brain, if you have time for me."

Pointing the way, Luster was more than accommodating, "Sure, go on in, you know where my office is. I have to go back over that bumper install with Tony. Be right back."

Alex slipped by the customer service desk and proceeded down the hall to Johnny's office and took a seat in one of two leather chairs at the front of his desk. While waiting, she glanced around the room at the numerous pictures gracing the walls. One in particular caused her to further investigate with a closer examination. Astonishingly, it was her mother kissing Johnny Luster, apparently just prior to his boarding the bus for basic training in 1943. Next to it was one of Johnny holding her in his arms on the field just after a football game. Sighing rather somberly, she whispered, "He wasn't lying and neither was Richard. My mom looks so in love."

"Those two pictures represent the only good I've had in my lifetime," informed Johnny in his loud gruff voice, jolting Alexandria out of her trance. "I've had other women in my life, but couldn't find that feeling again. Know what I mean?" He then sat in his high-back chair behind the desk asking, "What brings you here?"

Sliding back into the chair she had been seated in, Alex boldly revealed, "Since I can talk to you like we were in the corn patch, I came here to get some words of wisdom or maybe some help. I'm going to kill Willie Buchanan. Thought maybe you might know where he is hiding, or where I might start looking. Maybe some related advice."

Laughing out loud, he exclaimed, "I was wondering what you were waiting on; the tablets to fall? Anyway, he typically hides out at a warehouse right next door to Fingers Furniture on the Gulf Freeway. Been thinking about killing him myself to save you the trouble, but one more killing on your record won't matter at this point, especially one that would be so satisfying. From what I have gathered, Willie Boy may have several places, so make a visit to Tess's Lounge and convince one of them into showing you around."

"Does he usually have anyone with him during those times of hiding out? I need some details to help my plan of attack."

"Alexandria, I have a 1967 Dodge Coronet RT to finish so some Exxon CEO can take it to a big car show in three weeks, so I haven't had time to stalk Mr. Buchanan. Therefore, I have no extensive information to help you on that one. I wish I did, believe me. So, when do you plan to make your assault, or should I ask?"

Ignoring his question, she mumbled, "I guess I'll have to flush him out somehow. Might start with shooting up his hangout again. Maybe put a gun in one of the boys' mouths and trade information about Willie's whereabouts for the kid's life."

Pounding his fist on the desk, Johnny proclaimed, "Same thing I would do! But there's one difference. They're waiting for you. They don't know who I am. Whatever you do, do it soon, because Kinstley is on to you. In fact, I intended to make you aware of the possibility our bulldog detective initiating a monitor on all your actions."

"I better have a plan soon, I guess. Truthfully, my life is in shambles. I don't see how I could possibly fix it, because I can't live with myself if I don't kill Willie Boy."

Distraught, she continued, confessing, "Should have just stuck to teaching. Hell, should have taken a suburban school job. Took this inner-city teaching job thinking I was going to make some big impact on less fortunate kids. You know, pie-in-the-sky. I don't know how I got to be so messed up. Now, I'm looking at prison after I kill Buchanan. It would be my luck to get caught before I had a chance to kill that bastard…I better go; the longer I sit here, the more I get depressed about my meaningless insignificant loveless life."

Attempting to console her in a fatherly manner, Johnny offered, "You can't help being a champion of the underdog. You get that part honestly; that's the part of me you inherited besides the love of old cars. So, don't blame yourself for that. Blame yourself for not listening to Richard when he warned you about stepping over the line. And don't blame God, because he has sent you messengers whom you've refused their counsel. But you have to be who you are, not what somebody else thinks you should be."

"What about you?" She challenged. "You murdered Getty in front of people. Aren't you afraid of throwing away all you have built up right here?"

"Alexandria, I have pancreatic cancer. Doctors give me less than a year to live. And prison? I've been in prison ever since Frank McCord married your mother and raised my kid. The son-of-a-bitch took her while I was fighting Germans. I wasn't fighting for my country. I was fighting to make a safe place to live for the woman I loved. You know what got me through that horrendous Battle of the Bulge? A picture of your mother in my helmet. I got the Silver Star and two Purple Hearts. The love of your mother is the only reason I was able to crawl three miles to a farmhouse in France with three Gerry slugs in me. That was after the great shootout in the Ardennes Forest. Obviously, I lived. Frank McCord got what I earned. So, prison? I don't give a shit. Frank McCord needed killing. Go get Willie for taking the only decent person either of us has ever loved."

"Wow, I came here depressed and now I'm suddenly pumped up for action! Now, I know why I was led to come see you. Unfortunately, it's too late for us, isn't it?"

"Yep. That little brother of yours said you have a place to go where no one will ever find you. That's why I know you'll kill that shithead and never see prison. When you get to that place, tell your mother I still love her. Will you do that for me? Please, for me, so I can die knowing she knows I never quit wishing Frank McCord was me. After all, Alexandria, this is more than likely the last time we'll ever see each other again. Maybe in Heaven." He said that with tears in his eyes.

Alexandria began crying as she stood up, but managed to promise, "Yes, I will tell her in private. She'll probably be grateful. In fact, her heart probably needs that. Good-bye, dad." They hugged each other for the first and last time before Alex walked away.

Early Tuesday morning Alex wandered into the first period classroom well ahead of the warning bell and placed her satchel on the desk. Proceeding to the one window in the room, she opened the blinds, inviting in the morning sunlight to bring in some mood improving vitamin D. Having cried out the last available tears the night before, she sat on the front edge of the desk with a game-face ready and waiting to divulge the fate of Johnnie and his grandfather, Silas.

It wasn't long before students shuffled into the room, most barely cognizant of her solemn facial expression and lack of acknowledging their presence. But the ever-perceptive Scot Barton passed her desk and immediately sensed something was not right.

"Hope you don't feel as bad as you look, Ms. McCord," he remarked while turning to find his usual seat at the back of the room. Leaning toward Lee Zimmerli, sitting next to him, the big guy whispered, "Something really bad must have happened."

Lee replied, "I think you're quite correct. I hadn't noticed at first, but now that you brought it to my attention, she's got that look like her dog died."

Scot prognosticated, "Something has happened to Johnnie; that's my guess."

Lee returned not a word, but focused on his teacher as the tardy bell rang.

Never budging from her position, Alex related the news of Johnnie and Silas. “Class, I have a grave announcement. With unbearable sorrow in my heart...I must tell you Johnnie and his grandfather, Silas, were murdered yesterday. The authorities believe a gang called The Grimm Reapers is responsible.” Taking a deep breath, she added, “I can assure you, their killers will meet the Almighty soon. I personally will hunt them down like the filthy dogs they are and assassinate each and every one. Just spend this class time any way you wish. If you talk amongst yourselves, keep it to a low roar. I’ll be right here if you need to talk.”

Everyone was stunned on two counts; the murder of Johnnie and his grandfather, but more so by their teacher’s bold announcement of her intentions to personally execute the Reapers. Who was this woman with such compassion and tender caring for her students that she could on the flip side, become an assassin?

Zimmerli and Barton traded unsettling glances before Lee choked out, “Can you believe what we just heard Ms. McCord say? Did I hear her right?”

Scot covered his mouth slightly with his left hand saying, “I think Ms. McCord is a martial artist. I’ll tell you more at lunch. She might be leading two lives.”

“Now you really got me wondering. Forget lunch, tell me after class,” Lee insisted.

All through the rows of desks, students were buzzing more about Ms. McCord’s daring proclamation than the deaths of Johnnie and Silas. Meanwhile, Alex slid off the front edge of the desk and took a seat in her chair, pretending to scan the lesson plans, but all the while plotting strategy for carrying out the sentence on the Reapers.

As the class bell rang, everyone quickly gathered up their books and scurried into the hallway so they could voice out loud their bewilderment concerning Ms. McCord's unbelievable declaration of vengeance and spread the news of Johnnie's death along with his grandfather's. However, the statement promising retaliation was the highlight discussion, reverberating throughout the school.

Alex suddenly figured out she needed to make arrangements for Richard or Ms. Wok to drive Ricky home after school to accommodate her plans for attacking the Reapers tonight. Racing through the maze of students in the halls, she managed to grab him by the arm.

"Ricky, look for Richard or Ms. Wok out front. I cannot take you home today. I may not ever come home again, so you are now the man of our little family. There's no time to explain, but Richard will do that for me."

Startled, he replied, "Yes ma'am."

Nodding her head, she said, "Good, now run along to class. And remember, your entire future along with Sierra's and Cole's hinges on you getting a good education. They'll follow your example, so set a good one."

"I surely will. You can count on it," he responded while turning to head for his second period class, overwhelmed and confused at the drastic change of circumstances for both he and his siblings.

Watching him walk away, Alex made her way to Dr. Long's office and informed his secretary, "Amanda, tell Principal Long, he'll have to use my assistant to finish my classes today and indefinitely. I have urgent business to take care of."

The young secretary informed, "Dr. Long will be back in a few minutes if you'd like to talk to him yourself."

"No thanks, I'm in a hurry. I'm leaving campus immediately. He'll know why."

Alex motored home and immediately called Richard from her phone in the bedroom. "Unc, are both the cars at the hangar?"

Puzzled, Richard replied, "Yes, why?"

"I'm gonna need 'em. I didn't know how to tell you this last night, because I was so distraught and could not keep from crying: Johnnie and Silas were hung by the Reapers. Richard, they're dead because of me. I can't live with myself until I kill Willie Boy and every last one of the Grimm Reapers. That means I will not be home for a while. I would so appreciate it if you'd pick up Ricky after school today. He'll be standing by the flagpole. Please help Ms. Wok keep the household together, Unc. I'm sure I'll be on the wanted list soon. Hunting them down will be a full-time job."

"Alexandria, is there any way to talk you out of this? You're walking out on a lot of people."

"Richard, I did that a while back when I killed those drug assholes. And now, two wonderful people are dead because of me. They both begged me to mind my own business, but I didn't listen.

I'll never be any good for myself nor anyone else unless I avenge their deaths. Actually, Unc, even extracting revenge will not make me any good for anyone, ever. There's no way for you to know how torn I am. I guess we both knew someday it'd come down to this, especially you. Consequently, I'm stuck going back to Victoria forever, that is, if I can kill Mr. Buchanan and outrace the police to my freedom."

Sitting at his desk, Richard removed his glasses while rubbing his forehead. "Unfortunately, we knew in all reality you'd cross the line. Because you were in denial, you just kept getting deeper into everyone's business that was none of yours. It started out simple and innocent, and now you're a self-appointed assassin. I'll pray for you, Alexandria. May God be with you."

"Thank you, Unc. I'm really sorry it had to turn out like this. I guess my whole life has been a mess. Somehow, I just couldn't square it up. I can't let you go any further with me. I'll have to take care of the cars by myself and use the remotes for the gate and hangar doors. I gotta go, I'm just rambling."

"Alexandria..."

"Yes Unc?"

"Get 'em. Get 'em for all of us, especially you."

"I'll try, sir. Bye." She returned the receiver to the cradle and began sobbing while sitting on the side of the bed. She gazed around the room at the collage of pictures that compiled her whole life. There were snapshots of the great times she had with her mom and fake dad as an only child. They made sure Alexandria never hurt for companionship; took her everywhere they went. And then there were the images of her and the only guy she ever loved, Mike Koehl. He was the one she could never let go, denying herself of any adult romance.

Wiping the tears with both hands, Alex slid off the bed and marched toward the kitchen where Ms. Wok was preparing supper.

"Hello, Hua, it sure smells good in your kitchen. Looks like a feast."

"It's not my kitchen Ms. McCord."

Alex grabbed the keys to the Jeep and smiled, saying, "It's your kitchen now, Hua. I'm going away for a while, so Uncle Richard will be around to help you with anything you need. You are the head person in charge. Richard will pay you and give you money for anything you need." As she walked through the kitchen door toward the garage, Alex commented, "Hua, you are a Godsend."

Puzzled, Hua just stood speechless behind the island counter where she tied up her apron. Shaking her head in confusion, she proceeded to slice up some tomatoes.

Alex cranked up the Jeep and began backing down the driveway toward the street for what was to be last time. Ironically, it was the first time in her life the house was becoming a home; a place with children and a housekeeper. Just like her favorite TV show: *The Courtship of Eddie's Father*.

Chapter 16

For once, the ride down State Highway 59 south loomed uncustomarily lonely and unsettling. Gone was the adrenaline generated excitement; the anticipation of a mighty triumphant night's work. Present was the unbearable realization, with certainty, she was forever leaving behind the ones she loved and who needed her most. The foreordained moment had arrived and she was surprisingly apprehensive about this night of causing chaos and destruction, because Richard would not be there to offer his usual wisdom, comfort, and support. Most importantly, no one would be there to catch her fall, should that happen.

Guiding the Jeep through the hangar door, she closed it behind her using a remote which automatically turned on the indoor lights. Once inside, staring at her were the white 1971 Dodge Challenger with the legendary 426 Hemi and the 1969½ Plymouth Road Runner 440 Six Pack with all its armor-plated protection in key places. Richard had sprayed the latter entirely in "flat black" paint for nighttime stealth.

She ambled over to the driver's side of the monster Road Runner, admiring the Bird that had performed so impeccably during her previous devastating raid on the Reapers and their hangout. Peering into the open window, her two usual short-stock Remington 870s and their cartridge belts lay out on the front bench seat. On the dash sat a Colt military issue .45 automatic in a scabbard with six extra clips. Unc had left her more than prepared.

Moving through the door to the living quarters, Alex marched into her bedroom, and began slipping into that muscular suit looking navy-blue bullet-proof Kevlar suit. Sitting on the edge of her bed, she began to take mental inventory of the supplies that would be needed during what could be an exhaustive manhunt. An abundance of ammunition was a no-brainer which Richard had already provided, but enough food would help avoiding having to stop somewhere for meals. Cash too would be necessary in preventing the police from tracking her activity through debit card purchases. Once the destructive course begins, Dr. Long, Detective Kinstley, Farley Fontenot, and Buddy Hodges would realize Alexandria McCord was causing all the disturbances. Her absence from school alone would point the finger in her direction, therefore staying ahead of their collective pursuit was mandatory. The hunt may end tonight or may take days. Much past tonight, the chances of apprehension before the job is finished triples.

Wonder Woman stood erect and zipped up the Kevlar suit, grabbed the elbow length gloves, her mask, and helmet, while heading toward the small living room. There she sat on the much-used round ottoman and slipped into matching boots. Taking a deep breath to calm her nerves, she grabbed a workout bag and wandered into the kitchen, gathering several cans of tuna and pork 'n beans. She also tossed in a fork, spoon, and knife, along with a box of Ritz crackers, sardines packed in olive oil, several cans of Spam (Richard's favorite) and a can opener. None of the items required refrigeration and the fat calorie content would be more than satiating and sustaining. Once the bag was full, Alex swung it over her shoulder and headed out the door to the fire breathing rolling fortress of a car. After tossing the food supplies onto the rear seat, she took one last look around before slipping into the driver's side and closing the car door while firing up the engine. Flipping down the sun visor exposing the automatic door remote, our midnight marauder pressed the 'open' button, and moments later had the Bird roaring through the opening, heading for a final date with destiny.

Cruising the hangar road to the highway, Alexandria was fast becoming asphyxiated with melancholy. Ringing in her ears was Uncle Richard's frequent warning that someday the nightly crusades would go too far. Though it had already far surpassed simply going over the line, tonight could be the cou'de gra; the concluding chapter in her life unless she could accomplish this one last mission and escape the grasp of law enforcement long enough to reach Victoria. Approaching the highway, our girl used the remote to operate that ever-familiar gate. Once on the pavement, Alex began to focus strictly on strategy for tracking down Willie Buchanan with expediency and assassinating him with conviction, while ridding the world of evil.

The roar of the big block 440, along with the road noise from the window being in the rolled-down position, served as a symphony for Alex, further affirming Johnny Luster's claim to being her real father. By now the sun was beginning its descent, so she turned on the headlights and plugged in some old music, using the ancient eight-track tape player. Gracing all four speakers was an album by the legendary girl group, The Supremes, with Diana Ross singing "Baby Love," one of hers and Mike's favorites. Fence posts and gates flew by, giving way to large strip shopping centers and huge automobile dealerships leading to the city of Houston. Tess's Lounge would be the first stop where Armageddon would be thrust upon a small portion of the city, all along Navigation Blvd.

Cruising by Silas' grocery store was frightening, but pulling up to the curb in front of Tess's Lounge, more so. There were probably but half a dozen cars in the rear parking lot, as the evening was young; the fewer gang members inside the better. Willie Boy drove a red and white '57 Chevrolet Bel Aire two-door hardtop, but there was no such vehicle in sight. She'd have to hope someone would give away Willie's whereabouts while looking down the ever-intimidating barrel of an 870 Remington.

Alex eased open the car door and exited while grabbing her artillery. After sliding on her helmet, the guardian of the night strapped on the crisscrossing shotgun cartridge belts wrapping around her shoulders and buckled up the holster housing the .45 automatic. Moseying inside, she took note of seven gang members sitting at the bar and another four at a table off to the left, near the dart board. Slamming the door hard behind her drew their immediate attention.

As the guys all turned in her direction, she spoke through the electronic voice in the headgear, "Remember me, boys? It ain't over." Aiming the big pump gun in their direction, the nighttime crusader instructed, "One of you can take me to see Willie Boy, or you all can punch your ticket. I'm in no mood for talk."

Two boys at the far end of the bar immediately pulled their weapons, thinking they were secluded enough, but Alex fired four rapid shots their way, dropping both. Two more at the table stood to volley, but were a split second late, falling lifeless to the floor. That left two at the table still breathing and another five at the bar suddenly giving their tormentor the utmost respectful demeanor. Never losing eye contact with the group, she swiveled the other 870 on a strap from behind her neck, commencing to reload the one she just emptied. The electronic voice filled the air, "Having fun, guys?"

Making that universally recognized chambering sound of a pump shotgun, she reiterated, "Now, which one of you is taking me to see Willie Buchanan?"

After a seemingly long moment of silence, one tall strapping youngster closest to her felt insecure enough to answer, "He doesn't always tell us where he goes, honest."

"What's your name?" She demanded while pointing the shotgun in his direction.

Trembling, he answered, "Albert."

Without hesitation, Alex related, "Well, Albert, I'm running out of patience. Someone better take me to all the places he's likely to hangout, or I'll just drop all of you right here. I have no use for any of you otherwise, and neither does the neighborhood. The good people here will sing my praises. Your choice."

Convinced he was about to eat the next projectile, Albert volunteered, "I'll take you to some places. I can't promise anything."

Motioning to a gang member standing behind Albert, she tossed him some tie wraps, instructing, "Tie his hands behind his back. Make 'em tight or you won't live to see tomorrow."

As instructed, the lad secured Albert's hands behind his back, giving the wraps one last extra tug.

"Albert and I are going out to my car, and if I see anyone of you poking his nose out that door, I'll waste every last one of you," she promised.

Turning to Albert, Alex commanded, "Now let's go. Remember, I'd like nothing better than to drop you in your tracks."

Suddenly the bartender, who had not spoken up to this point, exclaimed, "You'll never make it to your car. Several associates of these guys are right outside in the street waiting for you. They'll let you shoot Albert just to hang you the way they did Johnnie and Silas. There will be some more at the backdoor, so you had better let Albert go and fend for yourself. It's your only chance. They'll be spaced out so you can't use your cannon as effectively as you did in here with everyone so close."

Stalling for time to think, Alex countered, "Why should I believe you?"

"No reason, except I'm not one of them. They pay me handsomely to keep this place open. Won't harm me, because they need a public place where legit customers come, which enables the gang to launder their drug money and other illegal donations they receive. All I have to do is know nothing and see nothing."

"Why then are you telling me this?"

"I don't want you or them to kill Albert. He's worth saving."

It was beginning to look like Alexandria had just spent the last of her nine lives. Seemingly, there was but one last glorious move to make – go down in flames by killing everyone inside, except for the bartender, and then proceed outside and chance surviving a literal slugfest. She pushed Albert aside, continuing to speak through that electronic voice, "Stay right here, and I'll spare your life. Poised to waste the others, she said, "You boys will not live to see me hang. Mister bartender, get down behind the bar, I'll spare you also."

Just as she spit out the last syllable to the bartender, the remaining Reapers began reaching in their jacket pockets and belts for their handguns. But they also were too late, as Alex began unloading one cannon and swiveling the other over her shoulder with the strap and discharging it with ferocity. Quickly, she grabbed her .45 from its holster while standing in a maze of gun powder. The return fire had ceased, apparently indicating the lightning speed of pump action had extinguished the remaining skunks inside.

Silence prevailed for several minutes as the smoke began to clear, and there was no evidence of movement from any of the bodies strewn across the floor. Albert had found a place to squat down against the wall to her right. She reloaded both weapons of mass destruction and pointed the .45 toward Albert ordering, "Get up, we have one more hurdle. If I don't make it, I promise, you too will not."

As the youngster managed to reach his feet, there was the sound of more big guns ringing that horrifying noise, unmistakably coming from the street just outside the door. Frozen in their tracks, she and Albert just looked at each other, mystified and feeling apprehensive. However, ignoring her fear, Alex nudged Albert through the door, stopping on the sidewalk. Once outside, they both observed a horrendous scene of scattered, blood-soaked bodies in the street. The bartender had been telling the truth. But now her attention turned toward the street along the side of the lounge, bracing for those in the back alley, who surely by now would be hurrying toward the front of the lounge.

No sooner had she refocused to that side street, a loud volley of shots rang out from behind her and Albert. Turning quickly in a panic and poised to return fire, she witnessed the bartender holding a .357 magnum revolver, while standing beside three more dead bodies; the ones who had been watching the back door. Upon hearing the gunshots out front, they rushed through the backdoor with intentions of gunning down Alex by surprise from behind. The bartender had courageously saved the moment.

Tapping the gun barrel on his chest, he softly informed, "I'm a free man if you get Willie. I'm a dead man if you don't. God be with you, whoever you are."

Again, speaking through the electronic voice, she asked,

"May I at least know your name?"

"It's Earl Doby. I'm proud to say I am the grandson of the great outfielder for the Chicago White Sox in the 50's, Larry Doby. He bought me this place when the neighborhood was made up of wonderful hard-working families. Tess was my mother, and she served meals here for those less fortunate. Alcohol paid the bills, but I never let anyone get plastered. My customers always made it home without an incident. This place is dear to my heart. Please get Willie Buchanan; for my sake, and the people in this area. Maybe kids can play in the parks again without fear of being forced to peddle drugs. It's about hope. And you are our only hope."

Biting her lip to keep from crying, she assured, "Earl, God uses people in mysterious ways to answer prayers. Be it His divine wish, I will end Willie Boy's life. There will be no lawyers getting him out of trouble this time. You have my promise."

Returning her vigilance to the street in front of the lounge, Alexandria finally noticed a black police-issued Ford Crown Victoria automobile, the kind police Detective Mike Kinstley drove, parked on the opposite side of the street. Unless her eyes were playing tricks on her, Detective Kinstley and Buddy Hodges were leaning against the front and back fenders, both holding identical 870 Remington pump shotguns and standing in a pile of shell casings.

Motioning Albert to step off the curb and weave amongst the bodies of his brethren, the two eventually came face-to-face with both imposing fellas who probably saved their lives for the time being. Leaving her helmet on, the electronic voice squeaked out, "I can't say I'm completely glad to see you two good ole' boys. I still have a job to finish if you'll kindly look the other way." Pointing her cannon in their direction, she added, "I can't let you stop me, so please don't make me take out your legs."

Laughing, Kinstley revealed, "Never intended to. If I wanted to stop you, I could have let these gentlemen lying in the street do that. Keep the headgear on, and I can't say I know specifically who caused all this carnage. Alexandria, it's almost ten o'clock. My resignation takes effect at midnight, so by the time all this mess has its paperwork processed, you are no longer my problem and I yours. I didn't want to apprehend you in the first place." Turning to Albert, he instructed, "Take her to Buchanan tonight, and I will not report you were ever here."

Puzzled, Alex asked, "You know Albert?"

"We have had some long heart-to-heart talks. Hasn't done as much good as I would have liked, but there is hope for him. Good luck to you both. Alexandria Luster, I hope all of this has been worth spending the rest of your born days in prison. The department will know undoubtedly, you're the one who has been serving all this midnight justice. They won't need me to tell them. You've left too big a trail. For the life of me, I can't figure out how you became so empty to this great big world we have."

Unmoved, Alex ushered Albert into the passenger's seat of the Road Runner, parked a few feet away, and swung around the rear of the car, climbing into the driver's seat. She fired up the beast and had the car roaring down Navigation Blvd.

Hodges looked at Kinstley, "I haven't felt this alive since I left Oklahoma City. I have you and that woman to thank. Now I have to figure out how to explain my whereabouts tonight to my editor. He'll want to know how I managed to be on the scene to get such an exclusive story. Not that he won't be thrilled for the Post to have such an exclusive on the biggest breaking news story Houston has seen in several years."

Kinstley replied, "How'd I get here to see this monster shootout right before retirement? That's my question to answer."

Hodges suggested, "Since the cops haven't shown up yet, why don't we anonymously just call it in, and go have a cup of coffee and something to eat?"

"You know, I can't do that. I have to stay here and give my account of what happened to the best of my knowledge. Of course, we had nothing to do with any of these killings." Handing the two shotguns toward Buddy, he instructed, "Hide these in your trunk; they're not exactly police issue."

Grabbing them, Buddy mumbled, "It's a good thing I decided to meet you here. These two pieces of incriminating evidence would place us in mighty hot water should they be found in your trunk…I guess I'll wait here with you. Be thinking of how it is we were so coincidently together."

Mike sarcastically asked, "Why are you going to wait here? So, I'll buy you something to eat?"

Buddy fired back, "OK, smart ass. I just want to see you squirm while swimming in lies. In fact, I wish Murphy was still your partner. That'd be really interesting."

Turning to Albert, while removing her helmet and tossing it

in the backseat, Alex demanded, "Where to from here? And I'm in no mood for the runaround. I'll kill you where you sit."

"The Fingers Furniture Store and warehouse on the Gulf Freeway. There's an older building next to it," Albert replied with cool confidence.

"What's there?"

"His hideout. Goes there to get away from everything. Usually plays high stakes poker, and has some strippers for real entertainment. There are video games and pool tables, plus a bar. Everything you need to have fun and de-stress."

"How many people might be there?"

"Depends."

"Depends on what?"

"How stressed out he is. Tonight, he's probably by himself. Gets like that when he needs to be alone to reflect."

Minutes later while guiding the vehicle onto the Gulf Freeway, she asked, "What's he got to reflect on? All the murders he's committed?"

Looking at Alex, Albert offered, "Doesn't quite understand how he got into a life of crime and became so inhumane. Knows he's in so deep, his time will be up. I think he has moments he wishes the law would end his life in some news making big shootout. Front page of the paper, you know?"

"Albert, he killed my parents ten years ago while they were visiting friends in a neighborhood that he continually robbed. Robbed the old folks of their social security checks and any cash they had. Did all his damage in the rundown neighborhoods that are unprotected. I've been hunting for him ever since. Have devoted my life to the cause."

"You're the lady who Willie confronted in the grocery store parking lot at Silas' a while back, aren't you? You're Johnnie's teacher friend, huh?"

Taken by surprise, she inquired, "How'd you know about that?'

"I was there. Truthfully, most of us are just looking for a place to belong. In the beginning, you don't really want to do people harm, but it just happens. None of us have a real family. I'm actually the only one with a job. I work in the Star Furniture warehouse, so I can live on my own. I rent a room with a small fridge and microwave. Even have a small bathroom with a shower. The others feel society owes them for not being fortunate enough to know how to read good enough for someone to hire them. It's tough when you think there's no other way out. Willie's parents were slaughtered in their living room right in front of him when he was eight years old."

"By whom?"

"His dad promised to testify against a Russian mob leader charged with numerous counts of murder, drug running, prostitution, and bribing local government employees. Before the FBI could get him into the witness protection plan, the mob did their dirty work. His dad accidentally witnessed something he shouldn't have. Ever since that day, Willie's been bitter toward everyone in every walk of society. CPS placed him in horrendous foster homes, schools, and at age 18, turned him loose on the streets to fend for himself. Not one relative offered a helping hand. Claims he prayed to God every night, but it did no good. His dad had worked a full-time job at a Folger's warehouse and served as pastor for a small community church. His mom scrubbed floors at night to provide money enough for the church to run a soup kitchen. Still want to kill him?"

Staring at the roadway ahead, she was touched by Albert's story about Willie, but however, was forced to confront Albert with, "Does that justify his hanging Johnnie and his grandfather? What did they do to him?"

Albert hesitated for a moment before admitting, "No, it doesn't. I'm just grateful I had no part in that act. The others laughed and cheered while the two begged for their lives. That's how far gone Willie and his gang have become."

"What's your story, Albert? What do you get from associating with their likes?" Alex inquired, exasperated.

"Some place to belong. Didn't learn to read very well myself, so I fell too far behind in school to catch up. No hope to make anything out of my life. Just felt like God had no plans for me. What I have with Willie ain't much of a life, but it beats being alone."

Continuing to probe, she asked, "What about your parents? What are they doing? No brothers or sisters?"

"My mom died giving birth to me. I was their first and only child. Dad blamed me, so he put me in a basket and placed me on the doorstep of my mom's sister, Aunt Holly. She had six kids of her own and was on welfare. Essentially, I got a roof over my head, a place to sleep and just enough food. When Aunt Holly no longer received money for me from the state, I had to go. Willie saw I was living in store-front doorways and alleys, and asked if I would like a permanent place. Of course, I said yes. About the time I decided a life completely like them was not for me, a 'Now Hiring' sign in front of a safety supply warehouse on Navigation caught my attention. Miraculously they hired me, and I was taught to use a forklift. I guess I showed up at the right time. The job enabled me to live on my own and just be a friend of the gang."

Slowing down the car, Alex pointed out, "There's the exit for Fingers. If Willie's car is there, I'll let you out so you can walk away. I'm tempted to leave your hands strapped behind your back, though. Don't need you turning on me or warning Willie."

Before Albert could say a word, Alex was steering the car off the freeway into the parking lot of the newest Fingers Furniture and warehouse. Back to the right side of the lot was a smaller warehouse once used to be for industrial storage. Looking straight ahead at a red and white 1957 Chevrolet Bel Aire hardtop, she asked, "That's Willie's car isn't it?"

"Yes ma'am. This is actually what he's been hoping for. If you'll be kind enough to free my hands, I'll drift back to my room on Canal Street. I did what you asked."

Wiping some moisture from her eyes with her left hand, she responded, "Albert, I'm sorry for you; for the plot life's dealt you… I can't believe this place is unlocked and has utilities."

The youngster explained, "We rent it. Please, this isn't the neighborhood to have your hands tied behind your back, especially at night. Honestly, I won't turn on you."

Alex exited the car and walked around the rear of the vehicle toward the passenger side and opened the door, allowing Albert to climb out. She took some wire cutters and clipped the tie wraps, freeing his hands, and quickly pulled the .45 from the scabbard, pointing it at the youngster. "I can't afford to trust anyone, so start walking. And may God be with you."

Albert nodded and started walking toward the Gulf Freeway. Alexandria waited until the boy was out of sight before jogging toward the warehouse side door. Between two cannons, their cartridge belts, and the .45 in her holster, there was more than enough firepower to take out Willie Buchanan. The very moment she had been waiting for the last ten years of her life was soon to be a reality.

Upon reaching the top steps to the door, Alex took a deep breath and slowly nudged it open, looking inside at the dimly lit path toward uncertain fate. Cautiously and quietly slipping along the left wall rather than walk out into the open, she traveled about ten yards before hearing a voice shout out.

"Hey, teach, looks like we're finally gonna have that showdown! Only one of us is gonna walk away; you know that!"

Acknowledging so, she shouted back, "I know, Willie!"

Further dialoging, Buchanan delivered, "You have everybody fooled with that suit you wear. Cops think they're looking for a man. I hate cops. That's why I wouldn't tell them they're looking for a woman teacher. That's funny, ain't it?"

Speculating he was hiding somewhere along the far-right

wall, Alex crouches down and attempts to keep him talking long enough to be sure of his location. "Did you buy this old warehouse?"

Laughing, Willie responded, "Why? What does it matter to you? You're gonna die right here, and I'm gonna call the cops and tell them, you broke in and tried to kill me. They'll call it self-defense."

While carefully focusing on the gaming tables midway on the back wall, Alex baited, "Why don't you show yourself so we can get on with this showdown?"

Unaware his stalker had an idea where he was hiding, Willie made a fatal mistake by darting out from behind an upright slot machine toward a pool table, while staying low to the ground.

Alex spotted the move and hollered, "When are you going to show yourself like a real man would do?" Patiently, she waited for an answer while continuing to stare at the pool table, but Willie did not respond. Now was time to go on the offensive and draw him into a shootout.

Crouching low, maintaining a slow steady "duck walk," she moved further along the wall on the left side of the entrance. The pool table where Willie shielded himself was dead center on that backside wall she was approaching. Her path would eventually put them face-to-face if Willie stayed right where he was.

An uneasy hush pervaded as Alex crept along the wall with cat-like moves, heart rate increasing with every step. Though on the prowl, and now within 25 to 30 feet of the pool table, she felt like anything but the predator. Willie seemed to have the advantage even as the distance between them was steadily shrinking. The upright video game in front of the pool table was blocking any underside view. Eventually, a low-crawl toward the center of the floor would be the only way to get a better angle to possibly facilitate enabling a first shot. For certain it would be a very risky move, putting her in harms' way unprotected.

Continuing the low, soft "duck walk" toward the center of the floor, she no longer had any cover, making it now necessary to belly-crawl toward the target, praying to get off the first kill shot. Belly crawling with the shotgun laying across her arms, she heard a sudden noise; the game machine was moving.

In a sudden burst, Willie unexpectedly sprang up from behind the video game and opened fire with his .357 magnum Colt revolver. By the grace of God, Alex feverishly rolled over on her left side unscathed and rapidly opened fire in his direction with all seven slugs from her shotgun. She immediately pulled the .45 from its scabbard, emptying that clip. The reciprocating volley lasted only a few seconds, but seemed an eternity.

Gun powder smoke blanketed the area, and Alex, hands shaking profusely, managed to roll over on her right side and slip the other cannon from its shoulder strap pointing it in the direction of Willie's previous gunfire. He must have been hit, because she lay out in the open, and there was no return fire. Plenty of time had lapsed for Willie to reload his revolver, so what was wrong?

Alex began pulling herself along the floor while on her right side, all the while pointing her menacing weapon in Willie's direction. Continuing to slide slowly and carefully along the floor through the dim light and hovering haze, she spotted Willie propped up against the rear leg support of the billiard table, blood pooling all around him and continuing to flow from all over his upper torso. Even the guy's right knee was ripped apart. Approaching closer, they met eye-to-eye.

In obvious pain and struggling to speak, Willie managed, "Well, teach, from the looks of things, you won. I guess I'll be checking out in the next minute or so. Gonna go meet my maker – the Devil. I'll fit right nicely in Hell, won't I? My life here hasn't been much different than what awaits me down there. What do you think?"

Laying her gun on the floor, Alex noticed she had taken a hit on the left side near the belly button, as revealed by a slight tear in the Kevlar, but with no penetration. The pain was beginning to make itself prominent as her adrenaline subsided with the sight of Willie. Wincing with pain, she continued crawling toward the lad and propped herself up on the opposite table leg. "Do you believe in Jesus?" she asked, almost feeling some compassion.

Willie hesitated, but managed to say, "Who doesn't? He just never cared for me. Nobody did." With that, he closed his eyes and was gone.

Head bowed, she was unaware her adversary was dead, so Alex offered without looking in his direction, "Willie, you may be surprised where you're going."

Just as she looked over at the young man, a rush of adrenaline exploded inside, causing panic and uncontrollable fear as never before experienced. Albert was standing with one of the shotguns pointed down right at her.

Staring up at him, trembling, she barely managed to ask, "Albert, why?"

Distraught, the youngster placed the barrel of the gun within inches of her nose, confessing, "I couldn't let you kill Willie. I walked a long way thinking he'd get you, but then I decided not to leave the outcome to chance. I loved Willie, but I got here too late. I'll never forgive myself, but I can avenge his death."

"Albert, I trusted you. I could have killed you."

Though visibly shaken by Willie's death combined with what he was about to do, Albert confessed, "You should have, for your sake. This won't take long. Close your eyes and it might not hurt so bad."

Alex remained looking up at her menace of death, watching his hand slide a slug into the massive chamber. Eyes closed, Wonder Woman awaited the awful sound of a detonated shotgun shell; one that would violently end her life. Albert, however, had a last second change of heart saying, "I can't do this to you. I've never hurt anyone." She never heard the boy's statement, because there was at that moment a rapid barrage of massive explosions echoing throughout the warehouse.

Reeling with panic, Alex looked up as Albert dropped his weapon to the floor and fell directly on top of her. Their eyes met just inches apart, before his closed for the last time, face falling limp into her chest. Having miraculously escaped certain death, the terrifying trauma caused her to blackout.

Chapter 17

When Alex regained consciousness, she found herself still propped up against one of the pool table legs opposite Willie Boy, with Farley Fontenot staring down at her from a sitting position atop a wooden spool housing steel cable. Bewildered, she looked up at him and then glanced over at Albert a few feet away to her left, lying face down in a pool of blood.

Before Alexandria could say a word, Farley explained, "I found a bathroom in this place and wiped your face with a wet paper towel. That's why it's a little damp. You'll find a dry towel on your lap."

Still in a fog, she managed to ask, "You must have shot Albert, huh?"

"You're quite perceptive, among other things. My deadly aim is the reason you are still here sucking up oxygen," admitted Farley rather sarcastically.

"So, what's going to happen now? Have you called the police?" She asked remaining propped up against the pool table leg.

Sighing, he informed with a disgusting tone, "No, I have not. With all the shooting, I'm really surprised they haven't already shown up. After all, you have been out for about thirty minutes. …Just in case you haven't already figured it out, you're in real serious trouble."

Barely above a whisper, she nodded her head affirmatively and questioned, "How did you know where to find me? Better still, how did you know I'd be involved in this to start with?"

"Detective Kinstley, that reporter guy, Buddy Hodges, and myself have had some long conversations attempting to put together scattered pieces in an effort to figure out who this nighttime marauder could be. In the end, all indications pointed to you. For a long time, we were at a loss for a candidate. This guy was quite entertaining, rescuing old folks from having their social security checks and available cash stolen. Kinstley really wasn't giving it much thought. After all, in the beginning, the guy never killed anyone; just left the bad guys wounded and tied up, waiting for the police. The public loved it.

"Then Paul Getty, the famous GEO for Lympko and Houston's most hated villain, was hit by rock salt in front of his team of lawyers. Kinstley even thought that was amusing, and the masked marvel gained legendary folklore status. There was no public outcry to apprehend this hero of the blue-collar world; middle America's crime fighter. However, the political machinery, beginning with the mayor's office, was becoming embarrassed. That's when the heat was turned up on Kinstley to find and apprehend this dangerous fella. The mayor attempted to convince the public, Captain America was a danger to those who elevated him to such a hero status. After all, elections were coming up.

"But our last great American Hero committed the unpardonable sin. He crossed the line and began to murder people; criminals that probably needed to check out anyway, to be honest with you.

"I'm sitting here now at a loss as to who killed Getty in gangland style. He drove a GTO; the other guy always drove a Dodge or Plymouth. The only connections were old muscle cars, and our once hero had threatened Getty. What was really confusing was the night a Plymouth and the GTO acted together. That really left us reeling. We're almost back to square one; more confused than ever.

"However, Alexandria, when you reported Willie Boy contacted you in the faculty parking lot, we all got suspicious. The day Kinstley informed you and Dr. Long, Johnnie and Silas had been hung, you blatantly told them both, you would kill Willie Buchanan. Tonight, you went on the attack. Prior to this rampage tonight, Kinstley did some background work on you and discovered the Grimm Reapers were responsible for killing your parents. That's about it. I'm not going to ask you who killed Getty. Don't care. I knew in my heart it wasn't you, and that belief was substantiated when the guy in the GTO worked with you the other night. If he doesn't strike again, Getty's murder hopefully will go unsolved. That jerk's loss is of no consequence; at least in my mind. Just another pathetic dirt-bag executive who cheats and steals from honest hardworking people who are loyal."

"If I had to say, all of this is why you never let me get close to you. There's just something about your makeup that drives you to help people solve their problems, at any cost. It seems to be your only goal in life. For most people, it's the pursuit of happiness and finding someone to be intimate with. But not you."

Again, nodding her head in agreement, she asked, "But you didn't answer my question: How did you know I'd be here?"

Laughing in disbelief, Farley divulged, "I received a phone call from someone who claimed to be your brother. He said I would find you here to complete your destiny, whatever that means. It sounded fishy to me, since you never indicated having a brother, not to mention the destiny part. Desperate, I let my better judgment step aside, while I drove over here feeling slightly the butt of a joke. To my surprise, you know the rest. Didn't tell Kinstley and Hodges, because you stepped so far over the line and are now facing at least twenty life sentences, if not the death penalty. Right now, those two bloodhounds are still trying to get information as to your whereabouts. And believe me, they're working as diligently and with a sense of urgency as I've ever seen Mike or Buddy work. You've managed to accomplish a lifetime of police work just tonight alone, if that makes you feel any better."

Wiping her face with the dry paper towel lying on her lap, she resisted telling Farley that Kinstley and Hodges helped her tonight. She simply asked, So I repeat, what now?"

"This is where it gets better than some science fiction movie. That weird sounding brother of yours indicated you had a place available, where you'll never be found. I don't quite know where that planet would be or what he meant. Maybe it's with Peter Pan and Tinker Bell. My suggestion is to get in that car of yours right now and go," he urged while intensely staring into her eyes.

"Why don't you turn me in? You're an ex-detective," she asked, hoping to hear Farley reveal his true feelings for her.

Shaking his head in disbelief, Farley bared his pent-up feelings, "My god, Alexandria, you still haven't figured out I'm in love with you?"

Alex paused for a moment, feeling ashamed, but managed to look up at him admitting, "I don't know why you would be. I certainly haven't been very nice to you."

Laying it all on the line, Farley opened up, "I know all about that Mike Koehl guy. Your uncle explained all that business months ago, when I went to him seeking some advice on how I could win over that hard heart of yours. He wasn't much help, but unfortunately, I'll never have that chance, because you have to leave right now. Take my gun with you, so I won't be nailed for shooting Albert in the back. I can't say, I was saving your life, because they'd ask why I let you get away. All I can do is claim to have found everything just like it is now with these two creeps lying here with gunshot wounds. Hell, I'll probably just tell the guys I saw a black van racing from the parking lot. At any rate, at least they won't think either one of us shot this guy you call Albert. They'll have a pretty good idea you shot Willie Boy, though. Albert's death will be the real puzzle, because there is no weapon here to match the slugs I put in him."

Maneuvering to her feet, she announced, "Well, I guess I better go. Is my car still there unharmed?"

"Yep," Farley answered, while standing up.

Looking into his eyes, she asked, "Would it be alright with you if I kissed you good-bye?"

"Only if it would mean something. I don't want some half-baked gratitude kiss..."

Before he could finish his sentence, she wrapped her arms around him and pressed her body hard against his, placing a kiss on him like there was no tomorrow. It was with feeling, so Farley pulled her in closer and returned the wet lip lock with passion. This is where the story should have ended.

Reluctantly, he pushed her away and ordered, "Get going. I'll need time to prepare how I'm going to explain the reason I happened to be here. Guess I'll just tell the others I received an anonymous tip. Actually, that part is true. Kinstley will know I'm lying about the rest, but he won't pursue it. The guy has unbelievable instincts."

Tears trickling down both cheeks, she said with feeling, "I could have loved you so much, Farley, but obviously it's too late. I'll never forget you." Turning her back, she began sprinting toward the front door of the warehouse.

Farley was left standing, forlornly, watching Alexandria disappear into the night, only to forever wonder where she went or what happened to her. Pulling himself together, he began walking toward the payphone hanging on a nearby wall, unaware Kinstley and Hodges had already had contact with their girl.

Just as Farley indicated, Alex found her car unharmed. She proceeded to unlock the driver's side door and slide in behind the wheel. Inserting the key into its ignition switch, she fired up the big block and roared out of the parking lot toward the Gulf Freeway, and eventually the all too familiar State Highway 59 South toward Victoria. Though that 1962 dimension was the only chance to avoid prison, her mind was swirling with all sorts of uncertainties. All she knew for sure was having to relive the horrible tragedy of Mike's fatal crash and the eventual shooting death of her beloved mother and now known step-father.

Cruising through Wharton, El Campo, and Edna on Highway 59, the often-visited landscape was dotted with the same rice and grain silos, cornfields, cotton fields, white wooden churches, and dance halls. However, they no longer provided wonderful memories. The scenery now was simply a reminder of the repeat of Mike's death, and her battle with heartache and loneliness. For she had followed the mighty Stingarees of Victoria High when Mike pitched against the high schools in these towns during the school week, and on weekends they attended these same dance halls together, listening to the music of B.J. Thomas and many others. Life had been a dream; a wonderful one at that.

In a fit of desperation and fear, she screamed out while pounding on the steering wheel, "God, I don't want to watch Mike die again!"

Mercifully, just moments later, the last magical moment occurred; the pint size cowboy appeared on the shoulder of the highway, causing the car to come to a complete stop. The little guy opened the passenger side door and climbed up on the seat, just like always, while Alexandria remained looking straight ahead. Glancing in her direction, he said rather solemnly, "You had no other choice. I knew you'd have to come, because you stepped too far over the line, letting hate rule you. Should have heeded Richard's warning; or shall I say wisdom."

Exasperated and never looking in his direction, she answered sharply, "Well, I didn't, so here I am! Can you please tell me how I am to enjoy the three years or so Mike and I have together, if all I can think about is his dying in that car wreck again? What then?"

"For now, just get back on the highway and head for the Jet Drive-In. The good news is, unlike your previous trips, you'll have no recollection of the life you are about to leave behind. In fact, it never happened. You'll actually be 14 years old again, in body and mind, attending Crain Junior High. When Mike dies, you'll be just as shocked and hurt as the first time. Because, for you, it will be the first time. You will not see it coming. Your lives up to that fatal night will be identical as before. You'll be in a dreamland."

Alex guided the car back onto the highway toward Victoria, while still never-so-much as glancing toward her little brother, but asked, "What happens after Mike dies? What do I do then?"

"You'll finish your senior year in high school and move on to Sam Houston State University in Huntsville, where you receive both your undergraduate and graduate degrees in history; just like before. Fortunately, you will land a teaching job at Victoria High School, and be a Stingaree again. You'll never teach at Centennial. You never had a life there. Everything you've gone through never happened because you were never there."

"I'll have to go through my mom and that Frank McCord guy being killed again?"

"I'm afraid so. But listen, you will also not see or anticipate anything. It will also be the first time. To you, he's your real dad who loves your mother in storybook fashion."

Frustrated, she asked out of desperation, "There's no other option?"

Continuing to stare in her direction, he said, "You know that answer as well as I do."

"So you're saying, if I cross this threshold into that other dimension, Willie Buchanan didn't kill Johnnie Wimbush and his grandfather, Silas? No one at Centennial High knows me? I'm not wanted by the police? Farley, Laura Reynolds, and the McWhorter kids know nothing of me? And Richard?"

"Alexandria, you were never there. None of that stuff ever happened. Look sis, let me lay this out for you. Once you cross over the threshold, you are instantly a fourteen-year-old girl asleep in her own bed. No one in Houston will have ever known you – you never existed there. Ricky McWhorter and his siblings live with their parents. They were never left alone. One of your favorite students, Scot Barton, went on to play football for the Texas Longhorns. His father never had a drinking problem and was Scot's biggest fan. Farley and Laura Reynolds married. Johnnie Wimbush turned down numerous basketball scholarships to help his grandfather, Silas, manage the grocery store. The lad could not be happier. He also is a part-time employee at the Community Center helping younger kids. Willie Buchanan was with the gang that murdered your parents, but afterward was never heard from. The gang never terrorized the neighborhood, and actually seemed to just disperse. You're actually helping all those people, not to mention saving some lives. You're saving yourself some horrible memories that would only serve to haunt you the rest of your life because, quite frankly, you caused some of it. You did not cause Mike's death."

"Paul Getty got away with his life, didn't he? All those poor people he ruined. That still happened didn't it?"

"Not entirely. Johnny Luster, bless his heart, put a rope around Getty's neck in the CEO's own home and had him hanging with his toes barely touching a chair. Told him the only way he could save his worthless self would be to call his Chief Financial Officer and order the jobs, bonuses, and pensions restored. But it had to be announced on the front page of the Houston Post.

"Getty's toes started cramping, and he began choking. When the dirt bag realized Johnny was going to let him hang to death, the Boss had a change of heart. Johnny cut his hands free so he could make the call, handing him the house phone stretched on a long cord. That was about eleven in the evening. The CFO called the newspaper, and the story came out the next morning. That's when Johnny cut him down.

"Luster threatened to kill Getty should the CEO report the incident to the police or rescind the agreement. The kicker is, Johnny was dressed up as the Joker character in the comic books of Batman. Getty had no idea who was doing all that to him anyway. Pretty cool, huh?"

Alex reflected a minute before saying, "Sounds like my dad. Obviously, that's where I get all this from. It all makes sense now. But what about Uncle Richard? We were so close. He'll remember me; he's family."

"Our Uncle Richard took over the ownership of what was once Johnny Luster's Mopar Restoration. Johnny died from pancreatic cancer shortly after his encounter with Paul Getty. Richard probably remembers very little about you from the last time he saw you at some family function. So please understand the concept here. Once you step over into the new dimension, no one in Houston will know you ever existed, including the police. You had no relationship with Richard at all, and never met Johnny Luster. I can't make it any simpler than that. Just quit being so stubborn and accept what you cannot change."

"So, I have only a few more moments to savor all those wonderful relationships with the people I love. I'm overwhelmed.... Oh my God, the four creeps in the Mercedes who harassed the kids at the Community Center! I forgot to get their worthless existence!"

"They never did any of that. Anything related to you exclusively never happened. Getty is the exception. He had nothing to do with anyone you knew...That was just a crummy business decision. And yes, the rest is overwhelming," he agreed nodding his head, sympathizing with her. "But how are you going to enjoy anything while in prison the rest of your life or waiting on the death penalty? Can you spend the rest of your life in prison blaming yourself for the hanging of Johnnie and Silas? Wondering what would become of the McWhorter kids? Could your conscience handle all that? The fact that none of that would have happened if you simply would have taken this opportunity sitting in front of you right this minute? Huh?

"And by the way, Albert was not going to kill you. He changed his mind, but neither you nor Farley heard him say he could not go through with it. He went on to manage the Boys' Club on Canal Street. That is, if you go to Victoria.

"Now, that you put it that way, Victoria looks real good. Who will remember me in Victoria?"

"Everyone who knew you before you left for college and returned to teach at the high school. You have friends there as we speak. Many people are expecting to see you tomorrow. Our parents, for example, not to mention Mike. Actually, they're technically your parents, not mine. Well, your mom and stepdad. But to you, he'll be your dad."

"What ever happened to Mike's parents? We kept in touch, when I first went off to college, but drifted apart after a while. Don't know why. I guess I got so wrapped up in my work, once I began teaching."

"Mike's father is still living in the same house. He's been really lonely since his wife died in a nursing home last year from

Alzheimer's. Many of his friends do not think he'll last much longer. So, if you enter that new dimension, they're both still alive, of course. You will see them age poorly after Mike's death. His mother will die of Alzheimer's and afterwards, his dad will die alone of natural causes."

Pleading, she asked, "Do I have a boyfriend? I mean, while I'm teaching at the high school?"

"No, I'm afraid not. You won't let anyone get close enough, because for you, Mike was the only one. No one can live up to him. People in town still talk about you two as if he was still alive."

"How does all this end up?"

"That part Our Father in Heaven didn't tell me. You'll just have to go live life. The journey deserves to be one day at a time, and you'll have to figure things out as you go and live with your decisions just like anyone else."

"Now, I feel lonelier than before. At least I had my students, Richard, Laura Reynolds, Farley, Dr. Long, and my real father with whom we could have made up for some of that precious lost time."

Losing patience with her procrastinating the only reasonable and fair decision for all concerned, the little guy shouted, "Alex, you have friends here and are involved with your students at Victoria High and the various school activities! You'll probably be happier than you have been! You'll have an honest life with an honest future! Won't always be looking over your shoulder!"

"Boy, I really messed up, didn't I? Deathbed regrets is about all I've accomplished; hell, living regrets. I'm smothered in them."

Reaching out and grabbing her hand, the little brother begged, "Yes. But please quit dwelling on what will soon be the past, and a past that will have never existed. Please realize there is no other way to repair the damage that you helped cause."

Seemingly acquiescing, Alex asked, "So, what do we do now?"

"I'll stay in this car with you until we arrive at the Jet Drive Inn restaurant. After you climb out, you'll be that same fourteen-year-old, asleep in your old bed at 1208 Anaqua. It'll be Saturday morning when you awake, and the only thing that will be of any concern will be that of seeing Mike Koehl that afternoon. You'll begin the day helping your mother with the chores as always, and later you'll attend the YMCA activity night, where you and Mike will dance to the music of the band called Honey & the Tear Drops. Other activities include swimming, basketball, ping pong and pool. You'll have a blast. It'll be the most fun and innocent time of your life. It will be the old days."

"No, Johnny Dee and the Rocket 88's?"

"No."

Forty minutes later, Alex guided the Road Runner into the Jet Drive-in restaurant parking lot. Both just sat in silence for several minutes without saying a word before Alex broke the ice.

"I feel like crying, knowing these are the last few moments

of my real life in Houston. God, I actually met my real dad. He's wonderful. There's a piece of me that'd rather go back and face prison."

"Remember, you will have no knowledge of Frank McCord not being your real father. You'll know nothing of his and your mom's rocky relationship. You'll still be oblivious to all their dysfunctions."

"I'm scared … This is a big decision."

Finally, at his wits end, her little brother threatens, "Alexandria, I'll sit here just two more minutes, while you ponder your decision. Once I exit this car instead of you doing so, the return to 1962 is revoked. You'll instantly be back at the warehouse you just left, with the police escorting you to a patrol car. You are my sister, so that's not what I wish for you. Honestly, it would break my heart. God is giving you a second chance, so please take it."

Seconds began ticking while Alex stared straight ahead, tears streaming down her face.

Printed in the USA
CPSIA information can be obtained
at www.ICGtesting.com
CBHW070410070824
12785CB00012B/387/J

9 798887 757223